Mary Grayer Clarke has been an avid reader since the age of three years. The first thing she had published was in the Newfoundland Magazine of 1984. She decided to start writing seriously when attending a creative writing course and having written several short stories and essays was motivated to try her hand at a full novel. She has also been involved in the production of several technical publications. Mary firmly believes that every cloud has a silver lining and that age is just a number.

Mary published her first novel, *Dark Regressions*, in January 2023.

With fond memories of my friends in Marchwood Writers' Circle

Mary Grayer Clarke

DARK REVENGE

AUSTIN MACAULEY PUBLISHERS™

LONDON * CAMBRIDGE * NEW YORK * SHARJAH

A CIP catalogue record for this title is available from the British Library.

ISBN 9781035806744 (Paperback)
ISBN 9781035806751 (ePub e-book)

www.austinmacauley.co.uk

First Published 2024
Austin Macauley Publishers Ltd®
1 Canada Square
Canary Wharf
London
E14 5AA

I owe so much to Austin Macauley Publishers, who gave me an extraordinary opportunity by accepting my first novel and now the sequel, which will hopefully turn out to be the second novel of a *Dark Trilogy*. My special thanks go to my son, Toby, who is always there to help Mum with her computer problems and his exceptional wife, Kay. Without them, I would not have had the motivation to complete any book let alone found the courage to send it to my very first, publishers. Finally, thank you to everyone who reads my book.

Prologue

Suzanne felt the air cool as a shadow passed over her. She turned. Beside her stood a tall man, clad entirely in black with the exception of a crimson cravat at his neck. She shivered and instinctively glanced away from him. This was a man she knew. Not personally but through Michael Deville's papers, that she had recently transcribed into a book.

"May I join you?" The mellifluous voice rolled over her like a warm blanket on a chilly day. "We have much to discuss, lady."

Suzanne knew better than to issue an invitation of any description to this character and it was with a deep feeling of satisfaction that she realised that at least she had learnt something of importance whilst conducting her promise to her now deceased, ex-husband. Together, with a sure knowledge that she must under no circumstances allow him to achieve eye contact with her, for to do so could place her under his control.

"NO!"

Suzanne raised her voice and people at nearby tables looked towards her. She rose and hurried into the teashop. When she looked through the window, the man known in this region as The Count, had gone, but she knew without doubt that he would be back for her…

Part I

Chapter 1

After an exhausting two years following the publication of her book, concerning the dark regressions of her ex-husband Michael Deville, Suzanne was to take a month's break. On her birthday in July, her boss, Boris Slovinski had offered her air tickets and a fortnight's stay at Hotel Orb de l'Or in the Swiss Golden Mountains. There had of course, been method in his kindness for he was very fond of this journalist, who had been the main reason his magazine, *International Viewpoint*, was now one of note. Before she had joined the magazine's permanent staff, Suzanne had worked on a freelance basis and provided several stories, which had kept it from remaining on the shelves of newsagents. Boris had been on the verge of having to close the business he loved so much, so he had eventually, persuaded her to join him permanently. Suzanne had brought interesting stories, which she had impeccably researched for truth and written with an enthusiasm that made the readers look for more. *International Viewpoint* was now up with the big names on newsagents' magazine stands and he could have easily moved to a more prestigious location in the city of London. However, this was not what Boris wanted; he was more than happy in the peace of the New Forest. Besides, he knew that Suzanne would not move from the place of her birth that she loved and his regard for her was more to him than she could know. Hence, a holiday in the mountains where Henri de Ville had been conceived in the seventeenth century, was a place that she had visited previously for only a noticeably brief time over five years ago. She had returned home the very next day after an encounter with the Count, who appeared to be connected to Michael's dark regression as Henri de Ville. Suzanne was not sure why she had been so spooked by this occurrence but instinctively knew that a strange feeling of fear was behind it. It was definitely out of character for the feisty journalist.

However, that was over five years ago and she wondered now, if maybe she had just been paranoid, after such intense involvement in Michael's records. She thanked Boris but asked if he minded deferring his kind offer until the end of

September, as she was already pretty fully booked for various things until then. He had shrugged but agreed to do so.

Still reluctant to take this particular holiday, Suzanne could not bring herself to risk offending Boris. However, before she left for this second trip to the Swiss Mountains, she met with Meg and Gerry, the friends she had made during her research at St Patricks. She explained about the holiday but also that whilst there, she proposed to investigate what might have happened five hundred years ago. They made sure that they were able to skype, which would allow them to converse face to face as it were, for a daily update on her progress. It would also enable Meg and Gerry to give her any information they may need to forage out for her. They arranged to do this every evening between 21.00 hours and midnight each day. They also agreed that should it for some reason, not be possible to Skype, then a telephone call sometime the following morning, would be made via their mobiles. This was just by way of an '*are you* okay' call.

~~

The journey to Billenbach was long and tiring. From plane to train and then by taxi to the hotel. It was late afternoon when she arrived and was grateful to shower, then fall onto a most comfortable bed, where she slept until nearly eight o'clock. Suzanne dressed and took the lift down to the dining room for an excellent and much needed meal, after which she skyped Meg and Gerry.

"We were wondering if you had arrived safely," Meg said. "What was the flight like? Is the hotel posh and the rooms nice? Have you got an en suite up there in the mountains?"

"Slow down a bit and give her time to answer," Gerry tried to silence his wife.

Suzanne was used to Meg's excitable manner. "Yes, Meg, the flight was great but it is a bit of a trek from the airport to the hotel, which incidentally is superb. The room is lovely with a view towards the clifftop, and way below, I can see the lights of the village. It's magical. I have an en suite bathroom and the bed is so comfortable I dropped off to sleep when I got here and slept until eight o'clock. Now, please I must apologise for being very brief but I'm not going to talk for much longer as that bed beckons." She directed her iPad towards the sledge-bed as she spoke, to confirm its quality.

Gerry intervened before Meg could get going once again. "What's your weather like there in September?"

"No snow has fallen but ice is already forming on the ground and the trees are decorated with frost gleaming like jewels."

Meg informed her, "It's been a glorious sunny day here, although it grew chilly once dusk fell."

They finally said their goodnights, promised to talk again the following day and Suzanne retired to the comfortable bed once more, where she slept until seven o'clock the next morning.

~~

She had decided to try and chat with the gatekeeper the following morning, to hopefully, learn more of the history regarding the Golden Mountains and in particular, the Convent of the Golden Orb. So, with that in mind, she walked to the gatehouse. As there was no one there, Suzanne continued her walk into the village, to browse through the shops and explore the neighbourhood.

Sitting at a table outside a small café with a large cup of coffee before her, was when Suzanne felt a shadow engulf her and gave a shiver of Déjà vu. She said aloud, "No," quickly finished her coffee and left to return to the hotel.

~~

The gatehouse keeper was back at his post when Suzanne reached the gates of the hotel and seemed very willing to chat with a visitor. He was a tall, sturdy man, anywhere between forty-and fifty-years-old, with rather long greying hair tucked behind his ears and falling over the collar of a worn green corduroy jacket, which boasted brown leather trimming and elbow patches. His jeans looked as though he might sleep in them and the loafers on his feet were scuffed. His beard was rather more luxuriant than the hair on his head and had it been of a more white than grey colour, would have given the appearance of an off-duty Father Christmas.

"Hello, my dear," he said, in pedantic almost perfect English. "You will be staying at yon hotel. Holiday, is it? Most visitors are only holiday folk, they ski, climb the mountains and cause all sorts of mayhem for the local rescue teams.

My name is Bartholomew, by the way, but you can call me Bart, all my friends do and I feel we shall become friends very shortly."

"Hello," Suzanne replied. "My name is Suzanne and yes, I am at the hotel for a while, but I'm a journalist, so am also interested in the history of the place, when it was a convent. The Convent of the Golden Orb, I believe."

The man looked around him, as though expecting to be watched, then in almost a whisper said, "Come into my cottage for a bit, I make better coffee than you will get in the hotel café and we can chat for a while."

Hmmm! Suzanne thought, *maybe I am about to learn the secrets of past lives*, and followed him into a warm cosy kitchen with an old refectory table and four wing-back chairs in the centre. The room filled the whole of the downstairs area, with a staircase in one corner leading to the floor above and a well-used leather settee along the side of it. Against the wall, to the left of the door was a cream AGA cooker that shone as though frequently polished, with a kettle steaming on the hob and a battered armchair to one side. Opposite the door was a full wall-to-wall and ceiling-high set of book shelves, crammed full of books. Along the top level were books bound in ancient leather, their covers originally decorated with gold-leaf tooling. These were now worn and the white cotton gloves placed near these tomes gave Suzanne a frisson of pleasure that they belonged to someone who cared about precious books as much as she did. The second shelf held larger reference books about insects, animals, plants, geology, anthropology and other subjects of an informative nature. Along the next two shelves were paperback books, mainly of the Lee Child thriller variety and the bottom one contained, what Suzanne assumed were Bartholomew's diaries and notebooks.

"I thought the books would interest you," said Bart as he turned from the AGA. He placed a tray on the table, containing two steaming mugs of coffee, a jug of cream, a basin of brown sugar and a plate of scrumptious looking assorted biscuits. "Help yourself," he said, adding cream and two heaped spoonsful of sugar to his coffee and dunking a shortbread biscuit. As Suzanne picked up her cup and sipped, he shuddered. "No cream and sugar? I could not drink it like that, too strong."

Suzanne smiled, "I always like the buzz I get from a good cup of coffee and you certainly make a good one. I must get your recipe before I go home, for it's better than I can make."

As Suzanne sipped her coffee, she looked around the large room. On the wall opposite the AGA was a desk containing a very modern PC, a lightweight laptop, and next to it a filing cabinet. Bart was obviously more up to date with technology, than his outward appearance would make one think.

"So, Suzanne, my young cousin Boris asked me to look out for you, we have the same surname, our fathers being brothers," he added. "I have read what you serialised in *International Viewpoint* and know for a certainty, that you should be aware that you may be in danger by returning to these mountains. The sensible thing for you to do, would be to cease looking into the past history of this place, return home and keep your head down. But from what I hear, that is the last thing you will do. However, please, for your own sake, try to stay at all times, in areas where there are other people and do not speak of our conversation to anyone. I am merely the guard at the gate."

He looked so serious and worried that Suzanne felt a shiver of apprehension and found herself looking over her shoulder.

"Yes. That is precisely what you should be doing, all the time and do not leave your door unlocked or your window open, not a tiny bit, even if you are hot. Do not sit out on your balcony and *do* keep those doors shut. I am not joking, Suzanne, as you will learn, when you understand the history of this place."

He is either very perceptive or paranoid, Suzanne thought. "You mean that there really is a character called the Count here in Billenbach? That I might have actually been able to see him when I was here before, it was not my imagination or paranoia?" Then, rather embarrassed, she told Bart of the feeling of Déjà vu she had experienced earlier that morning.

"Precisely why you should, no must, take notice of what I say." Bart advised.

He rose, putting on a pair of white gloves, ran his finger along the very top row of books and took down a large tome around three centimetres thick. He brought it to the table and sat next to Suzanne, passing a pair of gloves to her.

"I think we should begin with this one," he said.

Chapter 2

The book appeared to be a family bible. The names of the family dated back to the year 1021 and each family member appeared to be indicated, not by a Christian and/or surname but by the word Count, followed by the number one hundred. Thence forward, the last year noted, was 1581. Suzanne worked out that hence Count 100 in that year, could have been any age whatsoever but it appeared quite possible that he was 560 years old.

Therefore, the Count involved in the life of Henri de Ville in the seventeenth century, may have reached the end of his period of control, reign or whatever it was known as. This, possibly being due to the apparent fact, that Henri met his death in the caves, into which the Count could, or would, not venture. She pointed this out to Bart but he shook his head and suggested she look further into the great tome.

Suzanne remembered that the first words in the book of Genesis, King James version of the Bible, are:

Verse 1-In the beginning, God created the heaven and the earth.
Verse 31-And God saw everything that he had made, and behold it was good.
And the evening and the morning were the sixth day.

Which was where, with a gasp of horror, Suzanne noticed the total difference, between the Bible she knew so well and the tome, she had assumed to be a family version of that book. She turned the page back and read the title of the book.

The Family Book of Satanic Rights Statutes and Procedures

Turning forward again, she read the words on the first page, that was titled.

Satanic Practices. *These practices revoke all others mentioned in Jehovah's book of Genesis and are replaced by those of The Master of Mankind, that inhabit the world known as Earth, for perpetuity.*

This was followed by a list of regulations to be enforced by all human beings dwelling thereon, which Suzanne refused to allow to enter her mind.

"I know how you feel, Suzanne," Bart spoke quietly. "I felt the same when I first came across this book, and others, in the library of the convent, when it was closed. That was before it was taken over by the hotel company."

"What happened? Why was it closed and who is the new owner of the hotel? How did you manage to buy the books, for surely, they would have been of real interest to the Vatican?"

"The new owners are a group of higher-end hotel operators and there is no doubt they have done an excellent job here. The village has prospered, in a way it never could have done before they came. The Gelberger family, for instance, now own all the land that encompasses their farm, plus all the woodlands right up to the caves. They also, by virtue of a licence obtained from the local council, have the right to exploit the cave tours, car park, café and gift shop. Visitors can only go into the main cavern today though, the path to the top where the waterfall enters the caves, is considered to be dangerous, so it has been closed off.

As for the books I obtained from the library of the old convent, less said sooner mended as they say. This must stay strictly between the two of us, so before I reveal anything, you must give me your word, that you will never print what I am about to tell you."

Suzanne thought about it then came to a decision. "You have my solemn word," she said.

"The place had been derelict for about a year when I applied for permission to buy or rent this gatehouse cottage ten years ago. I was allowed to purchase it on a lease, for a maximum of fifty years, providing I functioned as security guard of the old convent, until such time as it might be sold. I love it here in the mountains, so I accepted the offer. It soon became my habit, to speed-walk the path to the hotel every morning, before breakfast, still do it, in fact. One day, I felt the urge to explore the environment of the old convent, so I walked around the building, peering through windows. That was when I discovered a door into the cellar, which was open. Being of a rather inquisitive disposition, I entered. No one was there to object, so I chose to explore the interior.

There were still the huge kitchen and not so-large cells, in which the nuns had slept, on the ground floor. On the next level, I found rather more luxurious rooms, obviously those used by the Reverend Mother and leading hierarchy of the convent. There was also a room that was presumably the office. On the floor above, I discovered the library, which was where I spent the next two hours. I sat at a table and speed-read through as many of the books as I thought to be of interest. It looked as though these valuable books had not been moved for any purpose, let alone reading, for many years. When I looked at my watch, I realised that it was gone ten o'clock and remembered that an agent was due to show a group of possible purchasers round the property at 11.30 am. So," and here Bart actually blushed, "I gathered as many of the great tomes as I could carry and returned to my cottage with them, planning to remove a few more the following day. I suppose that makes me a thief," he said, shrugging. "Anyway, I am not sorry for what I did, as when I tried that door again, it was firmly locked. When the hotel company took possession of the building, all the books and quite a lot of the furniture was burnt. I confess I nearly cried. Reminded me of what those dreadful Nazis did during World War Two.

Well, Suzanne, you know my secret now and are complicit with me." He added, with a wry look, "I hope."

"Apart from that, what made you apply for this job as gatehouse keeper to the hotel people, knowing so much about the dreadful history of the place?" She spoke without a breath and felt her face blush as Bart cut in.

"Slow down, Suzanne. Don't forget, I was already a sort of security guard for the property and it was the dreadful history, as you say, that made me take an interest in the first place. However, it is a long story and time flies as the parrot said when someone chucked a clock at it. If you would care to join me for lunch at about noon tomorrow, I will do my best to tell you all I know but it is now beginning to get dark, and I would feel happier if you were amongst the folk in the hotel. Don't forget to keep doors and windows firmly locked. I will walk you to the hotel. No, it is no trouble, just for my peace of mind," Bart said.

As they walked back to the Hotel Orb de l'Or, their conversation was general and friendly, as though they had known each other for many years. Suzanne felt it was reminiscent of her short term but firm friendship, with the vicar of St Patricks, Gerry, his wife Meg and the Cambridge professor, Roland Byatt.

Back in the foyer of the hotel, Suzanne once again felt she was being watched. She glanced around but could see no one, other than the receptionist, a dark-haired girl wearing a roll neck blouse of crimson under a golden silk jacket, with tailored black trousers. She was of serious countenance; her skin almost translucent, with piercing blue eyes, that looked as though they were made of crystal. *Was that what made me feel watched, was it the girl?* Suzanne thought. Then shaking off these unsettling thoughts, she requested her key card, walked to the lifts and pressed the button. The lift was about a metre square, its three walls being half mirrored, the remaining walls and door were made of bright stainless steel. Now, she felt like being watched by a clone of herself, who was not really just a reflection but someone entirely different, unknown.

The lift reached floor number 3, the doors softly slid open and with a shake of her head, Suzanne stepped out, silently declaring to herself that in future, she would use the stairs. Quickly walking to Room 307, Suzanne swiped her key card and entered her room, closing and locking the door with a sigh of relief. Finally, she checked all the windows and doors were firmly locked and gratefully snuggled under the duvet.

I wonder if my room was once part of the old library? she thought, as eventually the relaxing haze of sleep overtook her.

Suzanne had not expected to sleep well with her mind so full of questions but nevertheless, after eating dinner in the restaurant and taking a hot shower before cosying down in the undoubtedly comfortable bed, she closed her eyes, just to think. When she opened them next, it was to see daylight peeping through the gap in her drapes and looking at the bedside clock, realised that it was 7.40am. *I've been asleep for eight hours,* she thought, remembering that she was to meet Bart for lunch in his cottage at midday.

Chapter 3

Taking her time to get showered and dressed, Suzanne went to the restaurant for breakfast. It was of the bar variety, so helping herself to cereal with yoghurt and coffee, she sat at an empty table, overlooking the winding pathway leading to the cliff, where Isabelle de Ville allegedly descended to a cave, leading to what is now the visitor attraction and from which, she made her escape from the Convent of the Golden Orb and finally returned to England. There was much to think about.

It was not until she was in the lift with another three residents, that Suzanne realised she had decided to use only the stairs in future but she felt none of the strange, out of body experience, of the previous night.

At 11.50am, Suzanne joined a group of chattering visitors leaving the hotel and was able to discuss the contents of a brochure she had picked up from the reception desk concerning the caves with them. She recalled what Bart had suggested the previous day, about keeping with other people, as she made her way to his gatehouse cottage.

He was waiting and beckoned her into the comfortable kitchen she remembered. Suzanne entered, with a feeling of safety she had not been aware of, since leaving it yesterday. Sitting once again at the table, with a mug of strong coffee before her, she related her experience in the lift, expecting Bart to laugh at her. However, his expression was one of sincere concern.

"Suzanne, you are in more danger here than I had anticipated. The Count's powers appear to be much greater. Since the death of Henri de Ville, appearances and contact from the Count have apparently decreased, to such an extent that he has become merely a legend. For some reason, since your arrival in Billenbach, or more likely at the Hotel Orb de l'Or, his powers seem to have been revitalised and have increased exponentially since his shadow apparently engulfed you, outside that café. On that occasion, you did not see a person in the flesh, just his shadow, but you are aware of him, as he is of you. Do not sit outside that café

22

again, you might be safe inside, that is up to you. Did you do as I asked and make sure your doors and windows were firmly shut and locked and the drapes fully closed?"

"Yes. And I slept better than I remember for ages, a full eight hours."

"Did you dream?"

"Not that I am aware, as I said I slept really deeply. Was that not a good thing?"

"Tell me again, about your feeling the presence of the Count outside the café yesterday."

Having done so, Bart rested his chin on clasped hands. "So, you avoided looking towards this shadow that you say immediately gave you a feeling of Déjà vu. Is that correct?"

Suzanne nodded, "Yes."

"Good. You stood and said no in a very loud voice, causing the people at neighbouring tables to look in your direction. Right?"

Suzanne once again replied, somewhat embarrassedly. "Yes."

"Would you believe that those people saw and heard, only yourself? I have spoken to them and the café owner and they all say that you suddenly shouted no and raced off. They saw no one else, no shadow even, only you, and assumed that you had remembered something urgent, or experienced a mental aberration of some type."

Suzanne shook her head. "Am I going mad then, am I just seeing, imagining things?"

Bart placed his hand over hers. "No, my dear, but this is confirmation that the Count is back in action after all this time and we, you in particular, must be extremely careful."

Bart was silent as they sipped their coffee. Both were considering the short conversation that had just taken place. Suzanne broke the silence.

"Look, Bart, I'm here as a journalist. I am not just covering an ancient story, to confirm the provenance but it is also connected to me, through my late ex-husband. Perhaps, before you tell me more about the Count and this place, I had better fill you in on the events that brought me to Billenbach that first time."

When she had explained about Michael's regressions, which led to her book and the unexpected friendships with the Vicar of St Patricks, his wife and the university Professor Roland Byatt, Bart exclaimed, "More coffee, I think."

Once again, they sat in companionable silence, sipping hot coffee and this time, it was Bart who broke the silence.

"I have as I said, read your serialisation of Dark Regressions, so I know the story as you recorded it. Now, I also know your personal background with Michael Deville. My cousin, Boris, as I said previously, has filled me in regarding yourself and asked me to keep an eye on you. This is obviously going to be more complicated than I had anticipated. I thought I was going to enjoy the company of an attractive journalist, share some old history and rumours, then say goodbye, let us stay in touch. Your involvement is much deeper than I anticipated. I had no idea that you had been married to Michael Deville at one time, which completely changes the story. So firstly, do you have children with your ex-husband?"

"No," she replied. "That's one of the reasons leading to our divorce. Not that Michael wanted children, he didn't, but my not being able to, made me inferior goods—*seconds*. He regretted it in the end but by then it was too late and I had returned to my work as a journalist anyway. I had no desire to get back with him, especially knowing the state he was in. That became the province of Helena Rose, his new wife."

"Which must bring us back to the history of Henri de Ville and his mother Isabella," said Bart.

~~

"Okay," Bart continued. "Legend has it, in these mountains, that in the year 1021, there was an aristocrat known as The Count, who was said to have dealings with the devil. No one seems to know where the Count originally came from or if he was perhaps, the devil himself. However, it is told that he set himself up as leader of the community and built a castle into and on the mountain top, as his official residence, from which he proceeded to draw the locals under his control. The pathway from the village was closed, to all but visitors to the Count. His servant, Igor would make weekly journeys on a donkey, to collect provisions from the local inhabitants. It appears that these goods were by way of and here Bart made air quotes, 'the kind permission of the Count,' to dwell in their homes, some of which incidentally, had belonged to their great grandparents. But that was the control the Count developed over those poor people through fear. Every ten years, he took a virgin from the community, with the intent of producing a child with her. In all cases, the Mother miscarried, did not survive the birth, and if the child was a girl, it also did not survive. Unfortunately, or perhaps that should be fortunately, any boys, although surviving birth, did not appear to grow to more than five years old, before being overtaken by some form of ill health and subsequent death. This pattern continued until the year 1242 when the castle was transformed into a nunnery, known as the Convent of the Golden Orb."

During the telling of this history, Bart turned pages in the tomes, denoting the centuries that showed drawings of the Count, his castle and his virgin wives.

"Time for a break, methinks," he said.

"I'll make the coffee this time and I brought some pastries with me too." Suzanne walked to the AGA, feeling a real sense of belonging here.

"So, from 1242, the Count of that time was presumably living somewhere else?" Suzanne asked.

"On the contrary, local rumour was, that he continued to live in the area and was actually the priest, in charge of the convent. It was believed that he lived in the tower, on the western side of the convent and was said to have been seen standing on the parapet overlooking the village a thousand feet below, but this has never been confirmed. It was said that Sister Marguerite, the Mother Superior and she alone, was answerable to him. The nuns obeyed the Mother Superior's every order, as did she the Count's.

Nothing was documented about the Count, or governing priest, for two centuries. The Convent of the Golden Orb was kept in isolation, with absolutely no contact with the outside world. The locals assumed that the nuns grew their own crops, and kept chicken and animals to feed themselves.

However, after the Convent of the Golden Orb had been established for ten years, as in the past, at each tenth year therefrom, maidens would go missing. It was agreed amongst the community, that these girls had wandered on the mountains and fallen into a crevice. Whatever, they or their bodies were never found.

From what you have learnt from your ex-husband's regressions, the Count somehow found out that his birth-son, by Isabella de Ville in the seventeenth century, was in fact still alive, under the protection of the Prior of St Patrick's Monastery. Whether this was through a member of the monastery, maybe one of the nuns, or by occult means, is not able to be confirmed. This at first, would have thrown him into a rage but after calming down, he would have realised that Henri could be controlled in another way; a way that would interfere with all the good intentions of Sister Theresa and the Prior of St Patricks. So, it was that he subsequently infiltrated Henri's dreams and eventually appeared to him in person. Again, this could have been through occult means."

This was seriously something to consider, and Suzanne finally returned to the hotel with many notes written in her book, ready to transcribe. The next time she decided, she would take her iPad and make notes directly onto it.

That evening, she once again contacted Gerry and Meg in England, to update them. She told them that the following morning, it was her intention to take a tour of the caves and in particular, to study the waterfall, that emptied into the allegedly Bottomless Pool, through what the locals called the Devil's Eye. The pool into which Henri de Ville had allegedly plunged.

Chapter 4

After breakfast, Suzanne joined the minibus taking a group of tourists to visit the caves. Payment for this trip included the entrance fee, so upon arrival, those within the group were greeted by the tour guide, who turned out to be a member of the Gelberger family, Joshua. *So, a distant relative of the Josh who had married Isabella's companion and friend Susan Blessed,* thought Suzanne.

She knew from the Henri de Ville records Michael had originally produced that the Count for some reason could or would not enter the caves, so was reasonably comfortable to linger alone if necessary to conduct her explorations.

They were led into the cave entrance by Joshua who, as they progressed through the tunnel entrance into the amazing cathedral-like cavern, gave a constant explanation of the history and structure. Lights had now been inserted, giving an ethereal glow to stalactites and stalagmites. Over to the left of the entrance, a glittering waterfall cascaded a thousand feet, into what Joshua explained to his group of tourists, was known as the Bottomless Pool of the Devil's Eye. As he led the group on towards the far side, Suzanne remained standing quietly in the shelter of a stalagmite. When they were no longer close enough to see her, should anyone decide to look back, she made her way to the edge of the pool and stood looking up at the waterfall. This allegedly, was the one necessary to traverse behind, across a narrow slippery ridge, to reach the steep pathway leading down into the cave known as the Great Cavern. The one she assumed, through which Isabella would have been guided, from the ledge entrance to the caves. Splashes from the waterfall as they rebounded from the dark, malignant pool, were reflected like diamonds. As she gazed at the extraordinary beauty of light and dark, Suzanne found herself almost entranced.

What was that? Just below her in the pool of the Devil's Eye, Suzanne could see a raised hand. Then the head of a young man appeared above the water. He seemed to be in danger of drowning, his hand stretching towards her. Suzanne ducked under the rope, placed to prevent visitors from slipping into the treacherous water, and kneeling at the edge of the pool extended her own hand.

"Come on, try to take my hand so I can help you out."

The young man's hand still stretched towards her but nevertheless, he seemed to be trying to withdraw it, saying, "No, please no. He is…can't." His head disappeared under the water once again, hand still waving above it. As once again his head appeared above the surface, his hand reached closer towards that of Suzanne. She craned forward as far as possible. Then…

Their hands touched, clasped…

Suzanne felt herself slipping into the legendary Bottomless Pool of the Devil's Eye and heard the voice of the young man saying, "No. No. Don't."

She tried to free herself, but a force, no longer a mere hand but something which seemed to be not just pulling but also pushing her head under the water, was stronger than Suzanne. She was a good swimmer and held her breath for as long as she could, fighting to swim up to the surface but the force pulling her head under was almost supernatural and Suzanne could no longer fight against it. A voice filled her mind; a mellifluous voice that she recognised.

"Ah, my dear, I have you. Now, you shall be the carrier of the *Count's Revenge,* into the world that thought to reject the powers of the Master of Mankind. *My* punishment to those I despise and those for whom I care nothing, will all be destroyed…"

Suzanne fought once again to struggle to the surface, but felt herself still to be held under the water and as it finally filled her lungs, the last words she heard pleading in her head, was the voice of the strange young man she had thought to rescue, saying, "Oh, God in heaven, help us."

~~

As the tourists were escorted back towards the exit of the caves, someone said, "What's that floating on the pool? Looks like a coat or something."

"Okay, everyone stay here," said Joshua, quickly making his way to the pool. Then… "Could two of you men give me a hand please?"

All the younger men in the group stepped forward and Joshua said, "Just you two please," pointing to the nearest, fittest looking. Between them, they struggled to pull the clothing towards the rocky edge of the pool, realising now that within them was a body. It was the body of a woman and obvious that she was dead.

The group had no longer been able to retain their curiosity. They moved closer as the men turned the body onto its back feeling as they did so, a fine spray of water on their faces but thought nothing of it.

With a gasp, Tricia, who had sat next to her in the minibus, leaned over to confirm it was the person she thought it to be. As she did so, she felt an almost invisible spray of water on her face, licked her lips and wiped over it with her hand, saying, with a choke in her voice, "That's Suzanne, I was talking to her in the bus. How…? What happened…? She's a journalist and writer…"

"There is nothing we can do for her now," said Joshua. "So, let's get back outside where I can contact the authorities."

~~

The authorities duly arrived, just about all of them. Police, ambulance and crew, the owner of the site, Mr Gelberger, plus journalists, together with inquisitive locals and visitors.

Suzanne's body was taken to the hospital in Billenbach. The caves were closed until further notice and the police tried to find her closest kin.

News travels fast in a small community and Bart soon heard what had happened. He immediately contacted his cousin Boris Slovinski. Suzanne had worked for Boris for many years now and he valued her both as an employee and friend. Bart held his silence after giving the news, as he knew Boris would be very emotional. After a short while, he said, "Do you want me to call back later, cousin?"

"No." Boris drew a deep breath. "There is much for us to do. First of all, we must arrange for her to be returned to England. I'm not sure what she wanted in respect of a funeral etcetera, but I will deal with that. I do know she has no apparent relatives living but is close to the Vicar and his family at St Patricks. I'll phone them after we finish. What really happened, Bart? Suzanne would never have taken an unnecessary risk surely?"

"I do not believe so. I warned her about the danger, and she was convinced that the Count had already tried to connect with her, in shadow form. But we will discuss that face to face, not on an open line.

If you will contact her friends at St Patricks, have you got their number on record by the way?" Boris either had not or was in such a state of grief and confusion that he did not answer. "Okay, I have it here in the notes I have made during our talks, which in fact was only twice, although I feel that I have known her all my life. The Vicar of St Patricks is Reverend Gerald (Gerry) Cameron, and his wife is Meg." He gave the telephone number and address. "Did you get that down? Right. Perhaps you could discuss any necessary details, from the British side of things with them. Meanwhile, I will try and sort things out at this end and will accompany the coffin to wherever it has to be delivered.

Hold it together, my friend, I will be with you ASAP. There is much to discuss and to be done."

They said their goodbyes, to proceed with their various tasks.

Chapter 5

In Switzerland, the authorities arranged for an obligatory post-mortem. There was definitely water in the lungs, proving that Suzanne had drowned. No other injuries or toxins could be found, so the death was recorded as accidental. As the medical examiner, Otto Jurg, leaned across to pull a sheet over the body, he felt an invisible spray, like water on his face. He wiped his forehead with the back of his hand and thought no more of it, then continued to clear up after the procedure.

It was assumed the journalist had stepped over the restraining rope around the Bottomless Pool of the Devil's Eye, with the intention of taking a photograph of her own reflection and consequently slipped. The rest of the tour group being at the other side of the cavern, made it unlikely that anyone would have heard a cry for help. Her telephone had not been recovered from her clothing and it was assumed to be somewhere in the watery depths.

By the end of the week, Bart had gained permission to collect the deceased's belongings from the hotel and arranged for a flight to Gatwick Airport, the following Thursday. He would accompany the coffin, together with her belongings and would be met by Boris and Gerry at the airport. From there, they would proceed to St Patricks Rectory, where Meg had insisted, they stay as long as necessary. She would have prepared their rooms and one of her delicious meals. Gerry had contacted Roland Byatt and he was already at the Rectory.

~~

Suzanne's coffin was placed in front of the alter in the Church of St Patricks. Gerry had held a short service just for the five of them, as they stood around the coffin. The Vicar was at the head with Meg, his wife at the end. Bart and Boris were to one side and Professor Roland Byatt on the other.

After a silent moment, Roland said, "I would like to verify that it is definitely Suzanne in there."

"But we know it is," said Bart. "I personally accompanied her here, all the way."

"I do not doubt you, my friend, but we are dealing with a force greater than any of us, the Count/Man in Black. I do not feel able to trust anything to do with that devil. Remember that Suzanne returned the very next day, after her first encounter with him, five years or so ago. She told me how frightened she'd been and felt nervous even at home. She felt that she was being watched, albeit supernaturally. So, yes please, Gerry, I would like to check that the body we bury is indeed that of our friend Suzanne."

"Very well, do you all agree that we open the coffin?"

The response was unanimous, so the Vicar hastily returned to the Rectory to find a suitable screwdriver necessary for that purpose.

As the top was raised, an almost invisible mist rose from the body within. Roland was leaning over the body, which was definitely that of Suzanne, and was engulfed by it, but he hardly noticed. The others stood back out of respect for him, as the request to open the coffin as proof of identity, was entirely his. Hence, they failed to fully comprehend the vapour, which once freed from confinement of the coffin, spread quickly throughout the church. So it was, that inadvertently, they chose unanimously to ignore it. Once free, it separated, one portion to each group of pews, where it remained invisible, until it was time to be activated by the one who controlled it. Gerry said one more prayer, making the sign of the cross over the body, and as the coffin was once again sealed, made another saying,

"Rest in peace, Suzanne, and may you be protected by our Heavenly Father, Son and Holy Ghost…" To which the others responded, "Amen."

They returned to the Rectory, where after dinner, being exhausted, they agreed to retire for the night and fell into their beds, where surprisingly all five had a restful night's sleep.

The next day was spent organising Suzanne's funeral for the following afternoon. The Girls, as Meg referred to her twin daughters, arrived that evening and after a meal, they all decided it would be best to retire for the night, as Saturday would be busy and possibly rather traumatic.

~~

Bart was surprised at the number of people attending. There were, of course Gerry, Meg and their twin girls Kathy and Becky. (Adam their son, was studying in America and Ed, Gerry's son by his first wife Alice, who had died in childbirth, was living and farming in Canada, with a wife and children of his own). Roland Byatt from Cambridge, being the third person to whom Suzanne had confided the details of Michael's regressions, was naturally included. Also, members of the church, who had met Suzanne at fetes and services over the last few years. A number of villagers, who had also met and instinctively liked Suzanne, also turned up to pay their respects. Few of the magazine employees actually knew Suzanne; she had been a rather remote person, but Boris made sure as many as possible were present, in remembrance of their colleague.

The media had covered Suzanne's death from the beginning and made sure her funeral was also a newsworthy item. Since the publication of Dark Regressions, Suzanne's was a well-known face in many countries.

Only Gerry, Meg, their Girls, Roland, Boris and Bart, returned to the Rectory, for what Bart supposed was 'the Wake'. He was somewhat relieved, not being a believer in traditional send-offs. He supposed it was meant to be a time to share one's grief and remember various stories about the deceased, but in this case, they in fact, knew only what Suzanne had shared of her life with them. That mostly concerned her life since the death of her ex-husband and the contents of his box of regressions.

After a rather subdued dinner, the Girls departed to meet up with their friends in the village. As the five adults sat around a roaring log fire, contentedly full, with glasses of wine in their hands, Gerry proposed a toast.

"To our friend, Suzanne. May she rest in peace and may we, her only family, with God's blessing, be able to put to an end that devil the Count/Man in Black, on her behalf."

"I'll get some coffee," said Meg. "Then I suggest we each in turn, relate what we know of and from Suzanne and try to come to a decision as to what our next steps should be."

Chapter 6

They all knew the details of Michael's regressions, but Meg was able to tell what she knew and feelings she had received, from her friend.

"She was a very private person and an extremely conscientious journalist. She would investigate to the last item, before allowing anything to be put in print. I must confess, I was surprised when she returned so quickly after going to Switzerland, to research the Gelbergers and that Convent of the Golden Orb. It wasn't like Suzanne to chicken out, she was obviously very scared by that Count character. She was extremely serious but good for a laugh when she relaxed. When she helped out at the last Garden Party at the Rectory, she ran a book stall and sold all but three of them. Then insisted on putting the price of those three in the pot herself. When Suzanne stayed at the Rectory, she had your room, Boris, and left it as neat as a new pin. Her past: only that she was divorced, childless, lived alone and worked as much as possible 24/7. Other than that, I knew she worked for your magazine, Boris, *International Viewpoint*, I read it myself. Also of course, that the box of regressions was left to her by Michael Deville. Would you like to go next, Boris?"

"Not quite, thank you, Meg. I want to get some times and dates from my computer first if you will kindly excuse me. I probably know what Gerry has to say though, so perhaps while I check things, he might like to continue."

Whilst Boris retired to his room to check a few details, Gerry continued with what he had been involved in over the years they had known her. "I felt I had known Suzanne all my life," he said. "Or maybe in a past life because I now fully believe in the reincarnation theory. I do not however, wish to indulge in regression and will definitely *not* ever allow myself to be hypnotised."

Roland interrupted here. "Gerry, I have only lately become aware of your surname. Cameron, is it not?"

"Oh! You're wondering if there's a family connection between me and the James Cameron, in Michael's regressions. Well actually, yes. When I heard about his father's occupation of this very parish, I naturally looked into my genealogy. The connection is somewhat remote, but it appears that I'm a distant relation of a brother of James' father. Apparently, Ernest Cameron was anti-religion and brought his children up in the same fashion. Nevertheless, one of his sons married the daughter of a local vicar and one of their sons entered the church himself. That would have been my grandfather. My father was an insurance broker but I wanted to enter the church. So, my friends, here I am, vicar of St Patricks like a Cameron before me but one of the twenty-first century, where things are completely different from those days. Where's that coffee, Meg, and is there some chocolate cake?"

"Please, excuse me," interrupted Bart. "I will go and see what Boris is up to." He knew his cousin well and this long absence was unusual. He knocked the door and walked straight in. Boris was laying on the bed, his eyes red and face full of dejection and misery.

"It's all my fault," he said, voice breaking. "I was the one who sent her there, I even paid for the trip as a holiday, but I knew, in all honesty hoped, she wouldn't be able to let the matter rest. *I practically killed her myself.*" He broke down completely now and Bart sat on the bed, patting his shoulder and trying to comfort the distraught man.

"I loved her, have done almost since I first met her. She was so enthusiastic in whatever she did, and I thought that if she could close the only thing she'd ever retreated from, to my knowledge, she might—well, come to relax a bit and maybe fall in love with me too. No, that's not completely true, Bart, I know she was very fond of me. I was going to ask her to marry me when she got back. Now, she's gone forever." His voice broke again. Then Boris sat up, shook his head and swung himself off the bed. Standing, he stretched his arms above his head. "This is not good enough, I loved her, I sent her to those damned mountains, therefore I am to blame and must be the one to avenge her death.

I'm going to have a shower now, tell them I have a steaming headache or something, and am going to bed. Tomorrow is our final day here, so we must talk together and make plans for what is to be done before you and I return to Switzerland. Okay cousin, Bart?"

They shook hands, then relenting had a man-hug and Bart left, to return to the others and the cosy fire.

~~

Meg looked up as Bart entered, "Is he, okay?" she said.

"Not really, he blames himself for her death, because he arranged for the holiday trip, knowing full well that she would not be able to resist looking into what had happened before. No, no." Bart raised his hand to silence the protests. "I know Boris and he probably knew Suzanne better than any of us. He loved her and was going to ask her to marry him when she returned. How she felt about him, I do not know. But that is beside the point. What we have to do now, is form some plan to continue her investigation. We must leave your superb hospitality on Monday and return to our individual lives. Boris intends to fly to Switzerland with me, in an endeavour to continue where Suzanne left off, which is fine as he can stay in the gatehouse cottage. However, after the morning service tomorrow, perhaps we could all sit down and devise some sort of plan."

The others agreed to go their separate ways to bed and each think of what might be useful. Whatever they agreed, the important thing was that at all times they should be aware of what each of them was doing, so far as the investigation was concerned. They also agreed that they should plan to never make an investigation alone but work in pairs, whenever possible. In other words, endeavour to cover each other's backs and avoid any future potential intervention or accidents.

Chapter 7

Boris and Bart attended the morning service the following day but Roland was not feeling too good and Meg insisted that he stay in bed.

Once again Bart was surprised to see so many in the congregation, Gerry was obviously an extremely popular figure in the community, and he could see that with a wife like Meg by his side, it was inevitable. There was none of the serious droning that throughout his childhood, had turned Bart from religion. The younger children were in the vestry, where two ladies kept an eye on them, reading stories with a biblical aspect but without the old fashioned, rather boring way of telling. During some of the hymns, the children would join in, their young voices sounding like those of distant angels. The sermon Gerry gave was both apt and relatively short, the prayers sincere and the hymns joyful.

Meanwhile, the invisible vaporous mist had been released and was flitting up and down the pews, sometimes touching and remaining on a person, other times just touching and travelling onwards. No one saw, no one noticed. The service ended and refreshments were served at the rear of the church, with tea or coffee for the adults and fruit juice or fizzy lemonade for the children. The local Women's Group provided homemade cakes and the sense of friendship and camaraderie was evident. It had been an experience that Bart, to his own surprise, declared he would be delighted to repeat.

The Girls had returned to university by train, early Sunday morning and after lunch, the five friends sat down for a final discussion.

Boris was indeed intending to return to Switzerland with Bart, making it necessary to travel first to his home, in the flat above the magazine offices. He needed not only to pack for what he described as an indefinite stay in the mountains, but to gather together all the information he and Suzanne had accumulated, regarding the Henri de Ville regression.

Meanwhile, they would all go through the information they had managed to find out about the Cameron family. They hoped that by combining their knowledge, the connection would become more apparent, particularly, as Roland pointed out, Maurice Cameron had apparently married one Margaret de Ville.

They all agreed however, that there was a definite link between Michael Deville via the Cameron's and the de Ville's. Also, it appeared that St Patricks tied everything together in some way. But where on earth did the Man in Black or Henri de Ville's Papa Count, come into the picture? That was something they had to work out if that evil character was to be ultimately destroyed.

Roland was also to return to the university but as he was still feeling a bit under the weather, as he put it, had accepted Meg's invitation to stay until the following day. He tried to shake the shivery headache off, saying that it was only stress from the previous few days but had to confess that he had a head full of cotton wool. Meg insisted that he needed to rest and have someone look after him for at least another day, so it was, with more relief than he would have admitted, that Roland once again retired to his bed. So, saying farewell to Boris and Bart, he retreated once more to his room.

Little did they realise that this was indeed farewell, and they would not see Roly-Poly Roland again.

Chapter 8

The two cousins arrived back at Boris' flat above the shop, as he put it, just as the clock in St Thomas' Church chimed mid-day. Lymington was not exactly over brimming with visitors, which was something that happened every Saturday, when the whole of the main street was opened to market stalls, selling just about everything one could imagine.

"When the street is empty like this, it's hard to imagine Lymington High Street full of stalls and people. The colour and the noise. Suzanne loved it." Boris was silent for a moment. "She sort of came alive with the people all around her, would talk to the stall holders and visitors. But she was still in her own sort of bubble, as though it was all a story, that she was part of before she wrote it down. I was with her though and she came out of that bubble when she was with me."

"Okay Boris, my friend, even more reason for us to get a flight booked for Switzerland. I suggest we try and find one for some time Wednesday. It is late now, so I suggest we should go to the local pub for a meal and then try to get a decent night's rest. Oh, by the way, will you not have to arrange for someone to cover for you at the *International Viewpoint*, for an indefinite time?"

"I must confess that had slipped my mind, thanks for the reminder, Bart."

Boris picked up his phone, went into the sitting room and sat at the table overlooking Lymington Harbour, where he dialled the number of his head of editorial, Paul Holiday. "Paul? Boris here, I need a big favour from you."

"Yeah!" Paul replied. "What is it this time? You want several months off and yours truly to manage everything for you at the magazine."

"I always knew you were a bit of a clairvoyant, Paul, old chap. Yes, that's exactly what I want. Abigail, the magazine's infallible secretary, knows what's what, so all you'll have to do is to ensure things are signed off properly. Of course, printing will need an eye kept on it too, but old Pete is dependable and just needs the odd word of encouragement from time to time. All things legal, Abigail knows who to contact, those solicitors Vizard and Thomas in the High

Street near St Thomas's. You have my mobile number and please feel free to ring me if anything unusual crops up. I shall be in Switzerland, staying with my cousin in Billenbach."

"That's where Suzanne died, wasn't it? I might have known you wouldn't be able to resist investigating that rather suspicious occurrence. Fine, Boris, you know I'll do all I can to help, so don't you worry about *International Viewpoint*, nothing will change, and we'll publish as usual."

They said their goodbyes and Boris said, "What are we waiting for, I'm hungry." He took Bart to the Ship Inn, where after a delicious meal, with a bottle of wine, they returned home. Once there, Boris insisted they have one glass of his best brandy, before retiring for the night.

The following morning, Bart was introduced to the members of staff he had not previously met at the funeral and shown the workings of a modern magazine. Then excusing himself, he returned to the flat and booked the first available seats for the Swiss flight the next day, on his laptop. Then leaving Boris to finalise business at work, he set out to explore the area. There were several small coffee shops in Lymington and Bart discovered they also sold excellent homemade fruit cake, which after partaking, he thought *to hell with the weight* and ordered another slice, this time a rich chocolate concoction.

That evening the two men ate at a restaurant in the High Street, returned to the flat, made sure everything was packed for an early start the next morning and went to bed.

Part II

Chapter 9

It had been a long day; the flight was a good one but the journey from the airport was somewhat arduous. Bart hired a car and they drove for six hours before reaching Billenbach, stopping only once to fill the car and have a much-needed meal, with several cups of coffee, to help them stay awake. Eventually, arriving at the gatehouse, they simply unloaded their luggage, showered and fell into bed. Unfortunately, for Boris, he was obliged to make up the guest room bed, before falling into it with a sigh of relief.

When Boris woke after nine o'clock the next day, the first thing he remembered, was that he had not put his watch forward an hour, so it was in fact ten, not nine o'clock. How on earth did he manage to sleep so long? The second thing was the silence and he wondered if Bart had also overslept.

However, the aroma of freshly brewed coffee finally drew him from the warmth of a high-tog duvet. He quickly showered and dressed, then descended the stairs into the living space below. Bart was not there but he had left a note on the table, informing Boris that an early morning run had called him, and he would be going up the mountain to the hotel. Back in about an hour, he wrote, giving no indication of what time he left.

Boris poured himself a mug of coffee, which like Suzanne, he preferred black and strong. Then he foraged in the fridge and found the ingredients for a good old fry-up. By this time, it was 10.45 am. *Can't be much longer,* he thought, putting a small amount of oil in the pan and standing it on the AGA, to gently heat through.

Ten minutes later, Bart panted into the room, grabbed a hand towel and wiped the perspiration from his face. "Great!" he said, as Boris added bacon and mushrooms to the now hot oil. "Give me five minutes to shower and change, then I'll be ready for some of that. Did you find bread in the freezer? I like two fried slices with the eggs sunny side up, on them."

Boris waved two hands at him. "Go," he said. "Five minutes or it'll be over-cooked."

Over breakfast, they discussed the things they might need, for a possible two-day trek up the mountain and through the caves that were now closed to tourists.

"After breakfast," Bart said, "we will take a stroll through the woods, to the back of the hotel. From there, I will show you the pathway taken to the clifftop by Isabella de Ville and Susan Blessed, so you will know what to expect."

~~

Through the lower field and the woods, was a stiff climb. Bart, who was used to the steep pathway to the hotel, over which it was his habit to run on a daily basis, was hardly out of breath. On the other hand, Boris was used to spending a great deal of his time sitting behind a desk, his idea of exercise being, dashing around the office or walking to his local pub in the evening, for a meal. He was therefore, considerably out of breath by the time they reached the grounds at the rear of Hotel Orb de L'Or.

"For goodness' sake, cousin, before you return to England, I will make sure you are in a better state of health. Every day, you shall exercise and eventually you will be running up that path with me. We will even race. Though," he paused, "I suspect that even though I am older than you by nearly ten years, I will still be able to beat you."

"That's a challenge I look forward to," Boris panted.

"Well, if you have got your breath back, see that winding path going through the grounds and into the mountain ahead."

"What, that narrow track?" said Boris with a look of obvious reservations.

"Yes," his cousin replied. "That is the path taken by the two ladies back in the seventeenth century. It is known as the Serpent's Tail, the reason for which you will understand when we reach the top. See those giant rocks that look as though they are hanging over the side of the mountain, with two pine trees behind them, well that is where the Serpent's Tail will take us. I confess I have not climbed that track since just before I leased the gatehouse. That one experience taught me a lesson; that I am not a Superman.

Come, let us return to the cottage. We have much to prepare before we attempt the climb up the mountain and our exploration of the caves, following the same route as the Gelbergers. Although," he added, "there may well have been some rockfalls and other obstructions since they rescued the two ladies."

Bart gathered together a couple of sleeping bags, extra sweaters in case they were needed and fresh sets of underclothes and socks, for the same reason. Boris meanwhile, made sandwiches and soup that he put into two insulated flasks.

In two similar vessels, he poured coffee. Then, being Boris, he added a copious amount of individually wrapped chocolate biscuits. These he packed tidily in the two back-packs that Bart provided, together with four litres each of water.

"Should I add a couple of bottles of wine?" he asked, but the only reply he received, was a dirty look from his cousin.

"Tomorrow will be an exhausting day, so I suggest we eat now and retire to bed. Who knows if or when, we shall sleep in comfortable beds once more?"

Chapter 10

"Make sure you have water to hand as we climb and energy bars, for you will be both thirsty and in need of all the energy you can muster."

Bart ticked his checklist and Boris added litre bottles of water to their pockets, together with the suggested energy bars, three each in the opposite pockets of their anoraks. Then, finally locking the door as they left, Bart led the way towards the path they had taken the previous day.

~~

As the two men climbed the narrow entrance to the Serpent's Tail, it was as though they entered another world. Although they were going upwards towards the heavens, it was as though they had stepped onto the entrance to hell. The track was so narrow, Boris brushed either side against the rocks, as he climbed gingerly forward. As they climbed higher, there was the constant roar of a vast waterfall ahead of them, making it impossible to hold any conversation. This torrent of glacier water melt seemed to leap free from its frozen state, gleaming as it curved downwards over a thousand feet of mountain, pulled by gravity into what had become known as the Devil's Eye. This was a large crevice shaped like that of an eye, into which the water disappeared, falling within the caves, where it finally became one with the Bottomless Pool, within the main cavern.

Boris thought, *the pool must indeed be bottomless, for surely with the constant water filling, it would have overflowed. Did it reach the domain of hell? Perhaps*!

As Bart and Boris climbed, the twisting tail of the Serpent, it widened. This however, did in no way make their journey any easier, as rocks and rubble were strewn about, to be scrambled over or squeezed around. Finally, after negotiating the largest rock yet encountered, the two men found themselves on a small plateau.

"It must have been easier in Isabella's day," Boris commented.

"Certainly; do not forget that was over four-hundred years ago." Bart replied. "Incidentally, you do not appear to be so puffed. Perhaps, you are already getting stronger, although I find it strange. I would have expected you to be in a worse condition as we climbed higher. Thinner air," he explained.

"Pleased to have impressed you, old chap, but can we sit under those trees for a while and drink some water? Have you noticed that the noise of the waterfall is less up here, although we are closer to it. I imagine that would be because we were enclosed and it worked like a wind tunnel, with noise rather than wind."

They sat under the trees, feasting on sandwiches provided by the helpful Boris and drinking some of their water. Then moving carefully to the edge of the cliff, lay down on their stomachs and peered over, from which they could see a ledge, some two hundred feet below.

"The sun is beginning to set," Bart said, "and I want to abseil down to that ledge whilst there is still some daylight. Once we are down there, we can set up camp in the cave."

He tied one end of a rope he'd been carrying over his shoulder, to one of the pines and fixing it round his waist, swung over the edge of the cliff. When he landed on the ledge, he freed the rope and pulled on it three times. Boris retrieved it, following Bart's example and with less dexterity, abseiled down the cliff to join him.

The cave entrance was easily found but was blocked by an earlier fall of rock. It took them half an hour to clear enough space to enter and darkness had all but fallen by the time they had finished. Both men had already switched on their head-torches and now withdrew torches from their backpacks and found a place to set up their camp for the night.

They were protected from the outside chill but nevertheless, it was cold within the cave. However, Bart soon organised the camping stove, set a pan of water on it to boil and soon they were sipping hot packeted soup with ham sandwiches. "The flasks may be useful later, if we are unable to get the stove going," he said. After the meal, they settled down in the comparative comfort of their sleeping bags, with mugs of tea. Having made sure everything was tidily stashed, Bart and Boris lit a candle, extinguishing their torches, and settled down for the night.

Chapter 11

Boris woke up shivering in his sleeping bag and curled up, trying to find some warmth. He switched on his torch and looking at his watch, saw that it was six o'clock. Light was filtering through the narrow opening into the cave but it was a grey misty rain outside and seemed to make their shelter appear smaller. It was as though during the night, the walls had shrunk inwards, leaving only the two sleepers, with their belongings and one guttering candle between them.

"Are you awake, Bart? It's bloody well freezing in here."

"Yes. I too am chilled to the bone." Bart replied. "I will get the stove going for a hot drink, then we will eat a little and move to the next part of this exploration."

It was their intention to progress downwards, through the complex cave system, hopefully by the same route as Isabella de Ville had been led, some four-hundred years ago. Both of them, having put on an extra sweater and another pair of socks under their climbing boots, donned their backpacks and head torches, to commence their descent towards the waterfall.

Boris had managed to draw a rough map of the caves, which he devised from the various documents he had procured, via Suzanne's first visit to the Hotel Orb de l'Or, so they, hopefully, had some sort of guide as to which tunnels and passageways to traverse. However, four-hundred years is a very long time and during that period, there would have been many rock falls and general disturbances within the cave system.

On entering the tunnel, Bart and Boris both swung their hand torches ahead, to check a reasonably clear way. Then shining them on the walls, they drew surprised breaths.

"So, this is why the Count could not enter the caves," Boris said.

On either side, reaching to the roof where they touched, were carved Christian crosses. The cross beams, each about two metres across, also touched. Shining their torches further along the walls were another four such crosses, forming a Christian archway of six crosses all meeting at the centre of the mountain-roof. On the floor from the tunnel entrance was carved yet another cross. This time, the crossbeam joined the bottom of the first two crosses carved into the walls. The main long beam stretched from the actual entrance all the way to crosses five and six, to where their cross-struts ended.

"Do you suppose Josh Gelberger carved these, knowing the Count had to be kept out?" Boris wondered.

"Possibly, or maybe his father. It could have been Father and Son together, or even earlier Gelbergers back in the thirteenth century. Perhaps, that was why the Count's castle became a nunnery, in an effort to win back that obsessive control."

"Well, in that he nearly succeeded, but good overcame evil. Anyway," Bart continued, "there is no doubt that devil is trying to make a comeback and you and I have set ourselves up to stop him once and for all. So, forward my friend, we will proceed through the Christian Tunnel, as it shall be known. Are you ready?"

"Yes," was Boris' single reply.

The first of the expected rock falls occurred half an hour later, as they made their way down the tunnel leading from the entrance. A fall of rocks blocked the narrow path from side to side and almost to the top, from where they had fallen.

"Shit! What do we do now?" Boris said.

"Well, as I am so much fitter than you, I suppose I must be the one to scramble to the top," Bart said. "I will see what lies on the other side and try to clear a way for us to get over this infernal blockage."

So, saying, he removed his backpack and tentatively made his way towards the top of the pile of rocks, sending a few crashing downwards, making Boris retreat, dragging Bart's pack with him.

"Do not worry, cousin, they are only a few stones," Bart shouted, clambering still higher.

"Ahh!" Reaching the top, Bart could see beyond, a clear pathway. It would be easy to dislodge a few rocks, allowing them to drop to the far side, then there would be enough room to scramble, albeit with a little difficulty, over and onwards. He began moving the stones he could handle and after twenty minutes or so made his way partly back down.

"Right. Pass me my backpack and then yours. I will get them through the gap I have made and then follow them. When I call, you are to follow me. Okay?"

"Looks a bit dangerous to me, can we do it?" Boris was sounding as though the only thing he wanted to do was to return the way they had come and to the comfort of the cottage. He was not by nature, an adventurous or agile man. Then shaking himself, reiterated his declaration that he should be the one to avenge the death of Suzanne. "Go ahead, cousin, I'm right behind you." He passed the two backpacks up to Bart, who lifted first one then the other to the rim of the gap.

He is right, thought Bart. *It is very dangerous, and this is only the beginning.*

Reaching the top, Bart shoved the two bags over the edge to the far side and squirming round so he was feet first, slid, grabbing jutting rocks where he could, to join them.

"Are you ready, Boris? When you get to the top, make sure you turn so you come through feet first, like I did. I will be here to help you down."

Boris grunted his reply and carefully made the 10 feet ascent to the top. Having reached it, he looked through the gap, immediately feeling a surge of vertigo.

"Come on, man, turn yourself round and do not look down." Bart commanded.

Gingerly, Boris wriggled around, getting his feet through the gap and feeling with them for a foothold. Not an easy exercise, he discovered. He wriggled backwards a little more, which was when he stuck. Boris was not the wiry build of Bart and carried a deal more weight. He struggled but became only more stuck.

"Calm down, my friend." The relaxed voice of Bart, drove some of the fear from Boris (just a very little). "Now, move yourself forward again and remove your anorak. Then reverse again and drag the coat with you, that should give you enough room to squirm through." He put on the commanding voice again. "Come on, Boris, we do not have all of the day to mess around."

That had the effect required and Boris eventually managed to remove his coat. Then dragging it behind him, wriggled and squirmed his way through the small gap. Still gripping his coat, Boris slid practically all the way down the other side, where Bart finally caught him. He sat for a while with his back to the rocks, gulping the water Bart handed him. Then, they ate the last of their sandwiches and finished the now cooling coffee. Once again, putting on their coats and backpacks, the two men continued on their way.

Chapter 12

At the end of the tunnel were two more, one to the left, the other right. They debated for a while and decided to take the right-hand one, on the grounds that one should always take the *right* path through life. It was steep and slippery, with five paths leading from it, three on one side and two the other. The men stuck to the main path however, which led quite steeply downwards, and after walking for three quarters of an hour, found their way simply came to an end. They were up against solid mountain.

"It's tempting to try the side paths," Bart said.

"No. I now recall reading somewhere in Suzanne's notes, that whatever, one should always take the left-hand path, being the non-obvious one," Boris said apologetically, after a long silence.

"Oh well, back up we go then." Bart replied. "It will be more difficult going upwards, with such a slippery surface, it will surely take us longer."

"Yes, probably. One step forward two slides back. That chap Murphy has a lot to answer for," said Boris.

"Murphy? Who is this person?" Bart asked.

"Haven't you heard of Murphy's Law? No, of course, you haven't. Too much to explain now, ask me when we get home again."

It took them a full hour to retrace their steps, so they sat for half an hour, drinking water, eating energy bars and trying to foresee what the next obstacle would be.

~~

The left-hand path was less slippery but more rock strewn. However, they were able to help each other and only once had to remove their backpacks, carrying them to their sides to crabwalk for some hundred feet, where the tunnel narrowed.

"Much more of this and my stomach will be as flat as yours," Boris said. To which Bart responded with a chuckle.

Eventually, at the end was a wide ledge and a drop of about 8 feet, into a large cavern filled with stalactites and stalagmites, that shone and sparkled in the light of their head torches.

Boris fished for his hand torch and the rough map in his backpack, laying it on the ledge so they could both see it clearly.

"Looks like we've made it this time," Boris said. "It looks as though there is a tunnel the other side of this cave that leads to the Great Cavern of the Devil's Eye. That must mean that we are near to the waterfall cave."

Bart agreed and without more ado, gripped the edge of the ledge, swung himself over and down onto the floor, which they now named the Cathedral Cavern, followed this time, with determination, by Boris. The cavern was reminiscent of a great cathedral built in the thirteenth century. At one end was a great slab of rock not unlike an altar, above it a stalactite, which had spread over the top like a glistening cloth, draping down to the ground beneath it. Stalagmites stretched across the width and breadth before it, like a huge congregation, with stalactites appearing from the impenetrable heights, resembling so many hanging light fittings. What could be seen of the walls, was a mountainous rock surface with dark fissures, that could be entrances to more tunnels. However, the tunnel marked on the map, appeared to be directly opposite the ledge from which the two men had entered, so they made their way through, what they now thought of as the congregation. This entailed a convoluted twisting passage and they arrived nearer to the right-hand side of the wall than the middle. As they made their way back along the wall, many openings appeared.

"Which one can it be?" Boris wondered.

"I cannot say but would suggest we take note of the number of exits, as we walk the full length. By this means, we can make our choice of the one we are seeking."

They agreed this was the most sensible solution and having arrived at the altar wall, had counted no less than seven openings.

"So, as we return, the entrance we require will be number four," Boris concluded.

This tunnel, although sloping steeply downwards, was not slippery, being littered with small, crumbled rocks and although the passageway was considerably longer than the others they had traversed, they made their way to the other end in just over thirty minutes.

The men had expected to enter the cavern containing the Devil's Eye above, with the Bottomless Pool below and to one side of the waterfall. However, they emerged behind the waterfall, so close that within seconds, they were soaked. Looking up, they could see the eye shape through which the roaring waterfall entered, but to look down was not a possibility, as it would be necessary to literally lean out over the ledge.

"What on earth do we do now?" Boris shouted to be heard.

"Let us sit back in the tunnel where it is a little quieter, to discuss this problem," Bart shouted back.

They retreated 10 feet or so, sat down, drinking hot soup from their flasks followed by chocolate bars. As they ate, they talked over a plan to, as safely as possible, cross behind the thundering waterfall. The ledge, which it was necessary to circumnavigate, appeared to be no more than two feet wide and in places looked even less. They were aware that it would inevitably be slippery and that more people had met their deaths, since Henri de Ville's in the seventeenth century. This was what, after the death of two students a mere two years ago, had led to that part of the caves being permanently closed to climbers and visitors.

"Did you notice that big rock jutting out, just before the opening behind the waterfall, to the left of the tunnel?" Bart enquired.

"Yes, I used it to help me nearer that narrow ledge."

"That is correct, my friend. I suggest we attach a rope firmly round it and the other end around the waists of both of us, about 6 feet apart. That means, if one of us should lose his footing, the other has a chance of holding him. If that should fail and both of us drop over the edge, the rock will have us firmly tied to it, giving us a chance to fight our way back up."

Boris was not keen on this but having no better plan to offer, agreed. This time however, being near to the end of their perilous journey, it was decided to leave their back packs in the tunnel. So, each placing the last of their energy bars and the remains of bottled water in the pockets of their coats, made their already soaking and shivering way back to the ledge. Bart tied the rope round the chosen rock, being better trained at tying knots than his cousin, then linked Boris and himself together. He tried the strength of the knots, then with Boris behind him, slid crabwise and facing the cliff-face, onto the narrow ledge.

"Keep close and feel for handholds where possible, follow my lead. And, Boris, do not look down. Good luck." He bellowed above the roar of the falling cascade and began the treacherous crabwalk to his left, behind the torrential waterfall, which sounded as though it roared at them in anger.

An experienced climber, Bart navigated the ledge with reasonable dexterity. Boris slipped at one narrow point but was grabbed and held firmly by the other man. Eventually, they arrived at the side of the waterfall and saw with relief, a pathway down into the lighted cavern below.

The two men made their way as silently as possible to the entrance of the caves, which was now still closed, following the drowning of Suzanne. This was achieved by a rope on which was threaded the notice, hanging across the entrance.

"Just one moment, please," said Boris. "I need to take a photo of the pool." He fished his phone from a pocket deep inside his apparel and stood, where it was assumed, Suzanne had previously. Then turned it upwards, to photograph the waterfall in all its glory as it surged into the cavern, through the Devil's Eye. A moment of dizziness engulfed him, and he sank abruptly down, onto the rock on which he was standing. As he did so, something caught his eye in a crevice. He tried to recover whatever it was, felt that it was important to do so.

"Do you have anything fairly slim in your pockets, Bart, a screwdriver perhaps? There's something caught here, might be important."

"Will this old ballpen do?" He said, handing the object to Boris.

It just fitted into the crack and Boris was able to lever the thing that had attracted his attention, free. It was a mobile phone.

"If I'm not mistaken, I believe this will turn out to be Suzanne's, that they said had been lost in the pool. This might be the clue we were looking for."

They silently moved towards the entrance to the caves, checking that no one could observe them leaving and as discreetly as possible made their way round the outside of the car park. A half hour later, they were in the gatehouse cottage once more. Both immediately, gratefully stripping off their wet clothing and taking turns in the shower, at the very hottest bearable temperature.

Chapter 13

The two men were too tired to discuss the events of the past thirty-six hours, so after several cups of strong coffee and eating some soup with crispy bread, they toasted each other with a glass of Bart's excellent brandy and retired for much-needed sleep.

It was nearly mid-day when Boris awoke, to find Bart standing before the AGA, with a delicious aroma of fried breakfast simmering before him.

"Have you been for your morning run?" Boris asked.

Bart frowned. "No. Have you just woken up? I must confess I was only about fifteen minutes ahead of you. We had a very busy time, and both needed a well-earned, rest. Today, I shall skip the run and after breakfast, which incidentally is nearly ready, suggest we go over yesterday's findings. I have already nearly dried out the mobile phone, so hopefully we shall be able to see whatever is on the thing."

"How'd you manage that, did you leave it in the AGA oven overnight?"

Bart gave him a disgusted look. "I was trying to dry the thing out not cook it. Even you must realise the damage that could be caused…"

Boris interrupted. "I was joking. I imagine you left it somewhere above the AGA, so it could dry out as naturally as possible."

"Hmmm." Bart only slightly mollified, removed two hot plates from the oven and loaded the contents from the frying pan onto them, saying, "The least you can do is set the table."

Being well nourished and just a little guilty for his earlier comments, Boris carried the plates and cutlery to the sink, washed and dried them. Then all being tidy again, he refilled two coffee mugs and they sat at the table again with the hopefully dry, mobile phone before them. But the screen was blank.

"Damn," they said in unison.

"Have you got a charger Bart?"

"Of course," was the reply, as he rummaged in a desk drawer for the necessary piece of equipment. "I must have been inordinately remiss to omit the obvious. However, what did you think of the crosses at the entrance?"

"Well, it seems pretty obvious that they were carved there, in hope of denying entrance to the evil one. Did you notice other carvings in the walls of that tunnel, also the one leading to the waterfall? I took photos of as many as possible. Some were obviously from eons ago, back in the time of cave dwellers. There were Mammoths and Sabre-tooth Tigers, among others of stick people with long spears of wood, sharpened to a point at one end."

"I saw some carvings on the other side of that rock fall, which you had so much difficulty surmounting." With a grin, removing any cynicism, Bart said, "You may find it easier today, however, as I am sure all that exercise will have reduced your stomach. However," he continued, "the breakfast you have just eaten may reverse that slight advantage."

"Fine," Boris replied, "I have no intention of repeating that adventure again. Anyway, did you not notice the carvings? There was a Christ figure on the left-hand side, complete with halo."

"I was so busy trying to get to the next stage of our journey, that I confess I paid little attention as to what might be on the walls, the pathway was my sole concern at that time. When we took that right-hand tunnel, I believe, there were some carvings such as you describe but again, I fear I did not pay them much attention. My concern was for us to return as speedily as possible, not to get lost in that mountain."

"You are right, cousin, but at the far end of the rock-fall tunnel, there were crosses engraved on either side, plus one overhead. They were smaller than those at the entrance but might still serve to prevent access to those not of a Christian inclination. The cave-dweller drawings were in the right-hand tunnel, and I did manage to photograph some of those. However, I had no time to photograph any engravings on the wall of the left-hand tunnel as it was easier to negotiate and we covered it with alacrity, but my impression was, of much more recent carvings, and they were definitely more of a Christian nature."

"So, Boris, you are saying that those carvings in the tunnel leading to the back of the waterfall, were sculpted to make it impenetrable to the evil one."

"Yes. I'm pretty sure of it. They looked newer, not having had time to age like the others. Perhaps, the Gelbergers of the twentieth century did them, before the system above the waterfall was closed. I suggest we plan to talk to that family in the near future."

"There may have been recent carvings on or above that ledge behind the waterfall, but the torrent would have obliterated it. Whatever the case may be nowadays, remember that the Count would or could not enter from the clifftop in the days of Henri de Ville."

Time had seemed to race by, and Bart decided it was time to start preparing their evening meal. "We have missed lunch but eaten a late breakfast, Boris, my friend, so now I will prepare our food for dinner. Perhaps, you could check the mobile phone, to see if we can gain any useful information concerning the death of our cherished Suzanne."

"Okay, I'll do that but if it is working, I won't go into the contents until we can sit down together, over a glass of that fine red wine you have. Shall I fetch a bottle from your cellar?"

~~

Darkness had fallen by the time the two men could concentrate on the contents of the phone, which had belonged to Suzanne. Boris switched it on and having gone through the various emails, tried perusing the Apps for photography, which was where he discovered a video.

"We need to connect this to my computer," said Bart. "We shall get a clearer view."

Pulling one of the chairs over to his desk for Boris, he sat before the computer, plugging the USB lead, to the phone, they continued to watch whilst listening. The voice was somewhat faint and difficult to understand but it was definitely Suzanne, with the voice of a man speaking in the background, presumably that of the tour guide.

I have decided to record my impressions of these caves (perhaps I am getting like Michael and feel the need to cover myself). Having passed the ticket box at the entrance, we entered a tunnel leading to the Great Cavern. On either side, there are carved a Celtic cross and above them, carved into the arch, are the words in Latin, DEUS CUSTODIAT TE, which if I remember correctly, translates to GOD PROTECT YOU. Now, why would someone have done that, do you suppose? Certainly, something to discuss with Gerry and Roly Poly, when next I speak to them. As we walk below that rather ominous sign, the silence encapsulates us and people whisper, as though entering a sacred place.

There was a click as the recorder was switched off, then another as Suzanne continued.

We are now in the cavern, no longer a silent place. The great waterfall gushes and roars, as though in a great rage, droplets rising from the pool, into which it seems to deposit its wrath. No wonder, they call it the Bottomless Pool, for all that water must go somewhere deep within the centre of the earth. The rest of the party have moved on, round the circumference of the Great Cavern, with Joshua, the tour guide, explaining and embellishing the undoubted beauty, of the stalagmites and stalactites that seem to fill it. I have hidden behind one of them, my intention being to photograph the entrance of the waterfall, known as the Devil's Eye. I don't know what, if any, information this might give me but can only try and hopefully, by listening to this recording later, might pick up something of real interest.

There is silence except for the torrential roar of the waterfall, but the video continues to film towards the Devil's Eye above, where the waterfall thunders through from the water melts of glaciers high in the mountains.

"Wait. What is that just above the top of the Eye?" Bart moved the video back. "There, do you see?"

"I think so." Boris moved forward, so he was more directly in front of the screen. "Yes. It's difficult to see but when you pause. Yes, I can just make out what looks like another of those crosses."

"Right, my friend, which is what I see also. I will note just where to return, so we can check again later. For now, it would appear that both entrances to the cave system and also that of the waterfall, are protected by Christian crosses." Bart pressed the key, continuing the video.

I am now standing near the edge of the pool. It has been roped off for safety, but I can easily step over it, to get a picture that might give an idea of its depth. Hang on, surely, that can't be someone in the pool. Hey there, give me your hand and I'll try to pull you out. It's a young man, probably about early twenties, longish hair, good looking. He reminds me of Michael when I first met him. Oh dear! There's a young man in danger of drowning and here am I in journalistic mode, should be ashamed of yourself, Suzanne. Give me your hand, we can nearly reach. I'll have to put this phone down, might need both hands. No more filming but hopefully the recorder will still pick up.

The screen went black but indistinct voices could still be heard.

Come on, try and grip my hand so I can help you out
No, please no…he is…I can't…

Which was presumably, the voice of the young man Suzanne was endeavouring to rescue. There was a scream, then all sound was obliterated by the noise of the waterfall. Then a mellifluous voice that bearing what they knew about him, could only belong to the Count.

Ah, my dear, I have you. Now, you shall be the carrier of my Revenge Mist, into a world that thought to reject the powers of the Master. My punishment to all those I despise and those for whom I care nothing…

The next voice they heard, was the tour guide shouting for two men to come and help him, then complete silence.

"They must have unknowingly, pushed the phone into that crevice when dragging Suzanne from the pool and it was only by luck that you noticed it."

"Maybe," Boris replied. "Or perhaps the God in whom we both believe, was guiding our progress and protecting us, during our journey."

"Hmm! That is a reasonable decision, for we met some dangerous situations during that expedition and here we are, still alive and also with the mobile phone of Suzanne. That in itself, gives us evidence of her unfortunate demise."

"I've been thinking—no don't say it, I know that's a dangerous pastime. But seriously, Bart. You remember how Henri de Ville died, slipping off the ledge behind the waterfall, into the Bottomless Pool, whilst at home, Michael Deville died whilst clutching the box of final records, that he had compiled for Suzanne?"

Bart nodded.

"Well, man, think. The Count, or whatever that devil is called, can't get into the cave system, but his son actually died in there. One so evil and deeply involved in the occult for millennia, could have raised Henri for the very purpose of killing Suzanne, the one person to know the real truth of Michael's regressions. She was probably the only one, with the courage and determination to pursue him and endeavour to totally remove the influence he has enjoyed for over a thousand years. Also, the one person to totally reject and turn her back on him, walking away from him too. Can you imagine the rage of such a being, his chance of corrupting her, making her his to obey? I would put money on it, cousin."

"I agree, let us contact Gerry and Meg at the rectory to discuss our next steps."

Part III

Chapter 14

"Oh, Boris." Meg was sobbing as she answered the phone.

He heard Gerry in the background say, "Come on, love, let me talk to him," and after a short while Gerry's voice, "sit down, Meg, don't take on so."

"What on earth's the matter?" Boris asked.

"You haven't heard then? No, obviously not. Roland is dead."

"Dead! What was it, a heart attack?"

"No, much worse. It seems as though he had some weird disease, that the specialists are unable to name at the moment. But it appears to be spread rather like a cold, like getting sneezed on, you remember, he was definitely under the weather when you left and although he stayed with us another night, he was determined to return to the university the next day. He caught the train during rush hour and was then showing signs of actually being worse than he was willing to let on. He was very careful to cover his face when sneezing, but I saw him outside, just before we left and as he sneezed it was like a mist coming from him."

"But is that what killed him?" Boris asked. He had put his phone on speaker, so that Bart could also hear what was said and he now put in a question.

"You are trying to tell us, that whatever he had was passed to others in the carriage, through this misty sneeze?"

"Not everyone. Apparently, it was mainly those over the age of fifty, younger folk didn't seem to be affected. However, we were contacted, as Roland had our number on his phone, so the police were able to read his messages and saw that he had stayed at the Rectory over the weekend. They sent someone round here and stayed outside the door, to tell us the news. We were advised to isolate ourselves for a couple of weeks, to see whether or not we might become infected too. Since then, several of the villagers who were in St Patricks on Sunday, have become ill and are under strict observation."

"But you feel well at the moment?"

"We're fine but Meg's distraught at the thought that the Girls might have picked up something."

"Gerry," Bart tried to comfort. "From what you have said, the younger generation would appear to be unaffected by this strange thing and I would imagine that if you were to be infected, it would have shown by now. Nevertheless, do please take the advice given and stay out of personal contact with other villagers. Above all, I would recommend that you close the church and put a notice on the door, with some excuse for having done so. Please do not enter it yourself or allow anyone else to do so. If either of you start sneezing, then isolate from one another."

Boris and Bart stared at each other. Both had reached a similar conclusion. Promising to keep in touch and to tell Gerry and Meg what they had discovered about the cave system, Boris rang off.

Chapter 15

"Quickly, turn on the TV News Channel." Boris said urgently.

Bart did so and to their dismay, they saw that not only was Britain affected but other countries had also apparently been hit by this strange disease. It was now being described as a virulent virus, which appeared to activate through mist or vapour, against which there appeared to be no antidote, as so far, it had been impossible to retrieve a sample.

In Switzerland, the popular tour guide and resident of Billenbach, Joshua Gelberger, had succumbed to the sneezing infection, but duly recovered from its affects. However, it was proving to be a very slow recovery. At first, it appeared that he was the youngest person to be infected, until it was discovered that one of the men who helped him retrieve Suzanne's body from the pool, was some five years younger, being only twenty-eight. Vilko Makinen was touring Switzerland with his friend Jouko Koskinen from Finland and returned to his homeland just five days after the tragic death of Suzanne Deville, in the caves at Billenbach. He felt unwell the day before their flight and attributed it to the commencement of a cold. Whilst passing through customs at the Helsinki Airport, Vilko collapsed and was taken to hospital. He was suffering from a strange virus, that the doctors were unable to diagnose and upon tracing his movements over the past two weeks, a trainee doctor linked him to others on the same tour, with similar symptoms. Jouko Koskinen was duly contacted and requested to go into an immediate two-week isolation, undergoing various tests during that period, at the end of which he showed a clean bill of health. Vilko made a full recovery and was discharged from hospital. However, he like Joshua Gelberger, did not fully regain his previous energy levels for several months.

The other young man who had helped Joshua recover Suzanne's body from the Bottomless Pool, was a Russian, Leonid Smirnoff. He developed what he referred to as a mild cold, which he was sure he caught on the flight back to Russia. He dealt with it as one usually does a cold, dosing himself appropriately and going to work every day. Other people in his workplace also contracted 'a cold'. Some of them became very ill and were diagnosed with the strange virus. All seemed to be affected in a similar way, but the effects were much worse for some. Those badly affected, appeared to be the older members of staff and whilst some made various degrees of recovery, others were hospitalised and out of twenty-five employees, seven passed away in great pain and discomfort, including Leonid Smirnoff. Staff at the hospital reported, that as the patient sneezed, the mist from his mouth and nostrils seemed to envelope him, appearing to contract and squeeze him to death. The hospital staff treating these patients were all fully instructed and provided with hazard gear.

This information was passed through the World Health Organisation to all hospital and medical practices worldwide.

Later, other passengers on the Russian flight, were taken ill. Mostly, they were in the upper age group. Around half of those infected, were hospitalised and 95% of those died, in similar circumstances to those of Leonid Smirnoff.

Also, three older members of the cave tour, had died before returning to their homes in France, Italy and Zambia.

Tricia, the woman who had sat next to Suzanne in the bus and identified her body when it was pulled from the pool, had returned home to Britain but was feeling unwell during the flight. On arrival at Gatwick, she had collapsed and been taken to hospital, where she was quarantined. She was in her late forties and was apparently in a stable condition. The authorities were checking flights taken by the remaining five tourists, to establish their wellbeing and that of others on those flights.

Meanwhile, other news was being broadcast concerning the effects of the virus, reported from Japan, China and parts of Africa. The speed with which it travelled was terrifying and governments throughout the world, were meeting with the World Health Organisation in an endeavour to find what exactly the virus was. Until this was achieved, there could be no way of finding a successful antidote.

Breaking News, informed Boris and Bart that Otto Jurg, the well-known medical examiner for the region, had also met his death by the virus, and two of his assistants were both hospitalised in quarantine, very ill, with little hope of full recovery.

In its infancy, this virus had spread worldwide in less than a month and showed no sign of retreating. The media had dubbed it with the name of the

MistVirus. It had also matured, from a mere sneeze-spray to a mist, that appeared from the mouth and nostrils of anyone infected. From that point, it developed into a snake-like mist, which in turn seemed to have the strength of a circular vice, which could envelope the infected and squeeze the life from them. Patients in hospitals were incubated in intensive care and treated by doctors and nurses securely encased in hazard-suits.

"I suggest we have our evening meal, then sleep before discussing this matter further." Bart switched off the television and going to the sink, washed his hands and started to prepare the food.

"Good idea, we're both too tired from our time in the caves and traumatised by the dreadful news, to be able to think straight. If you don't mind, I'll take a shower while you do the chef bit. See you later, unless of course, there is anything I can do to help." However, he already knew the answer to that one. He was no use whatsoever in the kitchen, except perhaps for washing up.

Chapter 16

The following morning, having watched more news regarding the strange virus, Bart and Boris sat down after breakfast, with steaming mugs of coffee. Boris's was strong and black, Bart's well sugared and creamed but they both needed the caffeine fix, for what would prove to be a very interesting day.

"Before we start, I think we should note the changes in the effects of the MistVirus thing, or perhaps we should call it the Count's Revenge. It seems to have first started with some sort of mist that came from Suzanne, after they pulled her from the water. The effects were rather like a bad attack of influenza but that has changed. Now, the worse cases seem to consist of serious sneezing. The vapour, mist or whatever, then appears to envelop the patients and apparently, according to what we have heard, proceed to squeeze them to death." Boris looked at his cousin, eyebrows raised, for comment.

"Good point, Boris, I do not understand why this should be, except perhaps as it spreads, the Count has more control over the way in which it works.

However, we need to consider first, what happened following the death of Suzanne. From your arrival at the airport, what happened thereafter in as implicit detail possible. Would you mind starting, Boris?"

"Certainly, my mind will need a bit of a nudge to recall exactly. Right. Gerry and I arrived at Gatwick Airport around two thirty, to meet your plane at three o'clock. Because you accompanied the coffin, you and Suzanne's remains were allowed to disembark before anyone else. Am I correct?"

Bart nodded his assent.

"Please then, you continue."

"Well, I was allowed off the plane, as you say and escorted to where you, Gerry and a hearse, were waiting to carry the remains to St Patricks. On arrival, the coffin was immediately taken into the church. Then Gerry locked the church doors and took us to the Rectory, where we were introduced to Meg and Roland and shown to our rooms. I don't know about you, but I freshened up and joined everyone else in the drawing room. Which was when Gerry suggested that we might like to hold a brief service and prayer for Suzanne, at the church." He paused, looking to Boris to continue.

"If you remember, we stood around the coffin, with Gerry at the head, Meg at the tail, you and I on one side and Roland the other. After the short service, Roland requested that the coffin be opened, to make sure it was in fact the body of Suzanne therein, to which we all agreed. Gerry returned to the Rectory, to obtain a screwdriver to open the coffin. As it was opened, Roland leaned over to check and the rest of us stood a little back. Correct?"

"Yes, yes, of course. Do go on, Boris."

"Think, cousin, think. Do you remember anything out of the ordinary? I have been considering this moment very seriously and have remembered something rather strange. Shut your eyes, Bart, and recall, as accurately as you can."

Bart did as he was bid, then…

"Yes, of course, that weird mist that rose from the opened coffin. Almost like condensation. I remember Roland wiping over his face with the sleeve of his coat, like clearing raindrops. I suppose we all saw it but being otherwise occupied, failed to notice or comment on it. Afterwards of course, it was completely obliterated from our minds. From mine anyway."

"Right. The mist or vapour, whatever it was, seemed to disappear but I suppose it was just out of sight out of mind."

"You're thinking about what we heard on Suzanne's mobile. About Suzanne carrying the Count's Revenge throughout the world."

"Yes. Do you recall Joshua, the tour guide, the men who helped him pull the body from the pool and turn it, also the woman Tricia? They were all in close contact with the body and if they were struck by the same spray as Roland, would prove my theory to be correct. Joshua lived and one of the young men is now dead, but Tricia is in hospital and expected to recover."

We should aim to question her as soon as possible. Perhaps, Gerry or Meg might be willing to do this as they are in Britain. We still have enquiries to make in Switzerland."

Bart continued. "The mist/vapour that we saw rising from the coffin, where did it disperse? Somewhere in the vicinity of the church, most definitely. Is that mist controlled by the Count through occult means perhaps? Is that what he has used to infect Roland and others in the church, at the service on Sunday? This to my mind is possible. However, to conclusions, we must not jump. Until it has been possible to question the woman Tricia, this is only a possible theory.

Meanwhile, let us take a walk through the village. We may be lucky enough to meet a friend, who is willing to discuss the legendary Count. Someone like the local priest, perhaps. I know Father Emanuel is a bit of an historian, like myself and may well have been able to obtain books from the library of the Convent of the Golden Orb. Probably in a more honourable way than myself," he observed.

Chapter 17

Putting on warm coats and hats complete with earmuffs, the two men left the gatehouse cottage, into a fierce wind, that seemed to resent making it divert its power around them.

The village church was a ten-minute walk and after their severe buffeting by the wind, the two men were very glad to enter the welcoming warmth. It was dimly lit and took a few seconds for their vision to adjust and enable them to see the priest standing at the lectern.

"Bart, my friend," said Father Emanuel. "Who is this you have brought to this sanctuary today?"

"Good afternoon, Father Emanuel. This is my cousin, Boris from England."

The two men shook hands and speaking courteously, in impeccable English, the priest invited them into his quarters, the Rectory, which was attached to the side of the church, where he bade them to sit at the table whilst he made a pot of tea.

"I do hope you like chocolate sponge with cream," he said, "my housekeeper Villette makes the best sponges, and I am afraid chocolate is my favourite." He cut three large slices and after just one mouthful, Boris declared he was hooked and could she be persuaded to make one for him, at which the priest laughed and promised to ask her.

Then Bart explained that his cousin was the owner of the magazine, for which Suzanne had worked, also that it had been his intention to propose marriage, on her return from Switzerland.

"You will of course, have heard the dreadful news of her being drowned, in the Bottomless Pool within the caves. We both feel that it is unlike her to take the risk of stepping over the rope, set there just for the purpose of preventing such a mishap. Now, we have discovered something that proves her death was not an accident but in fact was murder."

"Murder?" Father Emanuel gasped. "Tell me first, what kind of proof you have, if possible, show me. When I heard of this terrible misadventure, I took the liberty of checking the details of Suzanne Deville on my computer. It was the surname that encouraged me to do this, and I was not disappointed to find that she was a journalist. Regarding the name, there was little or no information, except that she was divorced and had no other kin. But that name has recurred throughout the history of this area, whenever there has been mention of the Count. The final event at the Convent of the Golden Orb, concerned one Henri de Ville, who allegedly slipped and fell from the path behind the waterfall and was drowned in the Bottomless Pool. So, you will understand my interest."

He indicated the shelves of books and Bart recognised the bindings as similar to those he now owned.

Between them, the two men described their journey through the caves, from the clifftop ledge, behind the waterfall to the Great Cavern, where they had discovered Suzanne's mobile phone. They explained that having dried it, how once connected to Bart's computer, it had provided a video with speech.

"Do you have it with you. May I connect it to my computer to view the contents?"

"I do, Father. I have also taken the liberty of bringing a copy of Suzanne's book on the subject of Michael Deville's regressions, which I will gladly leave with you if you so wish."

"Certainly, I shall be delighted to read of these strange things."

Boris handed the phone to Father Emanuel, who made the connection to his computer, and they watched the unfolding story of Suzanne's drowning. The priest asked if he might watch it again and would they mind if he copied the contents onto a flash-drive. "As much for security as my own interest. If by some means, you might lose either what you have on your own computer or the mobile phone, then I have a third back-up that is completely detached and also under the protection of God's House."

"So, you agree with us, that in all probability, there are devilish occult means behind what happened."

"Yes. Let me take down just two of my books, which I confess to have removed from the library of the Convent of the Golden Orb, prior to its being sold to that hotel company."

Bart laughed aloud. "I am so sorry and do not mean any offense but I must confess to having done exactly the same thing. It seemed such a pity to think of all that history being discarded or going up in flames, which seems to have happened to the remainder. Perhaps, great minds think alike is the correct cliché."

Father Emanuel now joined in with the laughter and soon all three were doing so.

"It does not seem to be the correct time for frivolity, but sometimes a person needs to laugh. It clears the head of negativity and replaces it with positivity, which is exactly what is required to discuss the problem with which we are now faced. I imagine you have a fair idea of the history of the Count, up until the death of his son Henri de Ville."

The two men nodded, and Bart gave the priest a brief resume of what he had gleaned from them. He also told of what he had revealed to Suzanne and his advice to be watchful, as he was sure she was in danger after being engulfed by a shadow she was quite certain, belonged to the Count. Boris also told him of Suzanne's first trip to Billenbach and of her return in fear, the very next day.

There was the sound of a door closing and a cheerful voice saying, "It's only me, Father."

"Ahh, Villette. I have two visitors today. Could you please arrange enough food for three? Also, I fear your wonderful chocolate sponge has been completely devoured and my friends wonder if there is any chance of your baking an extra one."

"No problem, Father." Villette entered the room, a bustling person with the figure of a middle-aged woman. She was wearing brown corduroy trousers and a multi-coloured, hand-knitted jumper. Her dark-blonde hair had a touch of grey and the smile of someone whose face was invariably in that posture. She did indeed resemble her cheerful voice, and brown eyes twinkled with constant good humour. "Dinner will be served in one hour," she advised, as she moved with speed and surprising elegance, into the kitchen.

When she had gone, Father Emanuel asked, "Would you kindly give me a little time to run through the occurrences during the Henri de Ville regression? I want to skim through the diaries of those two ladies to gain more insight of the convent in those times."

As he read, Bart and Boris allowed themselves to relax by the fireside and close tired eyes. They were awoken by Villette, announcing that dinner was served and Father Emanuel smiled as he escorted them into the dining room.

Chapter 18

With an excellent meal inside them and bodies relaxed from sleep, the three men sat around the table, drinking coffee and liquors.

"You slept for almost an hour, my friends, which surely was necessary. It also gave me the time to read all I needed. At some point, Bart, I would value a perusal of your *Book of Satanic Rights and Procedures*, as I think I must have the one immediately following that. It gives in more detail, the lineage of the Count." The priest continued. "That book of sin, commenced in 1021 and supposedly, the first Count, was *family named* Count 100. However, it gets rather complicated from that point. Apparently, when a Count reaches the age of one hundred years, this appears to be the time when the ten-year-mating should commence. As you have said, a young virgin was taken, presumably to the Count's castle. He planted his seed within her and in due course, she bore a child, upon the birth of which she died, along with any babe who proved to be female. If the impregnation failed to work, she was taken as a servant for the remainder of her life, never being seen again and assumed to have been attacked by wolves or a bear, on the mountain.

To continue. It would appear from the diaries, assumed to have been written by Isabella de Ville and Susan Blessed, in the book you have kindly provided for me, that the missing girls may well have been imprisoned as servants, within the Convent of the Golden Orb. With the Count's hypnotic abilities, it is unlikely that the young women would have any memories or thoughts, other than that it was their choice to train as nuns. And so, they would have accepted their lot accordingly.

Michael Deville's recordings certainly tie in with what Suzanne was able to research, regarding the previous regressions and what has happened here in Billenbach, appears to confirm what happened in the seventeenth century."

He refilled their glasses and continued.

"It would appear that by the thirteenth century, the impregnation ritual had produced three Counts 100, who were duly entered into the book, as required. I shall refer to it merely as the Book. I do not like or approve, of the attempt to copy our Family Bible, it is offensive to me. Thereafter, no male descendants were born, or if any, they did not live long enough for the next stage to be implemented."

"The next stage?" Boris queried.

"Ah yes, the next stage." Father Emanuel said. "It is interesting for me to note that there had apparently been no success in this respect, until the birth of Henri de Ville. I suspect that was more due to his being removed, before his birth, from the confines of the Convent of the Golden Orb and spending the early years of his life under the guidance of the Prior, Father Gregory and Sister Theresa. Otherwise, I imagine things would have continued much the same as the previous four centuries. But allow me to read from the book covering the thirteenth to the sixteenth centuries.

'At the end of the year 1241, during which time three maidens had disappeared, the villagers held a meeting. Much discussion took place, and it was subsequently decided, that in future the maiden daughters of all those present, would be secluded in their homes, for the period of one year. That being each year ending with the number one, when female virgins from the village were wont to disappear.

Previously, these villagers had accepted the loss of their daughters, assuming the disappearance to be due to an unfortunate accident. However, no evidence was ever discovered, or the remains of their daughters.

There was, however, one amongst them of the family Gelberger, who having lost his fourteen-year-old daughter in the tenth year of 1241, determined to look into this matter further. It was he, who called for a meeting of all the families blessed with daughters, as yet unmarried, together with, should they wish to do so, their grandparents.

This was the first of such gatherings, called to discuss these disappearances, with the intention of trying to find a way to prevent them from occurring again in the future. During this meeting, the villagers learned that maidens had disappeared every tenth year, which ended with the figure one and that most families in the village, with an unmarried daughter of virginal status, had lost that child, in mysterious circumstances. Further discussions appeared to show, that these girls went missing at some point after the month of June. Some parents were of the opinion that the seclusion of these maidens, should be for a six-month period only.

There were heated debates between some of the families and Grigori Gelberger stood before them, knocking on the table with his fist, demanding silence so he could speak. Having achieved this, he asked for a vote by show of hands. Firstly, for those in favour of a seclusion of six months from June and then for those in favour of a full year. He then suggested that each family should discuss this first and they would vote a little later. He also recommended, they consider forming a council of villagers, perhaps one member of each family as representative, to enable them to regularly meet, say each month. In this way, any events occurring in Billenbach, whether good, bad or indifferent, would be passed to all the villagers.

The family of a goat herder named Gert Britt scoffed at the whole idea. They had only sons, all of whom helped their father on the mountains. Gert declared that the old belief, that girls either met with boys and were subsequently killed by bears, or got themselves pregnant and committed suicide, was the correct and reasonable one. They were shouted down by others in the room and asked to leave, which they did, still ridiculing the ideas put forward.

Of the remaining families, only two were in favour of the six-month protection, the rest all voted for a full-year protective seclusion for the period now upon them. Those two families who voted for six months both agreed to go with the majority, so the vote was cast.

Regarding a Council of Villagers, it was agreed by all that this was a good idea and unanimously requested Grigori Gelberger, to act as Chairman. A further meeting to discuss this matter, was arranged for the following week, when a member of each family would be put forward as representative. These individuals would, if duly approved by all, be sworn in as full members of the council, by the chairman.

The meeting was then closed, and Mrs Gelberger provided food and drinks for all present.'"

Father Emanuel closed the book, sighed and took a sip of his wine.

"Well, well," said Boris. "I guess that was the minutes of the very first meeting of the first Council of Villagers."

"That may well be the case," Father Emanuel replied. "But now I have to prepare for tomorrow's Mass. Could I prevail upon you to join me for lunch at one o'clock tomorrow, when we can further research, the conversion of the Count's castle to a nunnery, the Convent of the Golden Orb?"

So, it was agreed, Bart and Boris returned to the gatehouse cottage.

Chapter 19

The following morning, the cousins made their way once again to the home of Father Emanuel, where they were greeted by his faithful housekeeper Villette. She jostled them into the sitting room and provided coffee with homemade biscuits, in front of the crackling wood fire.

"Well, my friends," the priest said. "I thought we might be more comfortable in here." He pulled a large coffee table closer to the armchairs, opened a heavy leather-bound book, and continued.

"I have read through the period between 1241 to 1261 and it would appear that the villagers did indeed place their daughters in protective seclusion for the two following tenth years, being, 1251 and 1261. In the intervening years, the villagers seem to have formed a successful working local council and for that period, Grigori Gelberger was their leader, with the title of Chairman of the Council of Billenbach. This chairmanship took a large part of Grigori's time, and the running of the farm became largely, the responsibility of his wife Sonya. She kept the books concerning the farm and its animals and also with the help of Anita, her twelve-year-old daughter, looked after the chickens. Every morning before breakfast, Anita would collect the eggs and open the doors to the chicken run. These she always firmly closed at dusk, to prevent the local foxes from enjoying a satisfying meal of chicken. Young Anita was consistently dependable in her tasks and also took an enthusiastic interest in her schoolwork. It was her desire to study and learn about, not only the bodies of animals but also humans. This was her ambition, to become the person to whom the villagers could come for physical help, when and if needed.

Conrad and Felix were definitely going to follow their parents in farming, so whilst nineteen-year-old Conrad was responsible for the cows, goats and sheep, seventeen-year-old Felix's main interest, was in the horticultural side of farming. However, he did help his brother on a daily basis, to milk the cows and goats.

Thus, the Gelberger family prospered. The farm grew, as did the family, and when Grigori was finally obliged to retire, from what had become his main employment, as Chairman of the Council, he was replaced by his eldest son Conrad who was now married, with three sons and two daughters of his own."

Father Emanuel paused for breath. "I believe lunch is about to be served, my friends. I feel in need of nourishment."

"Right on time, Father. I'm about to put lunch on the table." Villette placed an appetizing casserole on the table and retreated, to complete other tasks allotted to her.

After demolishing the casserole, followed by a cream covered trifle, they returned to the sitting room where Father Emanuel called, "Coffee please, Villette." And aside to his guests, "Perhaps with a glass or two of port."

She duly arrived on cue, with a tray containing a bottle of excellent port, a jug of coffee, and all the necessary accoutrements.

"When you leave," she said to Bart, "there is a Chocolate Gateau for you to take with you."

"You are too kind," he replied with a smile, "but please do not change."

The three men relaxed for nearly an hour, discussing what the Father had read.

Then the priest suggested they continue, saying, "I have read much of this book and if you agree, will describe what follows in my own words, as it tends to become rather tedious reading."

It was agreed, with an option to ask questions if they felt inclined, to which Father Emanuel willingly concurred.

~

"So, it was, that life continued in the region of Billenbach, with only minor changes, until the end of the thirteenth century, when there was major climatic catastrophe in the area. This was caused by unaccustomed warmth in the mountains, creating serious ice-melt, culminating in avalanches. These destroyed swathes of pine trees, that had served as protection for the village for time immemorial. Following the melts came rainstorms of a ferocity previously unknown in that region, with land slips burying large areas and completely destroying the Gelbergers fields that were nearest to the mountains.

However, the castle at the top of the mountain stayed firm and once again, local inhabitants began talking of the Count. Superstition prevailed and rumours spread, that the Count was responsible for this change in the climate. It was mooted that he wished Billenbach, to be wiped from the face of the earth, together with all its population.

Ignoring local laws, a group of young men gathered together and climbed to the edifice that had been deliberately ignored for fifty years or so, with the intention of entering the castle and confronting the Count. They took with them, torches of fire and there was no doubt of their intention to kill the Count and burn down the castle. Twenty men climbed the mountain, of which only five returned. These men would never speak of what happened up there. Either they were too frightened and not willing to, or perhaps their memories had been expunged, making them unable to do so. No one would ever know."

Chapter 20

"The damage from the catastrophe gradually receded, crops flourished again and life regained normality. A meeting of the Council was once again brought to order and business was being done, by those who had thought to lose all future opportunities. The family of Gelberger, continued to run their farm, albeit in a somewhat different manner than previously.

Then one day, a carriage arrived, driving straight through the village and up towards the castle. The horses were unable to go very far along the mountain track and from the distant village no one was seen to exit the carriage. Villagers climbed the track to, hopefully, discover what could be happening, only to find that the horses had been freed from their harnesses and no one was in sight. They tried to peer through the windows of the carriage, but these were completely covered by dark curtains, with apparently no chinks, through which an inquisitive person could see.

So, a meeting of the Privy-Council was arranged, to discuss this peculiar occurrence. The Council members had just gathered in their seats at the round table, when the doors burst open and a man of short stature entered, with three companions, who were obviously his guards. He apologised for interrupting their meeting and introduced himself as Monseigneur Andreas de Villefont. He was greeted courteously and invited to join them, which he did, waving his men to the door, where they stood silently, until required.

He was then invited, to inform them of his reasons for this interruption. The Monseigneur told the Council, that he was representing the purchaser of the property at the top of the mountain, which had been acquired for use as a nunnery. It was to be known as the Convent of the Golden Orb. His object of intercepting the meeting was to enquire if labour might be available, to build a road that would enable a carriage to approach the dwelling, without the nuns being obliged to reveal themselves and having to make the difficult climb. After explaining all that was required in this enterprise, including the potential number of men, he advised that each of them would receive a wage, which the Councillors knew, was far above anything that could be matched within the village of Billenbach. There would be no difficulty in finding the amount of labour required. So, a meeting of the whole village was called and most of the men wished to be part of the team of labourers. However, ages had been specified as between eighteen and forty. General fitness was imperative, so the young men were chosen plus ten extra having been named as ready if at any time or for any reason, more might be required.

As work on the road progressed, it became obvious that so far as the farming industry was concerned, the energy of the young men was considerably missed, making the farm work, appear to be almost doubled. No young man wanted to continue with farm work, when he could make twice the money he had earned, by labouring on the road. However, each family benefited from the extra money and womenfolk took over many of the tasks, usually performed by the young men, whilst the jobs they could not manage, were carried out by men too old to labour consistently on the road.

~~

It took over one year to complete the road to the nunnery, as work could not take place when the weather was inclement. However, it was eventually completed and carriages, carts pulled by six oxen and barrows pushed by strong men, were frequently seen to proceed up and down the new road.

When this came to an end, the Monseigneur once again approached the Council. This time, he required a gatehouse cottage to be built, at the entrance to the new road. Once again, young men were required for the building thereof and this was agreed with the Council. However, this time, the Chairman of the Council of Billenbach, had discussed the matter with his colleagues and requested a payment for the land involved. This was agreed and the purses of the Council, were fuller than they had been for many a year."

Chapter 21

"The building of the gatehouse cottage was started at the beginning of April 1418 and was basically completed in September of that year. The interior took another six months. In April of the following year, the cottage was occupied by a young man named Lucca Brunner, who had acted as foreman for the road building. He had married at the end of the project and his wife Marie, was expecting their first child. In fact, the job turned out to be a bit of a sinecure and Lucca spent a great deal of his time organising the garden and keeping the pathway to the convent, in pristine order.

However, in the year 1421, the teenaged daughter of Francis Andir, disappeared. Phillipa had celebrated her fourteenth birthday on the fifth of July, with a party at the local Church Hall. She had said goodbye to her guests and her parents were clearing the room and washing the dishes. Phillipa was a good and helpful girl and offered to help them, but her mother insisted she return home to bed, as she was obviously tired. When they arrived at their cottage on the outskirts of Billenbach, Phillipa was nowhere to be found. Like those girls in the bygone centuries, Phillipa had completely disappeared. There was no indication of where she might be and nothing was heard from her again.

In 1431, two maidens disappeared and neither they nor their remains, were ever found.

In 1440, people were beginning to worry once again. Would more girls disappear in 1441, as they had done previously? A meeting of the Council was held to discuss what could be done about this and they debated whether or not to follow the example of the thirteenth century. But times had changed, it would not be so easy to force protective seclusion on the females of today. Nevertheless, it was decided to hold a general meeting of the villagers and suggest that they make the decision, as to whether or not those with maiden daughters, should put them under protective seclusion. Most parents who were affected were in favour, but others pooh-poohed the idea as rubbish. A handful stated that their daughters would downright disobey any orders, to stay within the precincts of the house, to enable them to be kept under protective supervision. They would simply ignore the rule.

So, it was left like that, in the hands and judgement of parents and in 1441, three girls simply disappeared, never to be found again.

This time, the Council brought in a firm law, which became known as the Protection Edict and although this rule was occasionally broken, the offenders were punished. Over the next two centuries, the Protection Edict proved to be effective and from 1451, no more disappearances occurred and life in Billenbach continued as a peaceful village should. That is, until the seventeenth century, when Isabella de Ville arrived from England at the Convent of the Golden Orb, with her trusted companion and friend, Susan Blessed."

Chapter 22

"Which brings us to the life and times of Henri de Ville," Boris commented. He continued.

"Would you like me to summarise, as I probably have more knowledge on that subject? I did after all, edit Suzanne's book."

Bart and Father Emanuel nodded their consent, so Boris continued.

"It appears that Isabella de Ville was ordered by her father to marry an older man, whom she disliked intensely. The reason for this is not really known, but is open for you to surmise. Because of this, she and her companion Susan Blessed, apparently decided to ask at the nunnery, which in those days was attached to the Monastery of St Patricks, that they might be considered to enrol as nuns. From there, the Mother Superior arranged for them to be taken to the Convent of the Golden Orb, in the mountains of Switzerland.

Are you with me so far?"

"I imagine the man Isabella's father had decided she should marry, was wealthy and that Baron de Ville was in need of financial support at that time," Bart commented.

"Yes, that is very likely, and the Mother Superior at St Patricks, must have had a connection to the Convent of the Golden Orb. Thus, both convents must have known and presumably been controlled, by the Count."

Father Emanuel frowned thoughtfully as he said this.

"Isabella would have been a bit older than the previous young women, but she was still a maiden, and the Count was anxious to continue his family in the old way."

"As I see it," Boris said, "it was the only way. For as we have worked out, it looks as though that particular Count 100, could in fact have been something in the region of 560 years old in the seventeenth century."

"But if that was the case," Bart commented, "there seems no reason why that could not continue. Unless of course, there was, is, a limit to the number of years available to each Count.

My feeling is that at the end of the life of Henri de Ville, something occurred which affected the lifeline. Perhaps, it was due to the fact that Henri died in the way he did. Whilst for some reason, Papa Count was unable to enter the caves with his son, had Henri succeeded in completely terminating the family Gelberger, as his Papa Count instructed him, then I suppose the circumstances would have continued. Also remember what Henri said, according to Michael Deville's records of that event.

I would suggest we now, break for the day. You have the book, Father Emanuel, and we have Boris' and Suzanne's notes at the gatehouse, so if we can arrange to meet again tomorrow, that will give us a chance to check the details. It is essential that we have all our information, as accurate as possible.

If you would care to join us at the gatehouse cottage tomorrow, I shall be delighted to return the compliment, by serving you lunch. After which, if you have the time, we can explore the Henri de Ville records in more depth."

Father Emanuel gladly accepted the invitation and as they stood to leave, Villette called to them, "Don't forget your gateau." She placed a box containing the promised chocolate gateau in Bart's hands, smiling widely as he leaned forward and kissed her cheek.

Chapter 23

Later, with mugs of strong coffee before them, the chocolate gateau, minus nearly half its original size and the table littered with papers from the records of Michael Deville, the two men sorted and discussed the contents. It was well gone midnight by the time they decided there was no point continuing, as the arms of Morpheus were calling.

~~~

Father Emanuel arrived promptly the following morning and as Bart had been preparing his second to none Chicken Risotto, since finishing breakfast, it was ready to put on the table within fifteen minutes of his arrival. A bottle of superb white wine was served with it. This was followed by a sweet of Boris' own invention. He called it Ice Cream Bowlers. This concoction consisted of large donuts (hole in the middle variety) with a dollop of ice cream on top, covered completely with liquid chocolate. Hence, the appearance of Bowler Hats. After the meal, Father Emanuel declared that both men had succeeded in presenting superlative recipes, such as he had never tasted before. Then, looking over his shoulder, as though someone might be listening, he said, "Please do not ever produce or discuss such a meal as we have just enjoyed with Villette."

"Well, I am quite sure that neither of us could produce a chocolate gateau such as she made for us," Boris said smiling. "I'm sure though, that we shall keep our culinary skills between the three of us."

Finally, with mugs of strong coffee before them, the men commenced their discussion of the life and times of Henri de Ville.

"Would you like me to carry on where we left off yesterday?" Boris asked.

The other two agreed with vigorous nods, so Boris continued.

"As you will have noted, Henri, during his occupation in London, became rather torn in two directions, after his visit to St Pauls Cathedral. Firstly, his loyalty to Father Gregory at the Monastery of St Patricks, who had raised him with kindness, as indeed had Sister Teresa. Secondly, there was a feeling that he *should* support his only blood relative, Papa Count. On this latter consideration however, he realised that it was largely due to fear of the Count, rather than familial loyalty.

However, Papa Count held a very strong hold over his son, who was necessary for the continuation of a prophecy."

Bart interrupted here. "We still do not know for certain, how it was that the Count could not enter the cave system. Although we can assume it had something to do with the Christian carvings at the entrances. It is something I feel we should keep in mind. Perhaps we may come upon a feasible reason as we continue."

"And" Father Emanuel added, "we do not seem to be sure of what the prophecy was, just how it was blocked. Sorry, please continue, Boris."

"Henri was given the task of destroying the Gelberger family, in its entirety. Apparently, the fact that he was born in England, plus the full circumstances of his birth, was kept from the Count."

"Not kept from him but the impression was given, that a boy child had, together with his mother, died in childbirth," Bart interrupted.

"Correct, cousin, but nevertheless the genes of his father in those early years, obviously ran strong in young Henri. I refer, of course, to his drowning Sister Teresa, at the tender age of five years, a tragedy that was considered just that, an unfortunate tragic accident. That was when Father Gregory, had Henri moved to the care of himself and the monks, within the Monastery. During that time, Henri proved to be intelligent but also mischievous and it was at that time in his life, that he began to have disturbing dreams. As he grew into his teenage, Henri became more adventurous and decided to escape the influence of Father Gregory. Thus, it was that at the age of fourteen, he committed his second murder.

Mother Superior, of the Hospice of St Patricks, became aware of something in the boy, that was not normal and after watching his daily behaviour closely, chose to inform her colleagues, at the Convent of the Golden Orb. This information was duly passed to the Count, who eventually, met his son for the first time. Henri was then nearly eighteen years of age."

"Which was when it was arranged, for him to leave the Monastery and travel to the City of London," once again Bart cut in.

"Quite, during that time, he was further influenced by Papa Count," Boris continued. "But he was also becoming a man, and don't forget, his early years bore the influence of Christianity, through the monks. His brain must have been split between good and evil, the latter perhaps, being the stronger of the two, as it was under the constant, somewhat fearful, control of Papa Count. Which I believe, brings us back to the task, set him by his evil father."

"Henri was very discomfited, by what he had been instructed to do and recalled memories he'd had whilst in St Paul's Cathedral. He fully realised now, that his choices were either with God or Satan." Father Emanuel added.

"That is so, Father, but fear of Papa Count, persuaded Henri to climb to the clifftop and to abseil down to the entrance of the same cave his mother had entered, nearly twenty years before, with his yet unborn self, in her belly. We all know of his journey through the caves, from Michael's records, transcribed in Suzanne's book; how he came to the waterfall, slipped and fell into the Bottomless Pool beneath.

Bart and I followed the same path, with a few different bypasses due to rock falls, and a great deal of care. When we eventually reached the pool, trying to surmise how Suzanne came to fall and drown therein, is where we discovered her mobile phone. We can surmise, that this had either slipped or perhaps been slid by Suzanne, as she fell, into a gap in the surrounding rocks. We have all seen what is on that phone and are now back to how and why, she met such a tragic and early demise."

Bart suggested they take a break for a cup of tea and the remainder of Villette's excellent gateau. Which they did, with pleasure and a deal of necessity.

During this break, it was agreed that the subjects of conversation, should be other than upon what they were previously engaged. So, as the MistVirus, now apparently covering the globe, seemed to be in some way connected to Suzanne's untimely death, they ignored that subject. It was not an easy decision as obviously anything connected with what they now considered as their mission, was uppermost in the minds of all three.

However, they chose to discuss the sad fact that Italy had beat England, in the latest football match. This was a subject that proved to be one of much debate. Time passed and as darkness had fallen, Father Emanuel declared it was time to take his leave, so they arranged to meet the next day, if possible and agreed to telephone him in the morning.

Chapter 24

The following day, as Father Emanuel was busy both morning and afternoon, they arranged to meet for dinner at eight o'clock at the local Chinese restaurant, the Golden Dragon. Its reputation was good, and Bart had frequented it several times in the past.

Meanwhile, Boris and Bart discussed how and when the Christian carvings might have been done. They agreed that it was obviously prior to the arrival of Henri at the Convent of the Golden Orb; the second time since his conception.

Father Emanuel arrived at the restaurant, to find Boris and Bart already seated at their table, with glasses of wine before them. As he joined them, the cousins could see that the priest was in excitable mood. Bart poured him a glass of wine and bade him speak.

"Last night I had a dream," he said. "Such a one as I have never experienced before in my whole life. When I awoke, I was actually trembling and having prayed to my God, I wrote the contents as I recalled them. One of the strange things that struck me, was the similarity to the regressions of Michael Deville and the way in which he chose to record each, as it occurred. My dream was similar. I suggest that we partake of our dinner and then return to the Rectory, as I would not wish anyone other than we three, to hear what I have to relate."

His companions reluctantly accepted his request and Bart beckoned the waiter to order their meal, together with another bottle of wine.

Just one and a half hours later, the three men were seated before a blazing fire in the Rectory sitting room, with bulbous glasses of brandy before them. Father Emanuel, took a deep drink and with a tremulous sigh, proceeded to regale them with the details of his strange dream.

I was in an 'out of body' state, in the company of Farmer Gelberger, his son Joshua, the lady Isabella de Ville and her companion, Susan Blessed, at the top of the cliff, from which we were to abseil to a ledge some feet below us. From there, we were to enter the cave system, within the Golden Mountains.

Joshua had allayed the fears of the two women, by explaining what he and his father had accomplished, to prevent the Count or his acolytes, from following them into the caves.

When Joshua had first declared his love for Susan and subsequently taken her to his parent's farm for safety, his father told them, that he felt it was time to tell them about the Count and his activities.

I now found myself, sitting at the table with Farmer Gelberger, his wife, son and Susan. Joshua had informed them of his love for Susan and their desire to marry. She was gladly accepted into the family. Mrs Gelberger and Susan had immediately, discovered a liking for each other and many things in which they held a common interest.

Father Emanuel was silent, looking into space, as though expecting to see people other than Boris and Bart, in the room with him. "Sorry, I felt for a moment that I was still in the farmhouse." He shivered, then continued.

"Joshua's father then told of the earlier years, from 1021 to the time that the Count's residence was apparently taken over as a nunnery, the Convent of the Golden Orb. I will skip that for the time being, as we are all aware of that period."

He waited whilst Bart refilled their glasses.

The cave system, particularly the cathedral cavern, with its beauteous stalagmites and stalactites, was used for occult worship. The waterfall from the high mountains, falls through, what became known to local residents because of its shape, as the Devil's Eye. This falls into the so-called Bottomless Pool and is believed to go right through to the centre of the earth, into Hell itself. Now, you may recall that Hell is assumed to be a place of continuous fire. It is believed that the Devil's Eye provides water, for those that dwell in that place and it is necessary for the Count, to drink from the Bottomless Pool, in order to continue both his existence and that of his male progeny.

"Do you mind if we take a break here? I need coffee, or fear I shall fall asleep."

Chapter 25

The three men drank coffee, leaning back in comfortable armchairs, dozing and yes; they all three fell asleep.

Bart was first to wake up, he was cold and shivering, rubbed his eyes, looking around trying to get his bearings, then realising he was still in the Rectory, stood up and put two logs on the fire. The noise roused Boris, who shuffled to a sitting position, whilst Father Emanuel, abruptly stood, saying, "Dear God, what is the time? We slept." Making them all laugh.

"Ah, you are awake at last. Come. Breakfast is on the table in the kitchen. You will soon warm up with food and hot coffee inside you."

Villette had arrived at her usual time of nine thirty, wondering why the light was still on in the sitting room. She listened at the door, through which she could hear someone gently snoring. Thinking it was the priest, she quietly opened the door. Upon seeing, not just one but three men, all sleeping she, smiling, retreated to the kitchen, to prepare a large fried breakfast for them.

Seeing the worried look on Father Emanuel's face, she assured him that there were no appointments in the diary for that morning, so he could sit with his friends and enjoy the food.

"You are indeed a priceless gem," he said. "Thank you so much, Villette."

So, it was, that that with full stomachs, Bart and Boris returned to the gatehouse cottage, for much-needed showers and a change of clothes, having arranged to return to the Rectory after lunch.

~~

Once again, Father Emanuel took up the story of his dream of two nights ago.

Having told his family of the occurrences during previous centuries, the good farmer made a proposal, which raised eyebrows. He held up his hand, to silence the many questions and comments, whilst myself, being invisible to them and presumably unheard, asked how on earth he proposed to achieve this. However, he had most certainly, thought the matter through thoroughly and explained how this was to be achieved.

The Gelberger family, was one of true Christian faith and the plan was to, with the assistance of his son and as many members of the church as possible, carve Christian signs, at both known entrances to the caves and if possible, on both the inside and outside, of the Devil's Eye. This action to be blessed by the priest, both before and after, the completion of these signs.

Having considered what shape these carvings should be, Mrs Gelberger suggested that they should, of course, be of the Christian Cross. Should more than one carving be necessary, to completely encompass the entrances, then they should touch, thus sealing them.

The priest was invited to visit the Gelberger farm that very afternoon and although astounded by what he heard, the Father agreed and said he would arrange for a meeting, of some members of the church, after Mass the following day.

"I did tell you my dream was a strange one and indeed everything I am telling you ran consecutively, although as you will note, there are sometimes more than one day between what happened."

At this point, the men broke for tea, returning after only a short break.

As Boris commented. "It's like having to put down a really good book, when you can't wait to get back to it, although one may wish never to have it come to an end. In this case, it seems to have continued for several hundred years and here we are in the twenty-first century, still trying to solve the mystery.

Sorry, old chap," he said. "Please do continue."

"I agree completely, but you will see in due course what occurred next." Father Emanuel settled himself in his chair and continued.

The priest had asked only six of his most trusted church members, they being skilful in the art of carving, to attend the meeting and having sworn them to complete silence, for reasons that would be explained in due course, he requested that Farmer Gelberger, should proceed to impart his plan. He retold all he had informed his family, whose complete discretion he confirmed they could rely upon, and having done so, put forth his decision to, God willing, effectively close entrances to the caves, in respect of the Count.

It was agreed that at least two men should be involved in the carving of Christian crosses at the lower entrance, two at the ledge entrance and two at the Devil's Eye. The latter was considered to be the most dangerous and Andre Blanc with his son Petri, who were both regular and skilful climbers, would be allocated this task. Hans Bremmer and Maurice Sacul, would be in charge of the ledge entrance and Frans Tunuc with his friend Gaston Lefevre, would deal with the main lower entrance. Grigori and his son Joshua would be available, wherever they might be needed. The priest would make a blessing for each site daily before start of work and again on its completion. An overall blessing would be carried out on the morning before the first commencement of the mission, from the church precincts, with a full service in the church upon its completion. It was agreed that the priest would attend and bless all three entrances, prior to commencement of the carvings, and together with the team members, made the rigorous climb through the Serpent's Tail, to the mountain top. Having blessed the Devil's Eye and entrance on the ledge, he returned through the caves that evening. At the entrance at the lower level of the mountain, the priest also made his blessing and finally returned, as did the eight men, to his home.

Carving would begin the very next day at all three sites. The priest had pleaded other tasks, which would prevent him from actually accompanying the men at the start and finish of each day. He quietly admonished himself, after the climb the previous day, to the ledge and back, he had no desire to indulge in such exercise twice daily. He therefore, arranged to meet with the men, before they set out to perform their tasks and would do so again on their return.

As it was, the team decided that the Devil's Eye should be first on their list, owing to the difficulty of the waterfall. Also, Andre and Petri could guarantee being free the next day, to perform this major task. Joshua would also accompany them, to assist if necessary. For the underside of the Eye, a rope was attached to a protruding rock, just outside of the fall of water. Hence, the surface was rougher than those within the torrent, which had worn their surfaces to a smooth rounded veneer. Both men wore climbing gear, complete with hoods and scarves as face protection, for they were well aware of the territory, into which they intended to enter.

Joshua Gelberger was in charge of topside safety, whilst Andre lowered himself, followed by Petri, to a small protrusion slightly to one side of the Eye. Petri was to do the carving of a Christian Cross, to the best of his ability, on the upper portion of the eye, whilst his father made sure that he stayed well balanced, within the small space in which he was working. After more than two hours, Andre called for a break.

Joshua helped them to the surface, where he had hot drinks awaiting them. After a forty-five-minute break, the two men returned to work and in another hour, Petri had finished his carving, so they took another break for lunch. Andre had insisted that he did the work on the lower side of the Devil's Eye, as the flow from the waterfall was more torrential in that area and Petri, being younger and stronger, was more able to keep his father safe, than the other way around.

Andre suggested, that owing to the fact of severe strain on them both, they should take a rest every hour. Joshua would pull sharply three times on Petri's rope, to indicate that an hour had passed and he was ready to help them to the surface once again. Meanwhile, he had been doing some carving of his own, to either side of the eye above ground. These consisted of single Angels, complete with wings and halos. His fellow workers would complete the topside of the Eye, the following day, again wearing their protective clothing. These carvings would consist of similar Christian Crosses, being held on either side, in the hands of the two Angels.

The priest welcomed them back at the church, together with the other members of the carving teams. He had not ascended the mountain, but prayers were said before they had left that morning and when they returned.

"So far, so good," finished Father Emanuel. "We should now assume that those carvings were completed and duly blessed by the priest.

I fear I shall not be available at any time tomorrow, but perhaps we can meet at the cave entrance in the car park early the following morning."

Having agreed to this, the three men parted company, with much to think about.

Chapter 26

Boris had made many notes and indeed taken portions of Father Emanuel's story, in his own version of Pitman's shorthand. He sincerely hoped he would be able to read it back, but knew that at least these notes would be a help anyway.

Leaving Bart to prepare their evening meal, Boris sat before Bart's computer, making an effort to decipher his notes. In actual fact, he was delighted to see, that although his Pitman's was not in every case, as short as it should have been, he was able to read his long/shorthand version pretty well. So, he printed three hard copies and after dinner, he and Bart sat comfortably with a glass of red wine each and went through the sealing of the cave entrances once more.

"Next time we meet, I shall take my recorder with me," Boris said, "I definitely do not want to have to struggle with my shorthand again."

With a chuckle, Bart asked, "Do you think you got the main details? That is the only thing of real importance. I think that tomorrow, we should go through what we have written about our own adventure through those caves, and perhaps, make some bullet points, to compare them with this latest information, to see if there are any similarities."

"The days seem to go so quickly, that when I think about what has happened it doesn't feel like a single day, more like a week. I suppose that's because we have so much going on, my head is over-full," Boris rubbed his head.

"I am much the same," said Bart, "which seems a good time to retire to our beds."

And on that note, neither of them expecting to sleep, settled on their beds and the next thing they knew, it was daylight again and time to begin another day.

~~

After an hour's run, in which unexpectantly Boris joined, much to the amusement of Bart, they sat down to a light breakfast.

"Do you intend to do that every morning?" Bart asked.

But the only reply he received was, "Hmmph."

Bart continued. "I think we should make a return visit to the caves today."

Boris looked somewhat aghast. "Why on earth should we do that? All the way up to the Serpent's Tail and…"

With a wave of his hands, Bart silenced him. "No, no, we will enter through the car park entrance; I need to see that waterfall and work something out that has been bothering me. The caves are still closed to visitors, so we should be able to enter the way we came out the other day. I will explain when we get there but hasten, be ready to leave in ten minutes."

Anxious to ask more questions, Boris managed to contain his curiosity, quickly gathering his digital recorder. Then donning his walking boots and anorak, he was in fact, ready in less than ten minutes and promptly joined his cousin who stood prepared to lock the door behind them. Bart carried his rucksack, having prepared with his normal efficiency for their requirements, including flasks of coffee and sandwiches (just in case).

There were cars in the car park, visitors in the gift shop or gazing through the windows and the café was nearly full. However, the entrance to the caves was not apparently overlooked and no guards appeared to be present. The two men made their way round the outside of the car park, keeping in cover of rocks and trees where possible. Eventually, with a final check to make sure they were not observed, they slipped under the ropes, through the entrance and along the tunnel to the great cavern. The only sound was the roaring of the waterfall, as it fell relentlessly through the Devil's Eye, splashing into the Bottomless Pool.

Bart led them to the end of the pathway they had traversed a few days ago and looking upwards said, "Yes, I thought as much."

Boris, who had maintained complete silence since entering the caves, expended a deep breath, unable to maintain his patience any longer. "For goodness' sake, Bart, it's time you explained why we are here. I've had enough of your abstraction, come on now, explanation time. Eh?"

"I am sorry, cousin, but I needed to see to be sure. You recall what we decided, before we reached the waterfall on our journey?" He didn't wait for a reply but continued. "Having found ourselves in blocked tunnels, we came to the conclusion that to follow the right-hand path, being the path of righteousness, was in this case misleading, so we then kept to the left and eventually found the waterfall."

"Yes, so what?"

"Look. Look, my friend. What side of the falls did we emerge?"

"From down here, the right-hand side."

"Precisely. Now, we retrace our steps and then facing the mountain, instead of with our backs to it, come down on the left-hand side." Once again, he waved his hands to silence Boris. "I am aware that the pathway on that side appeared to be far more difficult. When you consider, that was probably how Henri de Ville came to fall to his death. Nevertheless, we must retrace his steps of three hundred odd years ago if we wish to solve the mystery of the connection of Henri, to the subsequent death of our good friend Suzanne. So, are you ready?"

Boris could now get the gist of his cousin's reasoning, so with an affirmative nod followed Bart, to commence the climb, that would take them to the rear of the fearsome torrent of water, which as they drew closer, now precluded any ability to distinguish speech.

Chapter 27

The path they took, up to where the waterfall covered the ledge, was harder to ascend than it had been to descend on their previous trip. However, Bart, as ever prepared, on reaching the top, found a suitable rock just inside the tunnel, which was fixed firmly and had not been affected by the constant fall of water. Then, ensuring they were safely attached to each other, he proceeded warily along the wet surface of slippery rock behind the waterfall. Keeping as close as possible to the mountainside from which it protruded, Bart with Boris close behind, slowly made their way towards the middle of the waterfall.

The men gazed at one another in amazement. What they had expected, was a continuation of the slippery very narrow ledge. They found themselves in fact on a pathway protruding from the mountain, wide enough to take two men walking side by side. But the thing that caused their amazement, was an almost unnoticeable indentation in the mountainside, behind the cascade of water. The two men entered and by the light of their head torches, discovered it opened out into a small cave, large enough for them to stand upright. To their surprise, on the right-hand side was a jutting rock, about the size of a three-seater settee. But that was not what made them gasp, for on this seat was a worn remnant of material that could in some distant past, have been a blanket. Under it was an ornate metal box embossed on the lid of which, were the words HOLY BIBLE.

"This is proving to be so much more than I expected," Bart said breathlessly.

"What did you expect?"

"Not sure really, perhaps a ledge of about 2 feet with broken pieces, indicating where a man might have fallen. I don't know any more. Let us rest for a while, cousin, have us some food and coffee before we continue back downwards."

Boris as ever impatient, "Shall we go through what's in that box while we eat?"

"No." Bart was adamant. "We will take it with us back to the cottage and difficult as I know it will be for you, this box will not be opened until we are at the Rectory with the good Father Emanuel, tomorrow. No." He said again firmly. "I have one of my feelings that this box should be blessed before it is opened, and we may well find that Father Emanuel will agree. He may also wish to open it within the sanctuary of the church."

"Seems a bit over the top to me but this trip is your idea and I bow to your decision as to its outcome."

Bart thought he was going to have an argument over this point and gladly accepted Boris' acquiescence.

Refreshed after ham sandwiches and coffee, the two men left the cave as they found it, minus the box, which was safely stored in Bart's backpack. They continued in single file, still roped together for safety, along the wide ledge, which gradually narrowed until it led to the path leading down into the Great Cavern, with its wondrous natural artforms and noisy torrents of the waterfall cascading into the pool, this time arriving on the left-hand side.

With a nod towards the cave opening, Bart made his way towards it, followed by Boris. Having reached the ticket office, they now realised that darkness had fallen, the shops were closed for the day and the car park was empty.

They had left the cottage just before twelve noon. It was seven o'clock when they re-entered, and they realised with surprise, that this particular adventure had taken seven hours.

"This is becoming too regular an occurrence for my satisfaction." Boris commented, as they sat down for a perfunctory meal of beans on toast, for their evening meal. "I suggest we eat and go to bed. Tomorrow's another day."

Chapter 28

Another day it surely was, as the view from the cottage windows was a grey wet miserable one.

"Ah well, unfortunately, it's far too inclement for our usual run," said Boris with a wide grin.

Bart ignored him, picked up the phone and rang the number of the Rectory. After a brief conversation with the priest, he turned to Boris. "We are not to meet at the cave entrance as arranged, but in the church, at a quarter to twelve precisely," he said. "Father Emanuel is most insistent on this timing, for some reason he will explain when we get there."

~~

They entered the church through the vestry door at 11.55 hours, to be greeted by the priest decked out in all his regalia.

"Good. Good," he said, waving the two men further into the room, where over the desk lay two white cassocks of the type worn by choir boys. "Please remove your overcoats and if you are wearing them, your jackets and put these on," he requested, waving in the general direction of the cassocks. "We must be before the altar by twelve noon, or I fear we shall fail in our endeavours."

Looking at each other somewhat askance, Bart and Boris donned the cassocks, as requested. Father Emanuel bade them kneel and sprinkled their heads with holy water, muttering a prayer in Latin as he did so. He then silently beckoned to follow him as he entered the church. He led them to the altar and knelt before it, with Bart to his left and Boris to his right, both slightly behind him.

"Please pass me the box," he requested.

Bart, who had been holding it close to his chest since leaving the cottage, handed it over, with a clench of his stomach, as he realised how reluctant he was to part with the precious item.

Father Emanuel placed the box at the centre of the altar, between two tall white candles, that flickered with every movement. He sprinkled it with Holy Water, making the sign of the cross above the box, confirming the sanctity of their quest.

All was silent, until in the distance, the tower clock pealed at noon, twelve chimes. The priest, indicating that the two men should join with him, commenced the Lord's Prayer and upon the Amen, once again began to pray in Latin. Neither Boris nor Bart could understand his words but remained kneeling in reverent prayerful positions, repeating Amen each time the priest uttered that word.

Finally, Father Emanuel rose and faced them, raising his hand in blessing and saying, "In the name of the Father, the Son and the Holy Ghost, may God be with us." He once again made the sign of the cross. They remained with bowed heads in silent prayer until the tower clock once again chimed, this time the quarter hour, making Boris jump.

"Thank you for your patience, my friends," said Father Emanuel. "Now I feel, it will be safe for us to return to my study in the Rectory, to continue the tale of my strange dream and your discoveries behind the great waterfall yesterday. Today, Villette is remaining with her mother, but she has left a casserole in the oven for us, so when you are ready…"

~~

Back at the Rectory, the three men sat around the kitchen table, enjoying the meal prepared for them by Villette.

"This morning, or I suppose afternoon, doesn't seem real," said Boris. "I feel as though I'm in some sort of dreamscape from which, if only I can wake up, will find myself in bed back at your cottage Bart."

"Do not worry, cousin, I too feel as though I am outside myself, merely looking at what is happening."

"Enough." Father Emanuel broke in with a voice he might have used to recalcitrant choirboys. "That is exactly what I feared and why we have prayed in the church today. Come, we will retire to my study to continue this discussion."

Bart started to clear the table.

"Leave it. Come now." The priest's voice rang, still commanding.

In the study with the door and windows firmly closed, there was a similar stillness to that they experienced in the church. Just the patter of rain, blown against the windowpane by a howling gale. Father Emanuel nodded to them to stand before the fire and asked them to bow their heads once again, in silent prayer. He then made the sign of the cross before the door and two windows, before drawing curtains across them, spraying Holy Water over them in the sign of the cross and once again muttering incomprehensible words in Latin.

That done, he sat at his perfectly cleared desk, with Bart to his left and Boris to his right. "It is good to follow a pattern," he explained.

"A pattern?" Bart asked.

"Yes. As we were before the altar. The evil one does not like symmetry. So, shall we continue with my dream or are you eager to open that box first?"

"Well, naturally," Bart answered, "we are anxious to see the contents of the box, but bearing in mind what you have just said about symmetry, I think the sensible thing would be to continue with your dream."

"Very well, I have made a few notes."

Boris interrupted here, withdrawing the hard copies he had made and handing one to each of them. "I thought this might help, a sort of written record, like Michael Deville did. Hope you don't mind, Father. I also brought my digital recorder, so that we can just record what is said today. Makes it easier for me to transcribe than my rather indifferent shorthand."

"A sound idea, Boris, my friend. So, shall we continue?"

Chapter 29

"Well, now you see my reason for changing our plan to meet in the car park. I apologise but now we all understand why. Where did I get to?" The priest riffled through the pages before him.

"Ah yes, to continue.

The following day I observed, as Andre and Petri completed the carving above the Devil's Eye. The appropriate blessings for the day's work had been made in the confines of the church, as previously agreed. These carvings may well have been somewhat obliterated by the constant torrent of water but nevertheless, they will be permanently inscribed, as originally intended by the good people of the village.

~~~

On that same day, Frans Tunuc and Gaston Lefevre arrived at the main cave entrance at the foot of the mountain; the good priest joining them, to bless their work and clarify the purpose thereof. The two men worked either side of the tunnel entrance, carving Christian Crosses, each joining the next, from beginning to end. They worked with only short breaks for refreshment, for six full hours. Having completed this, they discussed the efficacy of a carved connection across the roof of the tunnel, thus leaving no unblessed way to enter into the Great Cavern. This was finally accomplished by two further crosses. Then Gaston carved Mary, the Mother of Jesus, with a lamb at her feet and Cherubim each end of the opening, joining those to either side and each cross joining in the middle. They had by then, been working a full ten hours and on exiting the tunnel, found the priest awaiting them.

He praised their work mightily and blessed the completion thereof, explaining again, the necessity of complete silence as to their task, to prevent the Evil One gaining knowledge of their plans.

~~

On the following morning, Hans Bremmer and Maurice Sacul climbed to the mountain ledge, through the caves and behind the waterfall. This was the final entrance to be secured by the blessing of God, preventing anyone of evil desire from ever entering the caves.

On their arrival at the ledge, they found Grigori Gelberger waiting for them. He had not been expected but explained, that so far, he had performed no part in the enterprise, and it was his firm desire to do so. He would do whatever he could to help the two carvers, and ensure that refreshments were available for them when required. They carved, as had the other members of the team, Christian Crosses, which joined one another at strategic points. Grigori Gelberger was no expert, so far as carving was concerned, but felt a need in his heart to make extra points of protection. He spoke of this to Maurice and Hans and the three men wandered further into the tunnel, where it curved. There, Hans carved a Christ figure on the left-hand wall, the halo above his head attached by carvings in the roof of the tunnel, where Maurice carved flying Cherubim. Grigori's contribution was a Christian Cross on the right-hand wall, held in the hand of one of Maurice's cherubim. Finally, their work completed, the three men descended back through the caves.

On reaching the main entrance, they turned to look at the mountain. The priest, who had not been involved with any of the carving, was waiting for them. As they looked up at the mountain before them, the priest held up his hand. He had not so far, carved a single thing of his own and felt in some way reduced, but now he would put the final touches to their mission. He bade them stay and taking carving tools from the bag Joshua Gelberger carried, scrambled above the entrance and proceeded to carve the words that can be seen to this day, DEUS CUSTODIAT TE (God protect you). His companions congratulated him, but he demurred, saying that it was God's wish and guidance.

They prayed together then, and the priest, once again, blessed this work and all that had been accomplished successfully during their mission. It had been fifteen hours on this occasion, before the weary men reached their homes. Tired but satisfied.

The following day, I found myself in the church amongst the men involved in the carving. A service was held and those present, swore before God to never speak publicly of what had been done.

"And that," said Father Emanuel, "completes the telling of my strange dream. Would you be so generous as to allow us to end our discussions for today? I know how much you wish to open that box, but we need our wits fully alert when doing so."

Consequently, it was agreed to meet really early the following morning and Bart and Boris departed to the cottage once more.

Chapter 30

Both men awoke the next day full of enthusiasm to make their way to the Rectory and, as Boris put it, "Open that damn box."

Phone safely in his pocket, Boris gathered his iPad, the notes he had typed up the previous day and his digital recorder, putting them in a rucksack.

"Are you ready, Bart?" he shouted to his cousin.

"Just a moment, I am placing our evidence in my safe. We cannot be too careful so far as this mission is concerned," he said, putting on his anorak and zipping it as he walked to the door.

~

They arrived just after nine o'clock and Father Emanuel led them directly into his study, where he proceeded to repeat the ritual and prayers of the previous day. The box stood on his empty desk. It projected a certain feeling of mystery and although eager to open it, the men hesitated to do so.

Boris moved first. "What are we waiting for?" He picked up the box and scrutinised the rust holding the lid firmly in place, then taking a small screwdriver from his pocket, ran it around the edge. He took his time, handling the box carefully. "Don't want to risk damaging whatever's inside," he said.

Eventually, with crunches and squeaks, the lid moved, and Boris was able to remove it. "Put a cover of some kind on your desk, napkins would do," he instructed the priest.

Father Emanuel left the room and returned with the altar cloth. "I still feel that the hand of God in this enterprise is necessary," he said, spreading the cloth over his desk as Boris held the box. He once again made the sign of the cross above it, indicated that Boris should replace the box and repeated the sign. When satisfied, he nodded. "Very well, let us continue."

This time Boris completely removed the lid of the box and with the three of them leaning over it, gently removed the contents. It appeared to be a parchment adorned with cramped writing. This was definitely English but was very difficult to read, as the box was small in width and depth, although the height was equal to that of the width. The parchment had been folded in half, then in halves again and once again folded, making it practically illegible along those folds. It required careful handling to prevent crumbling, or any further damage and Father Emanuel provided them with cotton gloves.

Finally, the parchment lay before them, open on the altar cloth and Boris, slowly and stumbling, commenced reading aloud, to record the contents thereof. Not an easy task under any circumstances but one they all thought to be imperative.

I am so very sory for my past sins He, Papa Count, my father, the devil himself, hath set me the task to dispos of the family Gelberger entirly He can continu to rule from his eyrie in the caves only if that family who helpd my Mama to escaep from the Convent of the Golden Orb is no longer living Upon the deths of these good folk all bariers at the entranfes of the caevs will be removd and the profesy will continu unchangd once mor I cannot do this dredful thing Under his influince I have killd the 2 people in my life to caer for me and to teech me the diferense between good & evil yet still I lisend to the All Evil One I call upon God in Heven to gide me now and to Sister Teresa and Father Gregory to forgiv me… I will not do as Papa Count commands. I will not… God forgiv your son in his last breths & taek him to your heven of peace, from the bottomless pool that now awaits me.

Henri de Ville

Father Emanuel read the parchment once again out loud. Bart then, with some difficulty, reluctantly did likewise. All three voices were now recorded, the last epistle of Henri de Ville now established by the three men. Father Emanuel indicated that he wished to add to that recording. Having crossed himself, he continued.

"The parchment found in the protection of a small cave behind the waterfall, by Bart and Boris Slovinski appears to be the last epistle, what today might be referred to as the last Will and Testament, of Henri de Ville. I, Father Emanuel, priest of this parish, together with Bart and Boris, have this day, November the fourteenth 2021 opened the said box and we have each of us, recorded the contents thereof in our own voices. I now confirm, with my hand on the Holy Bible, the absolute truth of this statement. May God be with us in our mission to combat Evil."

The three men stood in silence, each looking at the parchment before them and the old tin box in which it was contained.

Bart was thinking of the bravery of Henri de Ville, as he wrote and the courage it must have taken, to allow himself to slip down into the Bottomless Pool.

Boris held in his mind, Suzanne Deville, as she sought to rescue what appeared to be a drowning man, in that Bottomless Pool.

Father Emanuel considered the good and evil, attached to the resulting deaths of Henri de Ville and subsequently Suzanne Deville, in the Bottomless Pool.

Finally, shaking themselves from their reveries, the men moved and began to clear the desk. Carefully, the parchment was folded along its original lines and gently replaced in the box. The lid was once again securely closed, and Father Emanuel suggested they might consider placing the precious item in the Rectory safe, for the time being. It would be known throughout the village, of the attachment both Bart and Boris had to Suzanne Deville and through this, the priest considered it possible that the Count would be aware of their presence and intentions. Seeing the sense of this, it was agreed. Boris had the recording, plus photographs of the box, with its contents, the parchment, both open on the desk. It was agreed that keeping these items separate was a good security measure. Things being as they were, there was no knowing what evil could be opened around them. Was the Count/Man in Black, able to source information through the occult? Was there perhaps a villager, who was controlled by him?

"We do not know how this evil works nowadays," said Bart, "but I feel shivers up and down my spine, just thinking about it."

"God will protect us and good will prevail." The priest however, had a slight quiver to his voice.

When they left, the rain had ceased but the wind still blew strongly. As Bart pushed open the door of the cottage and gratefully switched on the light, he gasped and staggered back into Boris, behind him. The cottage had been trashed...

Chapter 31

The police had been called but nothing appeared to have been stolen. The usual questions were asked. Their names and addresses; and having learnt that Boris resided in London, England, they enquired as to why he was in Billenbach and how long he intended to stay.

He told them frankly of his connection to Suzanne, the woman who had been found drowned in the Bottomless Pool, of her position in his magazine and of their friendship. Boris also informed them, of his relationship to Bart and that they both wished to see the place their friend had died. He did not of course, inform them that this had already been accomplished. It was naturally assumed he was still in the area, awaiting the reopening of the caves and he would naturally stay with his cousin Bart.

The police requested they leave things as they were, until the SOCO team could process and hopefully recover fingerprints, to enable them to speedily arrest the culprits. Leaving spare keys with the police, they agreed to spend the night elsewhere and proceeded upstairs to pack overnight bags.

In Bart's room, free from the inquisitive eyes of the police, Bart opened his safe, which was hidden beneath the floor of his wardrobe. Its contents were still thankfully secure, so resealing it, closing the covering by pressing a hidden lock disguised as a coat hanger, the two men looked at each other, with considerable relief.

"Let's phone Father Emanuel," Boris suggested. "He must be made aware of our attempted burglary and perhaps he will put us up at the Rectory for the night."

"Good idea," Bart replied, taking his phone from the pocket of his coat.

Father Emanuel answered the call in short order. "Bart, I was not expecting to hear from you again today. What has happened?"

On being told of the break-in, the trashing of the cottage and the police presence, he immediately suggested that they return to the Rectory, where he would be happy to provide beds for the night. Bart gratefully accepted the invitation and he and Boris, carrying their overnight bags, said farewell to the officers still present at the cottage. Then Bart, ensuring that the police had a note of his mobile phone, they once again made their way to the Rectory.

~~

Villette had been called by Father Emanuel to assist. She had promptly arrived at the Rectory, where she prepared two rooms and one of her excellent meals. "It is only a simple salad, with some salmon I found in your freezer," she said, "but there is garlic bread in the oven. If you will excuse me now, Father, I must get home to my mother, she will need my help to get to bed."

She was leaving just as the men arrived. Bart squeezed her arm as she passed. "Thank you so much, for once again being available in our hour of need my dear," he said, smiling.

Villette returned his smile and with a nod, continued on her way home, which was a small cottage at the entrance to the church and Rectory.

"Let me show you to your rooms, my friends. Get settled in, then we will eat and talk over what has happened today." Father Emanuel left them.

It was only a short while before Bart and Boris, joined him in the warm kitchen of the Rectory, where he had set the table. As they joined him, he poured glasses of red wine, which revived them and after eating, the three friends moved to comfortable chairs before a blazing fire, in Father Emanuel's study.

Boris gazed into the flames, seeing pictures in his mind, of the Count in the centre of them.

"Why would anyone want to trash my cottage?" Bart wondered.

"Obviously, that has something to do with the fact, that you two are probing into the death of Suzanne. Whoever it may be, wants to know what you have discovered, and I can only assume, that there is something we have not yet cleared in our minds. Something of importance." The priest stared at his hands for some minutes. Then said, "We are all too tired to think straight at the moment, I suggest we retire for the night and continue tomorrow morning. I will ensure that after morning Mass, the rest of the day will be spent in the study with you gentlemen, when we will once again look and listen to what we have already perused. In the meantime, we should perhaps consider that as you are now staying at the Rectory, whosoever our enemy may be, will also be aware of that fact. We should all be wary, so lock your doors before you sleep and ensure the windows are also closed."

"That is what I told Suzanne," Bart said, shaking his head sadly.

They said their goodnights and heeding Father Emanuel's advice, Bart and Boris, despite their troubled minds, slept peacefully, until awoken by daylight creeping around the velvet drapes covering the windows.

Part IV

Chapter 32

It was in fact, after nine o'clock before Bart and Boris were out of their beds. They showered and Boris knocked on Bart's door. It was opened even as he knocked his knuckles on the wood and smiling, they said, "Good morning, cousin," at precisely the same time, smiles turning to laughter.

"I imagine we both slept soundly and woke at about the same time," Boris grinned. "Well, I certainly did, and it was 8.50 am when I woke up. Thought I'd better get a move on. Come on, I need breakfast, or at least some strong coffee."

Father Emanuel was waiting for them in the kitchen, toast was browning and the contents of the frying pan smelled appetizing. Plates were in the trusty cooker, warming. "Cutlery is in that drawer," he said, pointing to the cupboards on the left. "Please set the table," and as an afterthought, "tablecloths are in the drawer next to the cutlery."

Looking at each other, with no necessity to speak, the two men each opened a drawer, removed what was required and proceeded to lay the table. They opened a few cupboards to find pepper, salt, and Boris' favourite standby for virtually any savoury meal, tomato ketchup. Meanwhile, Father Emanuel had completed his job as chef of the day, by placing crispy fried bread onto the now hot plates and dishing eggs, bacon, mushrooms and tomatoes, on top. The toast was placed in its rack and another meal at the Rectory enjoyed by all.

Boris was delighted to note, that the Rectory boasted an efficient dishwasher and made it his job to load the dirty plates and utensils. "No point putting the mugs in yet, we shall no doubt be drinking a few more coffees," he said.

"Please put them in the dishwasher, Boris, we will have clean ones." Then loading a tray with the necessary coffee requirements, Father Emanuel led them to his study, to peruse the recordings and documents, concerning Henri de Ville once more.

It was a slow painstaking task, which he divided amongst them. They decided to read for an hour, making notes where they thought applicable, after which, those notes could be discussed, for as long as needed. Only the period covering Henri de Ville's time in Switzerland, seemed to be applicable. They would see what came of that and then progress to the second visit of Suzanne, leading to her death. Silence reigned, except for the occasional scratching of pens on paper, or the chink of a mug being returned to its coaster, until the mantlepiece clock struck the hour of eleven o'clock.

"Time for a break now." Boris laid down his pen.

"Good, I really need some coffee and there is nothing I can think of adding," Bart replied, with a sigh.

Father Emanuel, rose and poured three mugs of rather stewed, coffee. The three men sat, sipping their coffee in silence, each deep in his own thoughts.

Father Emanuel was the first to rouse himself.

"Time to discuss what we have found of interest, before going to the next stage. Shall I start and you two interrupt if there is anything I have missed?"

~~

"It appears, that Henri de Ville was first contacted by the Count, on his seventeenth birthday, when he was told of his paternal connection and from which time, he referred to the person previously known as the Man in Black or the Count, as Papa Count. However, prior to that, he appears to have been controlled through dreams, with no knowledge of the Count, only that they were disturbing ones, which he subsequently forgot."

"And after that meeting, he was still influenced by that creature, with no other personal contact, until he was eighteen," Bart interrupted.

"Quite so. Do you recall how Papa Count greeted Henri on that occasion?"

Boris responded this time. "He said, 'May our Master greet and guide you, my son.' He then told him, to prepare to leave the Monastery."

Father Emanuel continued. "Henri was taken to London, provided with lodgings and left to learn how to live in the real world. He eventually, set himself up as, and here I quote, THE GREAT MAGICIAN OF THE GOLDEN ORB, which is significant in its own right."

"During which time," Bart interrupted once again, "he made himself a small fortune, by tricking members of his audience with his conjuring."

"Correct, and then Papa Count turns up once more and tells Henri that he is to go to the Convent of the Golden Orb, in Switzerland."

"On his arrival there," Boris broke in, "he is told that it is his mission, to erase in its entirety, the family Gelberger, they being the reason for the escape of his mother, to England."

'Exactly', Father Emanuel agreed. "Henri de Ville is reluctant but afraid to deny his father. So, he enters the caves, taking the same route as Isabelle de Ville, with her companion Susan Blessed, Joshua Gelberger and his father, before Henri's birth. He enters, like them, through the ledge entrance."

Boris interrupted here. "He would have noticed the Christian carvings surely, but I can see no reference to them in his, or Michael Deville's records."

"Nevertheless, I feel they hold the reason, for Henri's later thoughts and decisions, when he reached the waterfall. God works in mysterious ways, my friends. Think of what kind of child and youth Henri de Ville was, despite the strong influence of his life in the Monastery. He was personally responsible, for the deaths of both, Sister Teresa and Father Gregory. Perhaps, the life he led in London, especially his visit to St Pauls, enabled him to understand the way of life outside the one he knew so well. There is no doubt, he was in fear of his father but could also see and feel the evil within Papa Count.

He followed the footsteps of his mother and her good, God-fearing friends. They were ultimately, responsible for his birth and education, in the security of St Patricks Monastery. Henri de Ville's genes were a mixture of good and evil and in the end, it would appear, that good finally won.

Now, I am hungry, so let us make some sandwiches and fresh coffee, before continuing our task."

Chapter 33

It didn't prove necessary to prepare their own sandwiches, as Villette had left both food and a bottle of wine, ready for when they were hungry. Afterwards, feeling refreshed, they returned to the study.

"Right." Bart spoke first, having pulled his stack of papers forward, tapping them on the desk, to perfectly straight alignment. "Perhaps, before discussing what we know regarding Suzanne, we should look more thoroughly, into our own excursion from the ledge entrance into the caves, to the one in the main car park. We endeavoured to follow the same path as that of Isabella and subsequently, Henri de Ville, but time and circumstances, inevitably made alterations to that route."

"Slight diversions maybe, but I don't see that could make much difference. We did effectively, make the same journey and as I see it, the main thing we learnt, was about the carvings. Perhaps, proving why the Count could no longer enter the caves, to what Henri called his eyrie. We still don't know why the Count needs to cross that particular threshold, his purpose or indeed, what may be kept within the mountain. Indeed, how non-egress affects, 'his way of the progression, of the so-called prophecy'." Boris made air-quotes for the final words.

"That is precisely, what we are trying to discover, my friend, what in fact is the prophecy. Nevertheless, I do agree with Bart. First let us look into the events surrounding your journey through the mountain." Father Emanuel looked questionably at his two companions. They nodded agreement and sat to their task of reading once again, the transcription carefully typed and printed, by Boris.

Twenty minutes or so had passed before Boris looked up and said, "Look you two, we all know what we did and did not do, whilst trying to get through that frigging mountain. Sorry, Father, excuse my language. We only half noticed, the carvings and I recall mentioning that there were other, much older ones, along some of the tunnels. I am the first, to oppose the suggestion of another such journey but nevertheless, I think one is really necessary, and I also feel that

Father Emanuel should accompany us this time. We know what to expect now, so it shouldn't be too bad. However, we must be prepared to photograph whenever and wherever possible, and to record our comments throughout the journey. Please think about what I have suggested, think on it for a while and then we will discuss our next steps.

And while we are on the subject of the caves, don't let's forget the small cave and what we discovered in it, behind the waterfall, on our last visit to the Great Cavern. No less than a letter, written by Henri de Ville himself; there might be other such hidden areas, just waiting for us to find." He grinned self-consciously, realising he was trying to ensure the others would agree.

"I agree." Father Emanuel was first to respond. "I also think we should start by being at the bottom of the Serpent's Tail, ready to commence this journey, as early as possible. Bart, you know the route, would it be possible for us to reach that point at first dawn?"

"Yes, it is possible but the climb up to and then along the Serpent's Tail, is a stiff one. Do you think you are capable of doing it in the semi-dark, Father? I recall Boris panted and puffed when we ascended from my cottage. This time we will have to bypass the cottage and make our way through the woods, backing onto the Gelbergers farm. But if you are willing to make the effort, then I agree that it is an adventure we should take once again."

Boris took charge. "Right, we all agree. Now it occurs to me that all our endeavours, are somehow being passed to others. Why otherwise, was Bart's cottage trashed? Bearing that in mind, we should not speak of our plans outside this room, and certainly not to anyone else. I suggest therefore, that we quietly prepare our own rucksacks, making sure they contain water and food, enough for two days. With luck, we shan't need it but you never know what will happen. Also, we should wear wetsuits, under our normal clothing. Bart and I have these, back at the cottage. For sure, we shall get wet whilst behind the waterfall and maybe in other places too," he added with a grimace.

Bart interrupted here. "I also have an old wetsuit, that I wore before taking an exercise regime. This may be of use for Father Emanuel. I will make a trip to the cottage to collect them after dark. I will not be seen by anyone, believe me."

"Good thinking, cousin," Boris said. "The food we will, with your kind consent, Father Emanuel, prepare whilst ostensibly getting our evening meal ready. Perhaps, you and I could be doing this while Bart sneaks back into his own cottage. Our rucksacks should of course, contain sleeping bags and polythene sacks, in which to keep our belongings dry. Certainly, as we pass behind the waterfall, for this time, we cannot leave our belongings behind. I suggest we each do this preparation in our own rooms when we go to bed."

"Understood, cousin," agreed Bart. "I think we should immediately set in motion our plans, then get some sleep for a few hours. We will need to be ready to leave no later than four o'clock and I therefore, suggest we eat a light breakfast before leaving. Then we should make our way to the woods, as silently as possible, so no speaking until we reach the start of our ascent of the Serpent's Tail." He held up his hand as Father Emanuel was about to question this.

"If someone or something is spying on us, they will know that we are staying at the Rectory. With luck, they may not have realised that Father Emanuel has a connection to our enquiries, but I would not put money on it. Do you both understand what I am trying to specify?"

Bart placed his hands, one upon the other, on the desk. Boris laid his hands in a similar position on top of Barts and Father Emanuel, understanding now, did likewise.

"Now, seems to be the right time for you to drop the Father," he said, "I am your friend and confederate, Emanuel."

A pact had been made and like the Three Musketeers, it was now One for All and All for One.

Chapter 34

As he walked back to his cottage to retrieve the wetsuits and a few other things he had in mind, Bart thought about the mist that seemed to be the original carrier of the unknown virus. He considered the men who had helped Joshua, the tour guide, pull Suzanne's body from the pool. Joshua himself, seemed to have recovered. Could that have been because he was relatively young or was it because he was a Gelberger? The Italian, Vilko Makinen, had also recovered but he was only in his early twenties—was that reason enough? On the other hand, the Russian, Leonid Smirnoff, had apparently not been really unwell, just a cold, which he had treated as one normally does. However, he had infected his workmates, seven of whom had subsequently died, including Leonid himself. And then there was the change in the effects of what appeared to be carried in a mist or vapour. Had the Count's Revenge mutated naturally, or had a controller successfully manipulated it, presumably the Count himself?

Bart stopped, in front of his cottage was a police car. It seemed unlikely, the police considered it possible, that the perpetrators would raid the same property twice. He slipped over the wall at the rear of the property, noticing there was no sign of lights within. His gut told him to keep his wits about him and to move slowly and quietly. So, crossing the garden, keeping close to the shrubs, he made his way to the door that opened onto a small, enclosed porch. He peered through the window but could see no signs of anyone inside, so carefully unlocked and opened the door. Slipping inside, he made his way towards the kitchen door, which was also kept locked, opening it quietly and stepping into the room. He looked into every space. For Bart no lights were necessary, he knew the layout of his cottage from back to front. Then he climbed the stairs, keeping carefully to the inner edge of each step, to avoid creaking. Those rooms were also clear. Switching on his torch and keeping it covered, he sorted those items he had come for, folding them into a canvass bag. The house was still a mess and several hours would be required to get it back to its tidy state once again. Stepping over the general disorder, Bart once again made his way out the same way he had entered, and as quickly as possible returned to the Rectory.

Food was prepared and as they ate, Bart described what had happened. "I cannot imagine why the police would put a guard at my gate overnight," he said.

"Not unless it is someone in the police who is spying on us," Boris suggested. "Whoever it might be probably thought we might return tonight and hoped to stop that. Anyway, you used your initiative, cousin, well done."

"Yes, well done, Bart. Let us get some sleep, we have a very early start tomorrow. Especially if we are to avoid the observations of, or on behalf of, who I can only imagine to be the Count." Father Emanuel looked serious, worried but also very determined.

Chapter 35

All went well and precisely at 04.00 hours, the three men left the Rectory, quietly and unobserved, having eaten a small breakfast, to ensure their energies were topped up but not overly so.

Father Emanuel, proved to be a great deal more fit than Bart had anticipated and Boris had definitely improved, since that first climb to the Serpent's Tail. Nevertheless, it took them an hour to reach their destination and as long again, to reach the top of the mountain. The rope Bart had originally tied securely round a tree, was still in place and after ascertaining that it was undamaged throughout its length, they were ready to descend to the ledge.

Bart went first, followed by Father Emanuel, who was helped into position by Boris.

I can do this as well as Bart now—well nearly, Boris thought to himself, as he swung over the mountainside and abseiled down to join his companions.

"Come," said Bart and led them without more ado into the entrance cave. "Have you got all your equipment ready, Boris?" he asked.

"Sure have. Shall we have a selfie before we start?" was the reply. "Don't look like that, I think we should film the start of our journey, showing the three of us and again when we reach ground level. Three in and three out, don't yah know."

Father Emanuel nodded his agreement. "I understand what Boris is saying. We should also explore this cave thoroughly before moving on. Make sure to photograph the carvings as precisely as possible and I imagine your recorder is voice activated, so for example, the roaring of the waterfall, should not cause it to operate."

"Absolutely. You're not just a priest and historian are you, my friend. Your general knowledge and abilities, keep catching me unawares. I guess people don't expect a priest to be anything but…a priest." Boris shrugged.

"Ah well, that story is for another day," was the reply.

"If you two have finished chatting, can we get on?" Bart sounded irritated. "Look at this."

He was standing by the far wall, where there was what appeared to be a lever, protruding from the mountain. It was about 30cms long and shaped like that of the horn of a large bull. The inner side of the curve held four indentations the size of a man's fingers.

"An invitation to grip and see what happens," Bart commented. "But first, photograph it and make sure your recorder is working, we must have a full record of this."

Father Emanuel, took a spray container from his pocket, saying, "No, this is not kitchen cleaner. I have thoroughly washed, disinfected, and blessed it, before filling it with Holy Water." He liberally sprayed the protrusion, praying as he did so in Latin. The others repeated his Amen. Then, as they stood close together, the priest gripped the lever and pulled downwards.

It was stiff but moved slowly, the grinding noise caused them to retreat, as the cave wall opened. Before them was another cave, about the same size as the one they were in but it contained a large oak desk, behind it a leather chair, cracked with age. But that was not what drew the eyes of all of them, for in the chair sat a grizzled skeleton. Its robes were rotting and as air filtered into the cave, they began to disintegrate. Held between the bones of the right hand was a quill, with which the person had presumably been writing on the parchment before them on the desk.

"Wait." Father Emanuel held up his hand, holding them back from entering. He sprayed around the doorway, still muttering prayers and moved towards the desk, his hand still raised to indicate that the other two should not yet follow him. After spraying the desk and remains, of whom they presumed in fact, to have been a nun, with Holy Water and uttering more prayers, he beckoned Bart and Boris to join him.

"It might be possible to read what is written on the parchment but do not risk touching it, for it may well do the same as her garments."

"You go first then, Emanuel," said Boris. "You have a better chance of interpreting any writings that we do. If it is legible, then please read the words aloud, so they are immediately recorded."

"There is writing, which appears to be in English, very faded but if I shine my torch directly, I should be able to read it. It starts; I am Sister Margarita, formerly Mother Superior of the hospice run by nuns, attached to St Patrick's

Monastery, in England and latterly, appointed Mother Superior of the Convent of the Golden Orb. This appointment was made shortly after the Lady Isabella de Ville and her companion, were escorted there for sanctuary.

I have assisted the Count for more years than I care to remember, and I accompanied him to this cave many times, through the secret tunnel, leading from the Convent of the Golden Orb to the ledge. I have also entered alone on occasion, to carry out tasks on his behalf. It was on one of these occasions, that I heard much noise within the entrance cave. I know not what it was, but since that time I have been unable to open the door. Following that day, I have not seen or heard from the Count.

I am growing weaker by the day and although I am able to obtain a small amount of liquid, no food has passed my lips for the last ten days. My end is near, and I know full well where my soul will be despatched. For this reason, I am leaving this letter for whosoever may eventually discover what is the secret cave of the Count. I know he has another place within this mountain, that he refers to as his Eyrie, but where that maybe I know not.

May those to whom I have done ill forgive me. I repent my sins.

Sister Margarita-Mother Superior."

Chapter 36

"So, that explains a bit more. It looks as though she was aware of the disappearance of the young girls, back before the family Gelberger intervened," said Bart.

"Aware of what happened to them, yes. That knowledge also explains how she came to become trapped in the hidden cave. The carvings were to prevent evil from entering the cave – they had not considered the leaving of them. She was in the wrong or perhaps that should be right place, at the ditto time," Boris said.

Then reaching for his backpack, he withdrew a plastic folder, carefully sliding it beneath the parchment and slipping it under until it was safely in far enough to gently lower the top cover.

"There. Still in one piece." However, he also found a card envelope and placed the precious find inside. "That should protect it, even if it proves impossible to read and at least the whole thing is in there, not just dust."

"Ever the journalist, cousin, I would not have credited you with such forethought."

Father Emanuel interrupted this teasing. "We shall find nothing else of interest here, so I suggest we continue. There is a long way to go, and we have yet to discover the Count's Eyrie."

Leaving the cave, they followed the tunnel leading to where there had been a rockfall. Bart led the way and as before, climbed to the top, where he had Boris pass him their rucksacks. Throwing them down the other side, he turned on his stomach and followed, small pieces of rock descending with him.

It was agreed that Emanuel should go next, and it soon became obvious that his short, rotund body would require the removal of more rocks, to provide sufficient space for him to squirm his way through. This was accomplished by himself, pointedly ignoring the offers of the others to do it for him, and in relatively short order, he joined Bart on the other side.

Boris, having achieved this before, apparently had no difficulty in joining his companions.

Making their way along the tunnel to the end, they decided to do as previously and took the right-hand path, but this time, Father Emanuel suggested they explore the five tunnels they had bypassed last time. They took the first tunnel, which was on the left-hand side, carefully marking their way by chalking on the wall as they progressed. This tunnel went only a short way, perhaps two hundred metres, before ending against the mountain. There were no indications of previous occupation, in the form of drawings or carvings, so the men returned.

The next two tunnels proved to be on the other side. Both were similarly explored and proved to be much the same as the first they had entered.

The fourth tunnel was the second on the left-hand side and again the men chalked as they traversed the pathway. It proved to be of greater interest than the three already explored, in that, there were cave drawings on either side, of both animals and humans. Their age was pretty much apparent, because of the animals portrayed. There were mammoths and sabre-toothed tigers amongst others that appeared to be of the dinosaur variety. Boris photographed all he could, including those of stick-figure humans, which seemed to be more of the chimpanzee shape, than that of later humanoids, their heads leaning forward and arms reaching almost to their feet.

"Does this indicate that the human race was around at the same time as when it is thought dinosaurs ruled the world?" Bart enquired.

"Not now," Father Emanuel said. "We will discuss all we find here today, when we are safely returned to the Rectory."

At the end of the tunnel was a large cave, in which they found bone remains of both humans and animals. The contents were duly verbally noted and photographed, before the three men returned once again to the original tunnel, to explore the fifth and final one.

This was a surprise too. The tunnel was just a very short entrance to a large cavern, that had the appearance of some sort of meeting house. At the far side was a large rock that resembled a table or altar, and above it, carved into the mountain, was a circle of approximately two metres in diameter. Around it and pointing outwards, were many straight lines. Around this were smaller orbs, some of them double or triple and between them were what surely had to be stars.

"I would say that is meant to represent the sun, plus planets and stars," Boris commented as he photographed it.

"But that would mean that some of mankind had knowledge that was not known to be apparent for eons thereafter. Perhaps, the stories of alien invasion of planet earth is true. Remember that a large amount of our early history, is what we have learned, from various man-made religions throughout the world. But once again, I say this is something for us to discuss in detail, when we are safely returned to the Rectory." Father Emanuel, turned to Boris, saying, "Have you all the information recorded?"

Receiving an affirmative, he continued. "Then let us progress to the next stage, which is I believe, back to our main tunnel where we are to take the left-hand path, as you both did previously."

Chapter 37

The return journey was made in silence. There was much to be considered and the way was both full of rubble, slippery and sloping upwards, needing them to concentrate on every step they took. Taking a rest after what had proved to be over an hour's climb back along the tunnel, the men sat to rest. Bart produced a flask of coffee from his pack and they each followed suit. Then they sat again in thoughtful silence, drinking their warm drinks, and eating sandwiches.

After twenty minutes or so, Boris suggested they make a move. "I remember this tunnel has a rocky pathway, that narrows for some distance. So, Emanuel, be prepared to carry your backpack at your side, whilst crab-walking. I don't think you are any larger than I was at that time, so we should manage. Okay?"

Knowing what to expect was undoubtedly helpful and they reached the wide ledge without any problems.

"The beauty of this cavern takes my breath away," said Father Emanuel, looking down. "It resembles a cathedral."

"Which is how we described it. Come, we must now lower ourselves down, to join the congregation. There should be no problem in choosing the correct tunnel on the other side this time Bart." So, saying, Boris swung himself over the ledge and down onto the floor of the cavern.

When joined by the other two, Boris made his way through the stalagmites to the far side, stopping before the fourth tunnel, which they had previously traversed. "We know what to expect when we reach the end of this one, but perhaps we should check the other six, before we get soaked at the waterfall."

Emanuel agreed. "That is precisely my reasoning. Shall we start with the far-left tunnel and work our way along?"

This plan was agreed, so making their way to the entrance, they proceeded along the tunnel, again marking the wall with chalk as they went, to be on the safe side. The tunnel was fairly level and after a while curved in almost a hairpin bend, apparently continuing in the same direction from which they had come.

This proved to be correct, as they exited from tunnel number two, back into the Cathedral Cavern.

"Well, that was an interesting half-hours' walk," Boris commented. "I wonder what the next one has for us?"

It proved to be not a lot, as after walking for three or four minutes, they were met by a rock fall that reached from floor to ceiling. It was decided to not spend the time trying to break through this for the time being and to continue to the tunnels on the other side of the one leading to the waterfall.

The nearest one led quite steeply down and after about fifteen minutes came to what looked to be the end. However, on the left-hand side was a narrow opening, maybe just big enough for a small child to crawl through. It was damp and from the roaring noise, could be assumed to emerge onto the waterfall ledge. So, they returned to the next tunnel entrance.

This one, like the first, was fairly easy access and after about twenty minutes walking, began to curve. However, this was not a hairpin bend, the curve consisted of what appeared to be a large, curved cave, the far side of which they would later find, did in fact, lead back to the Cathedral Cavern.

"I think we've found the Count's Eyrie," said Boris.

Chapter 38

This cave contained, what could only be described as a laboratory. Two long benches ran from side to side of the cave, covered with glass tubes and tanks. The latter were double tanks, with about a ten-millimetre gap between them. In the front one, there was a circular hole, large enough to receive the hand of a man. That was fitted with a tight glass cover, which appeared to make the tank completely airtight. The inner wall had a similar hole, connected to the outer by some kind of tubing and also sealed by a glass cover, apparently preventing the cavity between the two tanks, from becoming the recipient of whatever the inner tank held. In today's world, a person would insert their hand, duly glove protected, to enable the control of whatever it contained. Nothing could be seen within the tank but a slight mist, which did not appear to move.

Bart leaned forward, to see if anything else was perhaps concealed by the mist and as he did so, just touched the outer tank with his forehead. Immediately, the vapour swirled and twisted within the inner tank, as though trying to escape its confinement.

"Wow! That is scary." He jumped back, knocking into Emanuel, who had been looking over his shoulder. "Boris, does that remind you of anything?"

"The misty vapour that came from Suzanne's coffin when Gerry opened it."

"Exactly, and that seems to point to the virus infection Roland caught. Do you remember what we heard on Suzanne's phone? The Count saying, she would be the carrier of his Revenge throughout the world."

Father Emanuel drew them back. "This seems to be confined for the time being, but I feel we should withdraw from this eyrie. I will once again, with your permission, spray and pray both entrances to this cave, for almost certainly the exit, over there," he said pointing, "will lead us back to the Cathedral Cavern. The sooner we are back there, the happier I shall be."

Boris shook his head. "See, there is a clear way around the laboratory benches, and I feel we should explore that first. By all means, Emanuel, do what you feel appropriate in this area to start with, but we must walk round the walls of the curve in case there is something that might be of interest. We don't want to miss anything important," he added.

"Very well, but do not underestimate the grace of God, through prayer, my friends." Father Emanuel, proceeded to add the rights of Christianity over the benches, before the three men continued to walk around the outside of the cavern.

On reaching, what appeared to be the centre of the curve, there was a difference in the format of rock wall. Whereas the mountainside had been a relatively smooth surface, it now appeared to be raised in places and indented in others. Bart studied the area for a moment and reaching out to an obvious projection, tried pushing it to first the right, then left. This firm pressure had only the effect of making his hand smart, so putting both hands together over the protrusion, he pushed. This proved to be remarkably easy. It slid inwards, there was a click and with a loud rumble, not unlike an overhead thunderclap, the mountainside moved, opening upwards, like the sliding door of a garage.

As with the cave in which they had found the remains of the nun, Father Emanuel blessed the entrance before he would allow any of them to enter. There was a musty smell but to their relief, no remains, human or otherwise. There was however, a large desk-formation, made of sheer rock, behind which was a chair. At some time, it had been upholstered but now only mostly horsehair and tattered material of some kind, lay on the frame. Those were the first items the three men could see, for the cave was only slightly smaller than the laboratory cave and the rock-desk was front centre.

However, as they shone their torches round, there appeared to be on either side, a lofty arrangement of shelves, containing what they calculated to be hundreds of old books, which they decided to investigate at a later date. In between the shelves was a raised ledge, on which rested the fragmented remains of what they assumed was once a mattress and covers of some description. At the end of what they chose to call the bed, was another smaller ledge and on this, rested two partially burned candles in holders, a quill and container, that must have at some time contained ink. But, the most interesting item was a large black covered book, which the men assumed to be some kind of ledger.

"This would definitely appear to have been the Count's Eyrie," said Bart. "I don't feel comfortable here, so if you've got another envelope, Boris, please gather up that book. You have photographed everything as we saw it. Please,

Emanuel, spray and pray, no disrespect meant but I am frankly nervous being in here and I think we should get out ASAP." With that he retreated to the door.

As he did so, there was a low murmur, which grew to a crescendo. Boris sped to join Bart at the doorway, Father Emanuel followed quickly behind, literally spraying and praying as he ran. They exited, as the door in the mountainside dropped down behind them.

"The feeling you had that all was not right, has proved correct, cousin," said Boris. "I shall be more inclined to pay attention to your hunches in future."

"There must have been some sort of time-switch," Father Emanuel said. "However, that seems a little too modern a term. I suspect that the evil Count cast some kind of spell, to ensure that anyone other than himself, entering his Eyrie, would be imprisoned therein. We would have been incarcerated in that room, until death took us. However, we have escaped once again, and God has protected us. Also, for the future, our Christian prayers will hold the evil within. For further discussion and exploration, we must look to the future now. So, my friends, let us continue."

Chapter 39

They did indeed find that the far side of the cave led back to the final cave entrance in the Cathedral Cavern.

"We must now retreat back to entrance number four," said Bart. "That will take us to the back of the waterfall. However, we know the place to remove our outer clothes now, to allow the wetsuits to protect us from the torrent we can expect."

As before the journey along tunnel number four, took them just under thirty minutes to reach an area protected by jutting rocks. Stopping there, they removed their outer clothing, placing them in double thickness plastic bags and squeezing them into the back packs. Father Emanuel, once more insisted on blessing their next steps and the information carried by them in the now valuable backpacks, before moving forward to the rear of the thundering waterfall.

Speech was now impossible and Bart, having secured a rope to the same rock they had used on their first journey through the mountain, indicated by hand signs that they should now firmly connect themselves together for protection. This was harder than before as then they had left their rucksacks behind. Now, there were three of them, all carrying back packs. Boris remembered the process however, and with Father Emanuel between Bart and himself, they were soon ready to attempt the treacherous crabwalk behind the waterfall. Facing the mountainside, Bart led them along the ledge, to the pathway down into the Great Cavern. Again, with both Bart and Boris knowing what to expect along the ledge and with Father Emanuel and his prayers wedged between them, it took no more than fifteen minutes to traverse it to the pathway beyond.

Once free from the spray and roar of water falling rapidly down into the Bottomless Pool, the men, with great relief, untied the rope from around themselves and removed their backpacks. They each carried a small towel and hastily dried themselves as well as possible. Their clothes had indeed survived the trip in a dry condition and were gratefully donned over the wetsuits once more. Then, finding a safe rock on which to sit, as far away from the thundering waterfall as possible, they drank the last of the coffee in their flasks and nibbled chocolate bars, until regaining their breath and feeling somewhat revived, were able to continue.

"Well, that was worth the effort," said Boris. "Look what we have learnt, and we've found the Count's Eyrie to boot."

"I would like to take a look at the pool before we leave," Father Emanuel commented. "You found the mobile phone last time Boris but as a man of God, I may see or feel something you did not. After all, none of us expected this adventure to be quite so rewarding."

He stood and whilst Bart and Boris repacked the backpacks, made his way to the side of the Bottomless Pool. There, he looked up towards the Devil's Eye. It seemed to be glaring down at him with anger and Father Emanuel shuddered. Then flinging his arms wide, he prayed to God for his protection and guidance, in terminating all future evil, that the Count could inflict upon an unsuspecting world. As he did so, in the midst of the Bottomless Pool appeared the head and shoulders of a young man. This apparition spoke.

I am Henri de Ville. Please, Father pray for me. Tell God our father that I sincerely repent my sins. I tried telling the lady not to attempt to rescue me, that I was being controlled from afar by Papa Count, but she would not heed me. He used her for his revenge on the world and the only thing that can save all of humanity from his evil virus, is within the Eyrie laboratory.

With those words, he vanished beneath the water.

Meanwhile Bart and Boris had joined Father Emanuel by the pool.

"Did you see and hear him?" he asked.

"See who?" Boris said.

"Henri de Ville himself. Out there, in the middle of the pool. He begged me to pray to God for him. Oh! Obviously, you did not see or hear. Let us get out of this dreadful place, back to the Rectory. I do not feel at all comfortable within this great space."

Agreeing wholeheartedly, the three men once more donned their backpacks and made their way to the main entrance of the cave system. Boris photographed the exit as they left, paying special attention to the carvings. Father Emanuel prayed, and spraying with the small remains of Holy Water, asked for God's blessing and gave thanks for their safe return.

Chapter 40

On arrival at the Rectory, Father Emanuel suggested his guests go straight to their rooms to take a much-needed shower, with instructions to join him in the warmth of the kitchen within the next hour.

Taking another of Villette's casseroles from the refrigerator, Father Emanuel placed it in the oven to heat and made his way to his own room, where he enjoyed the comfort of a hot shower and change of clothes. Returning to the cosy kitchen, he discovered that the others were already sitting round the table, having made tea. Now warm and comfortable, Father Emanuel checked that the casserole was properly heated and removed it from the oven to the table, saying, "Please help yourselves, I have not got the energy to play the host and feel that we are now friends enough. So, just make yourselves at home."

Finally in the priest's office, sitting in armchairs with a glass of brandy each, they talked over how to progress. Boris started, by connecting his mobile phone to the computer and brought up the first of the photos he had taken. These were of their progress up the Serpent's Tail and proved to be of more interest than they had expected.

It had been assumed that this pathway up through the mountain, was named because of its twisting shape. However, all the way from bottom to top, along the right-hand side of the mountain, was carved the twisting body of a serpent. It proved at the top, to be not just the head of a snake, however large, but that of a dragon breathing flames. From below its head and long scaley neck, sprouted wings. These were only partially closed but clearly to be seen, were designs in circle and diamond shapes, which at some time in the distant past, had been coloured and time of course, had faded. It was very difficult to discern but looked as though on the left-hand side, had been carved a procession of prehistoric men. Unfortunately, these figures were mostly worn away with age.

"My word," said Bart. "I have climbed up that Tail four or five times now and have never noticed that amazing artwork."

"Understandable, my friend. That climb takes all of one's concentration to avoid a fall. Eyes in front of feet, not at side walls. If I'd not had my phone on video, we would still not have known about them. Do you suppose those characters actually lived in the caves in those days?"

"Almost certainly," Father Emanuel replied. "What better shelter was to be found? And if you think about it, they needed somewhere that would protect them from the wild animals. In those times, I am sure that animals hunted humanoids as they were themselves hunted, for food."

"Do you suppose there were dragons in those days, that these creatures were not just a myth?" Boris wondered.

"Well, it has been proved that dinosaurs certainly existed, and the Woolly Mammoth, so just because no fossils have been found, does not mean fire breathing dragons did not exist. However, I also think it is unlikely, that prehistoric man would have carved such a creature from imagination," commented Bart.

Father Emanuel held up his hand. "We cannot assume without proof, whether or not such things existed or whoever carved that magnificent creature, did so from personal experience or imagination. Also of course, there are still the Comodo Dragons, that do not breathe fire and have no wings. But who is to say that in the past they did not? That is not what we are investigating. At some time during our investigations, we may be in a position to fit this into the puzzle but meantime I suggest, we continue."

The photos of carvings at the top of the Devil's Eye proved to be as expected, so they continued to the descent, which brought them onto the ledge and the entrance to the cave.

Boris yawned. "Sorry, my friends, but I am tired and not able to pay proper attention. I'm sure you two must be in much the same state, so I suggest we retire and continue our perusals tomorrow morning."

Chapter 41

Again, the carvings just inside the entrance proved to be as expected. Nevertheless, the three men studied the photos carefully.

"What's that? There on the ground at the very spot where the entrance to the cave is," Boris exclaimed. "Look, it's worn away, but I swear that's another carving. It looks like writing. Your eyes are better than mine, Emanuel, can you decipher anything?"

"Just a moment." He pulled a magnifying glass from a drawer. "Yes. Indeed, it looks to me, like the carving over the entrance in the carpark. The carving though appears to be a Christian cross, with writing across the top bar. Only the outer edges of the bar are still visible, but it is still possible to read the letters at each end, where it has been protected from the weather.

"I wonder if the Count has inspected this recently," he commented. "I imagine not though, as the entrance is secured by what remains of the carving and those on the side walls and roof are still in place, so he would still be unable to enter."

They took turns at using the magnifying glass but could only just reveal the letters DEU on one side and what could have been an S. On the right could be seen quite clearly the letters T TE.

"Well, it looks as though you are right, Emanuel. The words DEUS CUSTODIAT TE have been carved into the bar of the cross. My word, the Gelbergers were determined to keep the Count out of those caves," Bart shuddered. "Just thinking about what he did all those years ago makes my skin crawl."

"We are the people who must shield, not just the village but the whole world from this evil now," Father Emanuel pointed out. "Let us therefore, continue going over what we have learned during our journey through the caves. The lever, can you bring forward your photo of that please, Boris."

He had photographed it from either side and the front. Also, Bart as he pulled the lever down, opening the hidden doorway to the cave. Boris slowly moved the video forward, revealing the skeleton of Sister Margarita sitting before the desk and the rest of the hidden cave. Then Bart, as he carefully secured the parchment letter in a plastic bag. There appeared to be nothing else of interest.

He then moved the video forward at a faster pace, until reaching the rock fall. This showed little that had been previously missed, the only comments being amusement, as first Boris then Father Emanuel made a somewhat less than elegant climb over them.

Boris fast-forwarded the video to the main right-hand side tunnel, from which five tunnels so far unexplored, led. The first on the left had proved to be short and showed nothing of interest. The next two were on the right and also proved to be short and of no interest. The fourth proved to be much more intriguing. It was longer than those previously checked and all along the walls were drawings of animals, of the dinosaur age.

"Look at that," Boris said excitedly. "A Woolly Mammoth, see those tusks. Is that a Sabre-Tooth Tiger? And there's that Dragon. It's surely breathing fire."

"Slow down, cousin, look on the other side. Those are humanoids and it looks as though they might be going hunting. See the pointed sticks and branches that look like knobkerries. They also appear to be organised in that they are in some formation. So, presumably the one in front is leading his men."

Father Emanuel interrupted. "You could be right, Bart, but as I said before we must not jump to conclusions. Those figures look half ape and half human, so perhaps they are Neanderthals. We cannot reach a definite deduction until the bones, that presumably come next on the film, have been officially tested by anthropologists. So, my friends, on to the cave of bones."

They had not entered that cave on their journey, just filmed it. Now, Boris forwarded the video slowly, as it scanned first the floor area and then the walls. At one end, the wall and roof were blackened, as though a fire had burned there. Scattered around were bones of all sizes and description, presumably those of whatever had been cooked on the fire.

At the other were two piles of skeletons that judging by the skulls, were humanoid. One pile appeared to be adult and the other children.

"That must have been where they stored their dead." Father Emanuel made the sign of the cross.

Benches had been hewn out of the end wall, on two levels.

"I imagine those were what the people slept on," Bart said.

"Let's get on to tunnel five, we all know what to expect there. But please, I'm dying for a cup of tea, so can we take a break, Emanuel, and return later," Boris requested.

Chapter 42

Refreshed, the three of them sat once more around the desk, switched on the video and continued watching the areas Boris had filmed.

The fifth tunnel was on the right with just a short entrance, which led into the large cavern that the men had assumed, served as a meeting place for the residents of the cave system. Boris concentrated first on the large flat rock that had the appearance of an altar. As he directed the view to the front of it, there was carved, the rough facsimile of a man.

"Well, I never," Boris said. "That is like mankind looks today. It's not like the drawings on the walls of tunnel four, for surely, they are pre-human. What do you think, Emanuel?"

"It seems more like a Christ figure. See the halo above its head, the way the arms are spread as though in prayer or blessing. Go above the altar, Boris, to that large circle. I think that is meant to be the sun surrounded by planets and stars."

He jumped as Bart shouted. "*Wow*! We didn't notice in the light of the torch but go back a bit and pause. There. Above the altar at the back. See what I mean? See, just below the big circle. Surely, it is a spaceship."

They stared as Boris enlarged the picture. It did appear to be, not one of the planets but indeed a flying saucer, such as those portrayed on television and film in the twentieth century. Tiny windows around the perimeter seemed to separate two large dinner plate shaped panels, whilst from the centre underside, were many lines that the men presumed were meant to represent the emission of air.

"Does that confirm that earth was first populated by aliens from other planets?" Father Emanuel asked. "But again, until these caves are properly explored by those more experienced than us, I think we should agree to keep our findings to ourselves. At least, until such time as we are quite sure of what we are potentially setting free in this world of ours. And indeed, until we have discovered a way to fight the Count's Revenge. Please, do we agree? If so, we must here and now make a pact of complete silence on this subject, except among we three and then, only when we are sure of complete privacy."

"I agree," Boris said, with a serious and slightly troubled look.

"And I," confirmed Bart.

The clasped hands in a circle and at the request of the priest, repeated as one voice:

We, Father Emanuel, Bart Slovinski and Boris Slovinski do promise under the guidance of God, our father in Heaven, to speak only of what we have learnt in the caves of the Golden Mountains amongst ourselves, and will reveal those findings to no other being, unless we three agree to do so.

"I am so very pleased that you two are sharing the Rectory with me at the moment, as I must confess to feeling a little nervous regarding our discoveries."

Bart agreed saying, "I am also much relieved that we are in a position to support each other, and I think we should continue to do so, both inside and outside this Rectory, for the foreseeable future. So, saying, will you shut down the computer for today, Boris, and if I may suggest it, perhaps we might disperse to the sitting room with a glass of your excellent brandy, Emanuel. Tomorrow is another day, as they say."

Chapter 43

They slept peacefully that night, well into the following morning and once again after breakfast, gathered around the desk in Father Emanuel's study. Boris set up the computer and pressing the icon for 'my pictures', fast forwarded to the Cathedral Cavern. The photos showed numerous stalagmites and stalactites, with a large rock covered by the latter, giving they remembered, the appearance of a cloth draped altar. The stalagmites formed, what they chose to describe as the congregation.

Looking at these, Bart commented, "That is why we named this cavern the Cathedral. It is so beautiful. But we are not here to show appreciation of the décor, so, Boris, please proceed to the far side where the seven tunnels are."

They had started with the far-left tunnel, which after walking for half an hour had turned in a hairpin bend, where they had eventually found themselves back at the entrance to tunnel number two. Apart from the pathway proving slippery with small rubble, these tunnels contained nothing for them to learn.

Tunnel number three was similarly unrewarding. After walking for three or four minutes, they had found the tunnel blocked from floor to roof and had decided not to attempt to clear the blockage. There were no carvings or writings on the walls.

The waterfall tunnel came next, number four, and they would return to that later.

"Was there anything special about number five?" Bart asked.

"If you recall, after only a short way in there was a small opening, too small for any of us as you can see," Boris pointed to a tiny gap in the sidewall, just about large enough for a small child. "Judging by the wet dripping down the walls, it had to be connected to the waterfall. Do you remember the noise?"

"Of course. Sorry, there is so much crashing around in my mind I am not thinking as clearly as I should."

"So, on to tunnel number six, which I am sure we all remember vividly."

Boris' photographs took them on the twenty-minute walk in twenty seconds, to where the tunnel curved, revealing the large curving cavern containing the equipment of a laboratory.

"Ah! The actual Eyrie," Bart said. "I know a little chemistry, studied it at university, until I changed to medieval history after the first year. Those tanks of vapour scare me though. It might be something achieved by mixing stuff from those bottles or jars. On the other hand, it could be a gas of some kind, though how or from where it comes, I cannot say. What do you think, Boris?"

"My feeling is that the mist or vapour is in fact, the Count's Revenge. Do you recall what happened when you bumped your head against the tank to try and see what it contained?"

"Yes, I do. It appeared to be an absolutely still vapour of some description, at the bottom of the tank but when the vibration went through the tank it moved, as though trying to get out. I felt as though it was trying to get me." He stopped short. "You are thinking about the mist from Suzanne's coffin when Gerry opened it. I remember saying when we saw the mist in the tank, that perhaps it was that which infected the Professor. Also, of course, there was that vapour in the church and some of the congregation went down with an unknown virus."

"Quite, and don't forget others were infected through Roland when he travelled on that train. Some family members of those in the congregation, were infected too. From what we saw on the news, that day we spoke to Meg and Gerry, some of the visitors who were in the cave at the time Suzanne drowned, were also down with the virus and they caused it to spread by passing it to other passengers on planes, trains or whatever, presumably via sneezes that contained this strange vapour."

Father Emanuel interrupted. "Remember what was recorded on Suzanne's mobile phone, that she would carry the Count's Revenge throughout the world. However, let us continue with our notes and photos."

Boris slowly forwarded the video around the perimeter of the cave, reaching the curve where they had discovered a protrusion that had turned out to be, when pushed, the opening mechanism to another cave. This one clearly showed the bookshelves containing many old tomes and manuscripts.

"Right," Father Emanuel said, "we did not have time to examine those books, but we did retrieve the Black Book from the rock desk. I suggest this might be the time to stop for a while, have something to drink and being refreshed, set ourselves to study it."

"I agree, but first we should discuss Boris's feeling of something not being right. What was it that got you, cousin?"

"I'm not sure but I think to start with, it was a gut feeling. Then I could feel a sort of trembling in the soles of my feet. The combination made me call to you two and retreat to the doorway. I do however, feel sure that Emanuel's intervention with his 'spraying and praying'." Boris made air-quotes. "I don't mean to be irreverent, Emanuel, but seriously, God was surely with us on that occasion. The rumble like thunder as the door began to close will stay with me all my life."

"On that note," Father Emanuel said, "let us have a break." He led them back to the welcoming kitchen.

Chapter 44

In the kitchen, Villette had just made fresh scones. They sat with her around the table, drinking coffee and having added fresh cream and strawberry jam to the still hot and delicious scones, relaxed as they chatted about normal everyday things.

Father Emanuel switched on the television, saying, "Time for the news, I wonder what has been happening in the world at large, while we have indulged in our own mission?" They soon learned as the presenter read…

The unknown virus, which appears to have started in Switzerland, is spreading across the world with devastating results. It seems to thrive in both cold and hot climates and the number of people that have perished from it has risen to millions. Younger people do not appear to be as susceptible to it as the older generation but that does not mean that they are totally immune. The World Health Organisation advises people to stay within their homes where possible and to keep doors and windows closed. This is because the infection would seem to be carried in a mist, which is only just visible and can appear suddenly. One reporter watched as the Mist struck. I will play his recording now; some people may find it disturbing.

I am sitting in my car, windows closed as advised. I am parked in an area favoured by dog walkers and will record what is happening as I watch. There are several paths leading through the woods, all clearly signposted and about half a dozen groups are setting out on their chosen paths. As I watch, a mist or vapour can be seen rising from beneath the bushes. I can see it from my position but I doubt if the walkers are able to do so. This report may very well not be believed—just some guy trying to get attention—they'll say. But I assure you on my father's grave, that what I am telling you is the whole truth. A mist is following each group, like it is stalking them. Some walkers are now out of my vision, but two paths are still clearly visible. The mist is now around their feet and a girl who has stopped way back and is without the area of mist, shouts to those ahead. I can't hear what she said. At the sound of her voice, the vapour speedily rises, so now those people and their dog, are hidden by the mist.

The presenter tells us that the reporter has stopped speaking for now but to be patient.

Quick, shut the door. I could not let the girl run into that mist, so shouted to her to stop, to come back. She turned, reluctant to pay attention to a stranger, but I managed to persuade her to at least return to the car park. Once there, I explained what I had seen and expected. Alicia is now in the car with me and is watching with horror, what befalls her friends.

First, we hear strangled cries. The people try to flee from the mist and the barking of the dog turns to squeals of pain. The mist or vapour seems to envelop them in something almost solid. Now the mist is lifting, disappearing. Alicia's friends all lie on the ground, some twitching, and others very still. She wants to go to them, but I prevail upon her the danger of doing so and have rung the services to deal with it.

This is Harris Montgomery, speaking to you from Denver Colorado, Reporter for RMBC. Please take care everyone and at all costs, look out for and avoid mists.

The TV returns to our presenter.

Well, that was interesting. It looks as though this unknown virus is carried by a mist, which appears as though it either thinks and acts for itself or is controlled in some manner. Now, we will continue with other news. A massive crash has occurred on the main road to Paris France…

Father Emanuel reached out and turned the television off.

"I think you should return to your mother, Villette, and stay indoors with her until you hear from me that it is safe to go out. Have you sufficient food in stock?"

"But, Father, I still have to clean the lounge and your study. And Mother and I probably have sufficient food for about a week, after that I am not sure."

"Right, Villette, take what you might need from the freezer and any tinned stuff from the cupboard. Bear in mind what I say. Pray, as will I and our friends here, and do not attempt to leave your cottage. Every day, we will keep in contact via our telephones, so each household is aware of the others whereabouts. Is that clear my dear?"

Bart intervened here. "Let us get the food packed and when you are ready, Villette, I will escort you to your cottage and see you safely inside."

"Oh, it is only a short walk along the drive, Bart. I can manage that, have done so for many years."

"Not with the danger of the mist, my dear, and I should never forgive myself if anything happened to you. Besides, those two bags will be much too heavy for you to carry."

So, having requested his friends to watch for his return, Bart and Villette hastened to the cottage at the entrance to the path to the Rectory.

Chapter 45

They reached the cottage in five minutes, having walked quickly, frequently looking around at ground level for any sign of mist. Villette opened the door and Bart carried the two heavy bags to the kitchen. Then he placed his hands on her shoulders, looking into those two dark sparkling eyes. "Please take care and pay heed to what the good Father asked. I would not have harm come to you, my dear."

Bart leaned forward, as did Villette and they experienced their first kiss. Then with a final hug, he opened the door and watched as the woman with whom he now knew he had fallen in love, closed it.

All around him appeared clear, so breaking into a run and keeping his eyes on the verges on either side, made his way back along the drive to the Rectory. He had taken only three minutes to return and had reached the rose bushes that grew on both sides of the path from the gate, when the front door flew open and Boris shouted to him.

"It's behind you, Bart. Run faster, it's catching up."

Without turning to see what was happening, Bart speeded up and almost fell in the door of the Rectory.

As Boris slammed the door, it was as though it had been hit by a large body. He firmly locked and bolted the door, then wiping his brow gasped. "That was a close call, cousin, I feel almost as exhausted as you look. Come, sweet tea awaits us, or at least, it should by now, Emanuel was working on it as I watched for you."

"Let's take this into the sitting room. You look as though you need to relax in a comfortable chair, Bart, my friend."

Father Emanuel, having poured tea, Bart stirred in two heaped spoonsful of sugar and taking a sip, replaced the cup and relaxed into an armchair. He waved his hand, side to side, indicating he needed to think over what had happened, breathing in through his nose for a count of six, holding his breath for two and exhaling for a count of six. After doing this eight times, he sighed.

"Thanks for your patience, I needed to relax and the best way I know is to breath slowly. I once read about that method in a book about mindfulness and it has proved effective for me many times.

Right. Villette has been safely returned to her cottage and fully understands what she has been told. If you will excuse me, I must phone, to let her know I am safely back at the Rectory. I would appreciate it if you will not tell Villette of my rather inelegant, entry back to Christendom. She will only worry and at the moment, she has her mother to look after. Meanwhile, I can confirm that we reached the cottage safely and so far, as I could tell, there was no sign of mist on my return. Thank you, Boris, for looking out for me."

"No problem, cousin, whilst you were gone, Emanuel and I checked all the doors and windows, including the outside one that leads to the cellars.

To get to that one, we needed to go outside, but all appeared clear. We then went to the church and made sure the doors were secure, also the ones leading from the vestry."

"I showed Boris the tunnel leading from the vestry to this Rectory. All possible entrances are now secure, including the windows and the one leading to the clock tower. I suggested Boris watch for your return whilst I made tea and from there you know as much as we do."

He continued. "With what we have learned since returning here from the caves, it would seem to prove that the Count's Revenge is whatever is in that mist or vapour. As we agreed before, there is something in it that contains a toxic which attacks specifically the human species, but it appears that animals are not necessarily immune. Bear in mind what I saw and heard in the Great Cavern pool. I firmly believe that it was a shadow of Henri de Ville, and do you remember what he told me?" He read from his notes…

I am Henri de Ville. Please, Father, pray for me. Tell God, our father that I sincerely repent my sins. I tried telling the lady not to attempt to rescue me, that I was being controlled from afar by Papa Count, but she would not heed me. He used her for his revenge on the world and the only thing that can save all of humanity from his evil virus, is within the Eyrie laboratory.

"There are two important things to note. One is that Suzanne's body was indeed being used to carry the Count's Revenge and the other, that the only thing able to save humanity is within the laboratory, which we now know is attached to the Count's Eyrie. You see what this information means, my friends; it is necessary, no imperative, that we contact all authorities that can help and tell all we know."

They sat mulling over this information. Then, Boris broke the silence.

"I agree that ultimately, we have to do as Emanuel suggests. In the meantime, however, we have in our possession, the Black Book from the Eyrie. If you agree, I think we must finish what we started here and make our decision as to what follows when we finish."

The others agreed, so after stopping for half an hour or so to make sandwiches and coffee, they returned to the study.

Chapter 46

Once again, the three men continued to watch the video Boris had recorded on his phone. This time, the hidden door to the Eyrie closing just as they had exited, was shown. The clang as it finally shut could be heard, then silence, followed by their gasps and comments.

"What do we think about that?" Boris asked. "Seems to me that the idea of a time switch is probable. Bear in mind that other things we have come across have seemed to be in advance of Henri's era, the flying saucer in the meeting cave for instance. So, perhaps if aliens are involved in this mystery, a time switch is not impossible."

"It appears no more improbable than an occult spell cast by the Count," Father Emanuel commented, "and as I said before, we should wait until there is positive information, after full examination by geologists and anthropologists."

Bart intervened. "You are right of course, Emanuel, but nevertheless, have you considered how long that would take? For example, most likely arranging for those experts, could take one or two years to get organised. They would probably take five years to collect and collate their findings, and at the end of the day, how far is the virus getting towards the end of mankind? We will never have the opportunity of stopping the spread of the virus, let alone the evil Count."

"Agreed, cousin. I have contacts through my magazine, who may well be interested in helping us solve that problem. Meanwhile, let's continue to the end of our video to discover what else previously skipped our notice. We also need to read all that is in the Black Book, as that may well contain the information we need."

The video continued round the outside of the laboratory, eventually coming to another tunnel. As predicted, this tunnel proved to be number seven, exiting once again into the Cathedral Cavern and containing nothing to remark upon.

"So," said Boris, "back to tunnel number four and the waterfall."

They studied the photos carefully for anything previously not noticed, but that thirty-minute trek was covered in less than three minutes, with nothing of interest. Boris slowed their crabwalk, complete with backpacks, facing the mountainside behind the waterfall. There was nothing to be seen but the mountain to their front and thundering water behind them.

Father Emanuel crossed himself. "Dear God, I would not wish to do that again," he said.

The video covered the Great Cavern and Bottomless Pool but had missed Father Emanuel's encounter with Henri de Ville. The final photographs were of carvings above and on either side of the entrance to the caves, but revealed nothing they had not seen before.

It was decided to leave the entries in the book until the following day, as it would undoubtedly require a great deal of concentration. Also, as none of them had ventured to look, it was felt that maybe the language would not be one with which they were familiar.

Chapter 47

Over breakfast the following morning, all three discovered they had not slept well, their heads being full of thoughts and memories of what they had experienced and what was still to be accomplished. They agreed that first of all a telephone call to Villette must be made, to confirm her safety. Bart immediately undertook to do this and disappeared with his mobile. On his return, he confirmed that all was well, which was after all, obvious by the smile on his face.

Father Emanuel, wished to go to his church, to check everything was as it should be and Bart volunteered to accompany him through the tunnel to the vestry.

Boris meanwhile, would email Meg and Gerry to update them. He planned to do so through a system which would disguise where the call came from and hoped Gerry had made the necessary encryption to his own devices.

The connection duly made, Boris attached copies of the second journey through the caves, together with a typed copy of their discussion. After he had sent this, Boris dialled Gerry's number to speak with him and to confirm the safe arrival of the information.

"Please delete all I sent as soon as possible, Gerry. This matter is becoming somewhat more difficult and decidedly dangerous. Please both of you, pay attention to what you see and be aware of the potential danger to yourselves."

"Don't worry, old chap, Meg and I are taking care, the twins are safely at university and we are in touch with them every day."

They spoke, being very careful not to say anything explicit and by the time the call was finished, Emanuel and Bart had joined him in the study.

Father Emanuel departed to make coffee and when they were once more sitting comfortably, he withdrew the Black Book that had been seized from the Eyrie, from his safe. Placing it on the desk he said, "Shall I take it from the envelope or…"

"Of course, just let's get down to studying the thing," Boris replied.

Taking care not to risk damage, Father Emanuel gently eased the book from the envelope and laid it on the altar cloth, which he had already placed on the desk for that purpose. "Gloves everyone," he said. "This may be very fragile and could crumble to dust, if we are not careful."

It proved to be in landscape format and about 1cm thick. The leather cover was embossed in the form of a coffin and was decorated with tooled gold, on the lid of which, was an inverted cross. Along the side was printed, also tooled in gold leaf, *THE LEDGER OF THE MASTER*. The cover was faded with age, the leather showing signs of cracking in places. Father Emanuel opened the cover revealing another replication of the embossed coffin on the outer cover. He carefully turned the page; the one to the left was blank, but on the right, written in large bold letters, were the words:

The Book of Satanic Rights the Ledger of the Master Count 100-1581

"Well, that certainly tells us something. That top line is the title of one of the books I rescued from the library of the Convent of the Golden Orb, before it became a hotel. It was a bit longer than that though, the title ended with Rights Statutes and Procedures. Suzanne saw it and was horrified, she thought it was a Family Bible, which in a way of course it was." Bart sounded both angry and disturbed. "We read the family bit—Count 100, followed by Count 100 etcetera but Suzanne never made it back for a further investigation into what else it contained. Probably, a good thing."

He shook himself, drank the rest of his coffee and continued. "Anyway, it looks as though we are about to have a chance to read what the Count had to say for himself, so let's get on with it.

Sorry, my friends, I got carried away there, give me a moment please, I will make some fresh coffee, if that's alright with you, Emanuel."

He departed to the kitchen, leaving Emanuel and Boris with raised eyebrows but fully understanding his distraction. They sat in silence until his return and remained that way until the three mugs of coffee had been consumed.

Returning to their task round the desk, Father Emanuel turned another page of the ledger.

~~

This page was headed **RIGHTS.** The print was faded, but not illegible and proved to be written in English. However, that might be so, but it was not an easy read.

Boris suggested he make notes direct onto his computer, picking out only those parts that appeared relevant. "Do you have a mobile with a camera, Emanuel?" Receiving an affirmative he continued. "Then, set it up and every time we turn a page perhaps you will kindly photograph each one. That way if at some point we are robbed or mislay the book, we shall have, hopefully, photos of the pages and my notes to refer to. All the information we have gathered must be separated, so no one can easily deprive us of the whole of our information. We will each take parts of it and as individuals, our responsibility is to keep that information safe in whatever way or place we see fit.

The first pages appeared to be a list of rights applicable to the Count, covering not only those appertaining to land and property owned by him, but also the control of similar items owned by the inhabitants of Billenbach. Those individuals were enabled to maintain their homes, land, and animals, only by donating a percentage of their total income (which appeared to be a double tithe- $2 \times 10\%$) to the reigning Count, on an annual basis. It went on to tell what would (and it appeared, was indeed happening at that time-*1581)*. If the tithes were not forthcoming, then all the animals were either taken or killed and the owners were advised to leave the area within two days. Failing to do this, their animals were slaughtered and the property destroyed by fire, completely razed to the ground.

Other rights entitled the Count to penetrate a virgin every tenth year ending with the figure 1, for the purpose of birthing a male successor. The three men were aware of this from reading the regressions of Michael Deville, in his life during the sixteenth and seventeenth centuries as Henri de Ville.

They had now turned the eight pages labelled as Rights and agreed to take a break. Father Emanuel locked the book securely in his safe, saying, "We should get some fresh air to clear our heads. I suggest we walk to the cottage just to make sure Villette and her mother are still safe and secure."

Chapter 48

Bart telephoned Villette, to let her know their intention. Together, keeping a lookout all around them, the three walked along the drive to Villette's cottage. She had been looking out of the window and saw them arrive, so the door opened as soon as they opened the gate.

"Come in, come in. Is everything alright?" she asked. "Have you had lunch? I was just about to get it ready, do please join us. Mother will be delighted to see you, Father." Villette rattled on in this manner, then, "Oh, I am sorry. Do please come through to the lounge and chat with Mother, while I see to things in the kitchen."

"Can I help?" Bart asked hopefully.

Villette smiled, "Of course. Another pair of hands will be very useful and you can tell me how the three of you are progressing."

As they disappeared into the kitchen, Father Emanuel led Boris into the lounge and introduced him to Villette's Mother.

The old lady was in her eighth decade, crippled with arthritis, but her eyes were bright and intelligent.

"Only two of the Three Musketeer's," she said with a mischievous smile.

"Is that your book of the week, Sara?"

"You know me, Father, I've read it of course, but at the moment I am into a good thriller. I know there's no point asking you for suggestions of good thriller writers, but perhaps your handsome companion might be able to do so. He looks the type of man who would enjoy a good adventure."

"Indeed, I am madame. My name is Boris Slovinski and I own a magazine known as *International Viewpoint*. Your lovely daughter may have told you some of what is going on in the Golden Mountains at the moment, but this particular adventure is one in which I would rather not be involved."

"Please call me, Sara, madame makes me feel shut out, old and ultimately useless. She tells me some but probably knows more than she speaks of to me.

Bless her, Villette worries that some knowledge, might upset me. She's wrong of course, but I know what is kept from me, is meant for my own peace of mind."

At that moment, Bart banged his hand on the tray he carried and said loudly, "Lunch is served."

~~

Villette had roasted a haunch of beef, served with roast potatoes and a selection of vegetables. Bart carved and Villette told her guests to help themselves to what they wanted.

After an excellent meal, they sat around the fire with mugs of steaming coffee and, having as previously agreed amongst themselves, that it was safe and the right thing to do so, told the two women of their mission and the potential danger to them all.

As he finished his tale, Sara said, "My and here was I looking to find fresh thriller writers. You three have an adventure far in excess of the pages I have read. Indeed, there must be a book in your mission, perhaps you should consider it, Boris."

"I told you earlier, Sara, that I own the magazine, *International Viewpoint*. In fact, the start of this mission was first published as a series in it, Suzanne's book titled *Dark Regressions*, appeared in the magazine before it was published as a book. You would enjoy that one I am sure and I will have my secretary send you a copy. Meanwhile, ladies, please take good notice of what you have been told. You are now fully aware of what you must and I repeat must, do to ensure your safety. Above all, keep your doors and windows firmly closed, keep in touch with us at the Rectory at all times and if you are in any way perturbed about, well, anything, please do not hesitate to phone us. I will make sure you have the mobile numbers of all three phones, so if one is not obtainable, you can ring the others."

Bart broke in. "If for any reason, you are unable to get a response from any of us, please no heroics. You are to doubly secure the cottage and if necessary, lock both of you in a room without a window. The bathroom perhaps, although that has a fan-vent, which I will make sure is firmly closed and covered before we go. Perhaps, you could take me on a tour of the cottage, so that I can see for myself that all mist-sized gaps are well covered."

They left the room and Bart took Villette's hand, as they checked every nook and cranny.

"My concern is for your safety, Villette, for when this is over, I hope you will allow me to entertain you, as someone who cares deeply for the beautiful lady before me."

She blushed but only nodded her reply.

When later, the three men left, Boris reiterated his instructions, adding, "You are to tell no one what you know. It would only add to your potential danger. Knowing no more than any of the villagers is your main safety net."

Chapter 49

As they walked, once again, the three men kept a careful lookout for any sign of mist. They had reached the lychgate to the church, Father Emanuel slightly in front, when almost simultaneously, Boris and Bart said, both in loud whispers, "Emanuel, to the side, look out." He turned slowly. To the right, mist was rising from beneath the trees edging the path, to the left it was snaking from under the hedge. But behind them, the swirling mist was further away but moving much faster.

"Quick, through the gate," he shouted, darting through, and holding it for the other two.

Bart was on the right and closest so slipped through. Boris followed and as he did so, the right-side mist, caught his foot. It was as though he was gripped by the hand of a strong beast. He twisted and pulled as hard as possible to release the firm hold on his boot, which was when Bart grabbed him by the arms. But he still could not move.

"Slip out of your boot," shouted Bart.

Boris wriggled his foot and just as he managed to free it felt a tug on his left foot, as mist encircled the heel of his boot. With the right foot now firmly on the ground before him, he withdrew his foot and stumbled as Bart half dragged him through the lychgate.

Meanwhile, Father Emanuel had unlocked the church door. "Quickly," he yelled.

The two men ran to the church, just reaching the door, held open by the priest, as the swirling snake of mist to the rear, shot under the gate, now joining with the other two and forming a larger and rising mist, almost waist high.

As they flung the door shut, bolting it top and bottom, the thump on the outside was reminiscent of Bart's return to the Rectory, after seeing Villette safely to her cottage. It was as though several large creatures, had combined to prevent its closing.

All three men walked unsteadily to the front pews, all genuflecting before the altar and crossing themselves. Father Emanuel, uttered prayers of thanksgiving, Bart and Boris adding their Amen.

"Those were Ferrigami boots. Very expensive," Boris complained.

"Better lose them than you. Just thank God we were next to the church when the mists appeared. Had they touched your skin, I doubt you would be able to escape. We now know how the Count's Revenge works. It crushes the life from its victims." Bart shook his head. "Emanuel, my friend, let us go through the hidden tunnel to the Rectory. I need a strong drink and Boris needs a hot shower to warm him, plus something to put on his feet before they freeze."

Chapter 50

Finally, sitting around a blazing fire, with glasses of wine in their hands, the three men discussed the events since their visit to Villette and her mother at the cottage.

Bart asked, "Do you suppose those two ladies are safe in the cottage or should we try to bring them to the Rectory?"

"As long as they do what we advised, and I have no reason to think they would not, they are probably safer there than to risk the short trip here. Think of what has happened on the two occasions we have made that walk. Villette is sensible and anyway her mother finds it difficult to walk. Also, we will keep in constant touch with them and they will have our prayers to protect them," Father Emanuel crossed himself and nodded to Boris to continue.

"It looks as though what they are calling the MistVirus is getting stronger. Remember those walkers in the forest, they were all enveloped by the mist and apparently crushed to death, including their dog. The woman, who for some reason had lagged behind was able to escape, presumably out of reach of the mist. It seems as though this mist is able to think for itself but in my opinion, the Count is manipulating it in some way." Boris led the discussion. "That would account for the earlier sneezing experiences. Roland for instance, was unwell for several days before he succumbed and among the other passengers on the train, some were infected and others not. Then things progressed, with apparently the first person to be crushed, being a patient in hospital. The doctors and nurses in attendance, fully protected by hazard gear, were able to report that the mist arising from his sneeze, could be seen to envelop him."

"And no one appeared to even make an attempt to help him," Bart commented.

"In all honesty, cousin, would you have risked trying to enter that mist? You'd most likely become the next victim."

Father Emanuel interrupted a potential debate. "Whatever the case, there is no doubt that the MistVirus is very strong, as we can confirm by the strength of it against the church door, the Rectory door also for that matter. One thing to note though, is that although the mist collided heavily with the doors, it seems unable to creep through gaps and cracks. Strange, do you not think? However, that may well be to our advantage and something we should seriously consider. What we must do, is search through the Black Book found in the Eyrie laboratory, to try and discover what the late Henri de Ville tried to tell us. So, I suggest we return to my study and continue our research."

"Agreed, but I'm going to need coffee, lots of it. Shall I make it while you two set up things in the study," Boris stood, assuming the answer would be in the affirmative, and Father Emanuel with Bart returned to the study.

Whilst Father Emanuel opened his safe to retrieve the Black Book, Bart stoked the fire and by the time Boris returned carrying a tray of the essentials, all was ready to commence once again.

Chapter 51

The next heading revealed was **STATUTES.** The rules and regulations were many, the main one of which appeared to be that nobody was allowed to do anything whatsoever, without first consulting the Count. His decision was to be final and absolute.

"Great," said Boris. "That gives '*himself*' complete control over the whole of the village, including its inhabitants. Effectively, the statutes confirm the rights. Do you consider we need to expand upon each one, or shall we take them as read and continue to the Procedures bit?"

They voted to first continue photographing each page, then return to Rights and Statutes if it seemed necessary to do so.

So, to **PROCEDURES.** The rigmarole they hoped would guide them to the plans of the Count, during the sixteenth/seventeenth centuries and what his aspirations were to the present day, some five hundred years later.

These were written in the format of a diary, presumably by the Count, commencing from 1581, when Isabella de Ville and Susan Blessed first appeared at the Convent of the Golden Orb. They were easier to read but nevertheless, the three men decided to continue as originally agreed. So, turning the recorder to voice activated mode, they continued.

"I read the first part," Father Emanuel said. "So, perhaps you would like to continue, Boris."

"Not for the moment," was the reply. "I want to make sure the photographing of each page is to my satisfaction. Bart, you continue the reading please."

"Very well." He made himself comfortable, coughed to clear his throat and commenced reading.

"Today, I have received information from the Sisters of Solitude, attached to St Patricks Monastery in England. Mother Superior Margarita has advised me that recently, two young women turned up at the gates to the nunnery, asking for refuge. She has ascertained, that the younger of the two is no more than sixteen years old and knowing of the problems here in Switzerland, is asking permission to send the two young women to the Convent of the Golden Orb, accompanied by Sister Madeleine, for my appraisal. I have concurred to this request and now await the arrival of my next potential Bride.

Two weeks have passed and still my Bride has not arrived. How much longer does Mother Superior think she can keep *me* waiting, just because she is far away in England?

There would appear to be another period of waiting for the Count and judging by the scratches of his pen and ink, his temper keeps erupting."

Bart stopped reading here and drank some coffee, "Ugh! This is cold. Do you feel like making another pot please, Emanuel? This is thirsty work."

Later, his thirst duly quenched, Bart continued.

"It has taken nearly four weeks but at last, today Sister Madeleine with her two charges, arrived at the Convent of the Golden Orb. I shall, of course, not reveal myself until the time is right, but the lady Isabella is of great beauty and high birth. Her father is the Baron Dominitus, a man well known to myself, for many reasons.

I have ordered the separation of the two women, after seven days. The companion is of no relevance and will be conducted to the kitchen, where she can work with the other women. These women are those who failed to become pregnant; those with the temerity to produce a girl-child, all succumbed to the Grim Reaper, together with the babe during the birth. Those unable to produce a male child for me to educate as my heir. To become the next Count 100.

His anger shows here, not only through the bitter words, but he has underlined whole sentences."

With these words, Bart poured himself more coffee before reading on.

"I have appointed Sister Aureole, to attend to all everyday requirements of Lady Isabella. She will when the time is right, be brought to my room of Procedures and Celebration, at the top of the Convent of the Golden Orb, where I will perform the necessary daily procedures, to establish her right to become my Bride and to bear my son and heir. This time, I know that she will produce a male heir and he will live.

Six weeks have passed and the time draws nearer. Today, Sister Joseph has reported to the Mother Superior, that she witnessed Lady Isabella's companion fall from the clifftop, which could only have resulted in her death. I can now proceed with confidence, my plans for Lady Isabella.

The procedures for my Bride will commence today. She will be taken to the office of Mother Superior, who will apprise her of the death of Susan Blessed, due to her falling from the clifftop. Tomorrow, I will visit Lady Isabella in her cell with words of comfort. She will be hypnotised on that occasion and from that moment, will be completely controlled by her Lord and Master. Just seven words *'Be still, my child, and hear me'*. Following those words, my Bride will only hear my voice and her memories will be those I wish her to remember.

Once more, I have control of the mind of another, to do with what I will.

I, The Count, answer only to one Master – Lucifer himself.

My Bride answers to her one and only Master – I, The Count."

Bart shook his head in disgust. "I have had enough; I wish to stop this now."

Chapter 52

Once more in the kitchen of the Rectory, Father Emanuel gathered together the ingredients for a chilli-con-carne with rice. Boris washed their mugs and the coffee equipment. Bart sat at the table, head in hands.

"God help us. That man is evil personified." He said despairingly.

Boris poured him a glass of red wine. "We all agree with that, cousin, but unless we have some idea of his planning, there is no way forward for us to terminate his latest plan for our world. We can only hope to find the antidote to the MistVirus, if we fully study the contents of the Black Book thoroughly."

"I know," Bart replied. "The antidote is held in the laboratory within the Eyrie, as '*the ghost*' told Emanuel. We are obliged to take so much on faith and seem to have so little proof. Yes, yes, I know, Boris, the proof will be contained somewhere in that damned Black Book but that makes it no easier to cope with."

"Meanwhile," Father Emanuel broke in, "the food is nearly ready, so if you two would kindly set the table, perhaps we can eat in peace and try to forget our quest for a while at least."

As they ate their meal, it proved almost impossible, for all three to dispel thoughts of what they had so far read in the Black Book. They sat with long frowning faces etched with despair and eventually, gave up trying to enjoy the meal, pushing remaining food to the side of their plates. More wine was poured and was gulped down.

"At this rate, we are not going to be able to return to our study of that book. We shall all be drunk. So," Boris said raising his glass, "I suggest we do just that. Let's get drunk, for that might well ensure our finding sleep this night."

The others concurred, Father Emanuel pointing out that severe hangovers would most certainly be their punishment in the morning. "I have just the right antidote for that problem, however," he said.

So, they returned to the fireside, this time with an extra bottle of red wine and settled for whatever may come. As it happened, they relaxed in comfortable armchairs and fell asleep, having only sipped one more glass each.

~~

Boris stretched, saw the time was nearly six o'clock and made his way to the kitchen where he set the coffee machine working, with a very strong mixture. By the time it was ready, both Emanuel and Bart had joined him, rubbing their eyes. There was apparently no need for Father Emanuel's hangover-zapper, strong coffee did the job satisfactorily.

With a self-conscious grin, he confessed that coffee was in fact his antidote and making toast for a simple breakfast, suggested they showered, then return to the study and the Black Book.

Chapter 53

"Right, are we ready for another session with the Procedures?" Father Emanuel asked, opening his safe and placing the Black Book on the desk. They had agreed that he should be the reader of the next section of the Count's writings.

"The initial ceremony will take place this very day. She will be prepared and laid upon the altar in my room of Procedures and Celebration, at the top of the Convent of the Golden Orb. I shall say those words that give me total control of her mind. '*Be still, my child, and hear me*'. Thenceforth, she will be unaware of what is happening and will hear only the words of sacrifice, being sung by the Convent Choir, to the Master. She will not of course understand those words, as they are in a language unfamiliar to her.

Then, for the next five days, a similar ceremony will be performed. The sung words to the Master will vary, as time draws nearer for the penetration of my Bride. At last, will come the seventh day, the Day of Penetration. The day my son and heir will be impregnated into the body of Lady Isabella. I will train my son into the ways of the Counts 100 and at last will rest, until time comes once again for my rebirth."

~~

"These days have been recorded in Isabella de Ville's diary, which we have all read and I believe understood."

Having absorbed more strong coffee, it was now the turn of Boris to read from the Black Book. So, he commenced, first making sure the recorder was working properly and photographing each page before turning to the next one.

"I make a point of visiting her every day, always repeating the mantra for control. I have also ensured this through Sister Aureole, who is to remain in charge of Lady Isabella, making sure she is completely compliant. This is achieved by a drug prepared by myself and the kitchen staff insert it in the milk prepared for her.

At last, after eight weeks of anxious waiting, I am today assured that my Bride is indeed pregnant. I feel sure that she carries my son within her and nothing will now prevent the succession of my family as preordained by the Master himself."

Boris skipped the next few pages, as they were only boastings of the Count's abilities in several exploits, but concentrating on the one uppermost in his mind at that time.

"I have no inclination or intention of reading that stuff and nonsense," he commented in disgust. "Please pour me another coffee, Bart, black this time please, I need a strong caffeine hit."

~~

Yet more coffee having been consumed by all Boris continued.

"Well, well. It appears that the Count had no idea that Susan Blessed was still alive. He believed like everyone, that she had fallen to her death off that cliff. The next entry is some four weeks later, Isabella must have been about three months pregnant. He has just learnt of her disappearance and is extremely angry. There are scratches, scrawls, and ink blots. Also, some strange drawings that might well have an occult meaning but we will look at those on the computer later. Meanwhile, I will continue trying to read what that devil has written.

She has gone. My Bride has left the convent. Where in the name of Hell, has she gone with my son. When I catch her and once, she has birthed my son, she will be sent to Hell by me, personally.

I have learned that when Sister Aureole collected her empty cup, she was apparently asleep, curled on her bed facing the wall. Sister Aureole checked the room, picked up the empty cup and shut the door of the cell behind her. There was no reason to lock the door as to all intents and purposes, there was nowhere for her to go. This morning Sister Aureole went to shake her awake at six o'clock, only to find that what she had assumed to be Lady Isabella, was in fact a pillow.

I have removed Sister Aureole from her comfortable cell to one of those used for the kitchen novices. These have no windows, are small, dark and uncomfortable. She is to be put to the most menial tasks in the kitchen and everyone has been forbidden to speak to her. They all fear their Master, *me*, so will not dare to disobey.

I have ordered a thorough search of the grounds and mountainside, with special care to check the cliff-top where her companion, Susan Blessed, fell to her death.

The rest of this page is left blank." Boris turned the page and continued.

"*DAMNATION AND MAY THEY ALL ROT IN HELL.* Begins the page, following two more blank pages.

Since the time of the carvings, some three to four hundred years, I have not been able to personally enter the cave system. The Gelberger family are responsible for this. I need to gain entrance to my Eyrie and above all, the laboratory. Meanwhile, I have to rely on my Demon to make entries in this book. That in itself is not a problem, as this creature is entirely run by my own brainwaves. Demon is merely an automaton that fortunately was left within the Eyrie before the caves were closed to me. I plan to use it on all necessary occasions.

The following page is also left blank but turning over continues…

I have heard from the Reverend Mother of St Patricks Hospice, that a child was recently birthed there, to a woman who is apparently the daughter of Baron Dominitus.

Shortly, after the birth, I called at the Monastery of St Patricks, where Brother John, advised the Prior of my presence. We met in the chapel and the Prior, who obviously saw some advantage in this meeting place, advised me that the birth had resulted in death. I have accepted this, assuming it to mean both Mother and Child are dead.

One Sister Teresa attended the birth and duly reported that both Mother and Child did not survive. On the following day, a Farmer's Daughter also gave birth in St Patricks Hospice. This was the result of a relationship with a Romany, who had now moved on with his companions. She did not survive but the boy child apparently did and Sister Teresa has obtained permission from the Prior, Father Gregory, to raise the boy within the precincts of the Monastery. He is to be named Brother Henri.

Here follow more scrawls and scratches, also many words that I am unable, to not only decipher but would not wish to do so if I could. They appear in capital letters and the sight of them brings shivers down my spine." Boris stopped reading and turned off the recorder.

"We begin to learn more," Father Emanuel said with a sigh. "Perhaps, we should put this back in the safe until tomorrow, for I feel unable to cope with more of this evil."

Boris agreed. "It gets into your very soul doesn't it, Emanuel? Let's hide the dratted thing away for the time being, then perhaps you would be kind enough to say a prayer to clean the atmosphere around us."

This done, the three men agreed to retire to their rooms until it was time to prepare dinner.

Later, they ate a relatively silent meal and retired in the hope of sleeping peacefully but with little real expectations of doing so.

Chapter 54

The following day found the three men back in the study early. None of them had slept well with so many things on their minds. It was once more Bart's turn to act as reader, a task he had not looked forward to. He took a deep breath and commenced.

"The following page, going by our knowledge through Michael's regressions, is apparently revealing what happened after Sister Teresa drowned, when Henri was four years old.

The next page is blank, which I presume is a period before the Count found out that the boy, whom he had accepted to have been the child of the farmer's daughter, was in fact the son of Isabella de Ville. His own Son and heir. The writing in the book continues…

I am of a more optimistic frame of mind today and have instructed my Demon to enter more information into the Black Book in my Eyrie. Mother Superior, at the Hospice of St Patricks, has advised me of the death of Sister Teresa by drowning. I understand that the boy-child was with her in a boat at the time. It has been assumed that he could not swim, and he encourages this belief, but one of the Sisters of Solitude, close to the Mother Superior, has observed him actually doing so. I shall now keep an eye on the boy, to confirm my belief that he is the son of Isabella de Ville.

Here follows another blank page, which I imagine, is a period when the Count does not require his Demon to write in the ledger. Then…

I have watched this boy through the past years. He is assuredly my son. Such a character. He has the monks eating out of his hand, though the Prior tries to control him. Imagine, inserting a rat in the habit of one of the brothers, one with a real fear of the creatures. Such a face of innocence too. It is nearly time to enter his dreams, to influence his future actions and begin training him, to follow in the footsteps of his honoured Father.

Papa Count is watching you, my son. You are now thirteen years of age, growing fast and maturing too. I have started to influence you through dreams and find you responding just as I wish. You are thinking of life at the Monastery as religious nonsense and I am so proud of your successful termination of the Prior. There is for the time being, nothing to restrict your absences from that prison in which you are held. But I will continue my training through your dreams for a while longer.

Time has passed, nearly three years and it was the eve of your sixteenth birthday. You were indeed surprised to find me in your room on that day but following my prayers to the Master of Mankind, soon came to understand that I am indeed your Papa Count. You will now be trained by direct communication with me when I so desire it.

After two years had nearly passed, I commanded him to move to the City of London, where he would perform the conjuring of a Magician. Learning to deceive by sleight of hand and make himself rich in the process. Ah, my son, you learn well.

After some months, I am now ready to have my son brought to Switzerland. To the Convent of the Golden Orb, where he will be given instructions by myself, for the total destruction of those responsible for the closing of the entrances to my Eyrie in the caves. The family Gelberger will be no longer and with their deaths, the sealing of the cave entrances will become void.

We now know what happened to Henri during his presumed attempt to crab-walk his way behind the waterfall," Bart said. "I suggest that we now break for lunch and continue thereafter. Boris, it will be your turn to continue the readings, if you are willing."

Chapter 55

Lunch completed and sitting round the desk again, Boris continued.

"Why am I always the one to get landed with the unpronounceable words? I'm sure they're not fit for the ears of responsible, God-fearing people. Also, I'm scared that if I were to repeat them, I might have quoted some curse or other and will cause us all to explode or disintegrate. Anyway, after all that rigmarole, there are a couple of pages full of scribblings that might be either words or drawings."

Bart and Emanuel looked carefully at the pages referred to, then shaking their heads and after carefully photographing them, suggested Boris continue the next writings that he was able to decipher.

"He writes as follows.

Oh, my son, my Henri, what did those religious maniacs at the Monastery teach you? Did you not learn from your Papa Count, the way forward? You were my heir, my future, the future of our dynasty. I am now unable to either enter the caves to my Eyrie and laboratory, or to send the Gelberger family to dwell in Hell.

I must now await the coming of one who is able to, in a later age, bring forth my Revenge. That may be many hundreds of years whilst in the meantime, I must hide until He Who Once Was shall again appear upon the Earth."

Boris mopped his brow. "I assume the Count did indeed hide himself as he prophesised. It looks as though Michael Deville was, 'He Who Once Was'. It would appear, that his regressions were the doorway, through which the Count or as in Michael's earlier lives, the Man in Black, became a visible force on the Earth once again. He must have been secluded in the Convent of the Golden Orb, until it became the Hotel Orb de l'Or. At that time, the regressions were completed, both Henri and Michael were known to be deceased and my magazine was preparing to print *Dark Regressions* in serialised format, prior to the publishing of Suzanne's book, which is where the Count has his Demon continue writings.

There are more blank pages that appear to have at some point in time, been marked and either erased or had drawings compressed upon them. Can either of you discern what they might be?"

"Let us come back to those later," Father Emanuel suggested, and this being agreed Boris read on.

"My Master has informed me of one Michael Deville, a man of interesting psychopathic character. He is regressing into his previous lives and is the one, for whom I have waited all these years of tedium. He commences by going back through his time, from conception to birth and early childhood. Ah! There is one time, he pitches a young friend into a ready dug grave, leaving him there until such time as he is rescued. Splendid! What an excellent start to life for him.

Is it necessary for me to travel those regressions with him, I ask the Master? DAMNATION!

His response was in the affirmative. I have no choice but to obey my Master's commands. I must confess, however, that I like the manner in which Michael chooses his wife and following the marriage, proceeds to control her in the same way as I would.

My Lord and Master has chosen to regress this man, who is assuredly sick to death, from a time close to his lifespan in the twentieth century. This to be followed by the nineteenth century, the eighteenth century and finally, to the life and times of Henri de Ville in the sixteenth and seventeenth centuries.

I must pay great attention, for as my Master requires me to follow Michael Deville's regressions, there will be items of note within, which it would be unwise for me to miss."

Father Emanuel interrupted. "This would seem to be a good place to take a break until tomorrow morning. I feel in need of nourishment, as I am sure you, my friends, do also. Shall we adjourn?"

It was with sighs of relief that Bart and Boris agreed with him, so locking the Black Book in the safe, they made their way to the cosy kitchen.

Chapter 56

"I don't feel that I've been away from this desk for the last ten or twelve hours," Boris said as they settled down around the desk, to commence reading from the Black Book once again.

"I feel much the same and fear it is my turn to read today," Father Emanuel said grimly, as he opened the safe to retrieve the Black Book and continue his endeavours to decipher the writings of the Demon, in the Count's ledger.

"Michael Deville—I remember that individual from my time as a psychiatrist. An arrogant young man, who was of the opinion that it was not within my power to hypnotise him—stupid fellow. He went through all those young women in an endeavour to make one of them his wife. *OF COURSE,* Suzanne! I bow to the wisdom of my Master, for surely the jogging of my memory, after all those centuries has proved necessary.

Then came Peter de Ville, a soldier through the instrument of the Man in Black. He proved to be a weak link and also, disobedient. Next was the Cameron boy, son of a vicar who was of the opinion that his son would follow in his footsteps. I, of course, instructed him, in my persona of the Man in Black and made sure Theodore Blount duly influenced him. Both those young men came to a sticky end as I recall.

At last, we come to Henri de Ville, my son and Heir. Ah! Those were the days, Master. Lady Isabella de Ville, daughter of the Baron Dominitus, already a man controlled by myself and a worshiper of the Master of Mankind.

Isabella, a young lady whom her father proved to be unable to control. She thought to escape by becoming a nun. She was of course, unaware that the Monastery of St Patricks, was drawing closer to the control of my Master than the Prior knew. The Hospice was at that time, attached to the Monastery and run by the Sisters of Solitude. Mother Superior of that convent was controlling it on my behalf. It was she, who arranged for Isabella de Ville and Susan Blessed, to be escorted to the Convent of the Golden Orb in Switzerland.

'*Be still, my child, and hear me*' were the words I spoke to my Bride, as we carried out the Procedures.

The companion, Susan Blessed, was separated from her mistress after one week and I thank my Master, for his removal of her from the scene, in a timely manner.

But DAMNATION…NO! NO!"

Father Emanuel paused. "Once again, we have those words, some of which I am able to translate but have no wish to do so. I appreciate that the readings are frequently prolonged, because of the difficulty to decipher the writing and understand that it becomes somewhat tedious. So, my friends, at this point, I suggest we take a break for coffee and maybe some food."

Chapter 57

It was three hours later that Father Emanuel once again took up his position at the desk and commenced reading. The three men had spent the hours after their meal, discussing how they might deal with what was to be learnt from the writings in the Black Book, supposedly completed by the Count's Demon through his control.

"She has gone! My Bride has gone! The one to bear my son is gone! I will have the heads of those responsible. Bring Sister Aureole to me now. No. Gather all, including kitchen staff, to the Room of Procedures and Ceremonies. I will inform everyone of what will be done to recover that bitch and the punishment to be inflicted on those who enabled her to escape.

Sister Aureole swears that Lady Isabella was asleep in her bed, when she collected the empty mug from her cell. I have had this traitorous sister thrown in the dungeons below. With no food or comforts of any kind, she may rot throughout her journey to serve our Master of Mankind, in the depths of Hell.

It is only because the kitchen staff are necessary for my comfort, within this convent in the high mountains, that they are to be allowed to continue their work."

Bart interrupted. "Did I not see in Michael Deville's regressions that Sister Aureole was set to work in the kitchen, and to live as the staff there? Did the Count actually write that she was to be thrown in the dungeons or does his Demon sometimes write his own version?"

"I can only read what is written, Bart. We have no way of knowing the true validity of it." Father Emanuel continued reading.

"My investigations show that she exited through the door in the kitchen and that she must have had help. The grounds have been searched, including the cliff top from where her companion, Susan Blessed, was seen to fall. However, there is no sign that my Bride has suffered the same plight.

Although I have been denied access to the caves and to the village below, I can with the help of my Demon, be shown what is happening within the caves. Therefore, Demon has enabled me to see my Bride being escorted through them, from the ledge entrance, behind the waterfall and into the Great Cavern, finally exiting through the entrance at the foot of the mountain. She is accompanied by Joshua Gelberger, his father and a person who appears to be, the woman assumed dead, Susan Blessed. May the Master of Mankind curse them all. Demon cannot tell me of what occurred once they were no longer within the caves but I believe my Bride was given refuge, by the family of Farmer Gelberger.

There is another blank page here, once again followed by words, which I am beginning to think are the work, not of the Count but his Demon. It is perhaps the fact, that Demon does not always stay in a state of hibernation when not required to write or observe, on behalf of the Count but acts upon its own behalf."

Father Emanuel took a deep breath. "There are more pages here, with scrawling, scratches and words that must not be spoken. Then come another two blank pages, which I assume denote a period during which the Count is no longer in contact with his Demon.

Let us stop for lunch now."

Chapter 58

This time, lunch was a simple one of sandwiches and coffee. The men reassembled in the study in less than one hour and Bart had agreed to continue the afternoon reading.

"I am pleased to say that unlike Emanuel, I have no idea, concerning the translation of any of the words of the Demon. Thank God." Bart sat before the book and opened to the page marked with a bookmark.

"The Count, having been taken through Michael's regressions, appears to be repeating some of his previous writings. We know what happens regarding that, episode, so I will skip the next few pages and will continue from where the Count next has communication, from the Sisters of Solitude."

"Hang on," Boris said. "Let me photograph those pages first."

Having done so, Bart continued.

"My wrath is great. It is only by the termination of the family Gelberger, that I shall once again be able to continue the Rights Statutes and Procedures of the Counts. Circumstances make it impossible, for me to be able to achieve this through my own actions or those of a member of my family. May they be damned, I have no heir."

"There are no further writings by the Demon, so we can assume that the Count made no communications with him over the next few centuries. Then, with only one blank page, the writings continue."

~~

"We are aware of the life and death of Henri de Ville, so will skip the details but to recap, he does indeed join Papa Count at the Convent of the Golden Orb, where he is duly inducted into the wishes of his father. He is instructed to terminate the family Gelberger on behalf of his father and enters the caves. During his journey, following the footsteps of his mother, Henri has a St Paul type epiphany and asks God, for forgiveness, as he falls into the depths of the Bottomless Pool.

There are no more writings until we reach the twenty-first century, when the Count becomes aware of Michael Deville's regressions.

It is now the twenty-first century, and my Master has instructed me through the regressions of Michael Deville. I am, thanks to the one and only Master of Mankind, been enabled to form a plan to once again, resurrect the reign of He Who Will be obeyed. I, The Count, will control the dynasty of Counts 100 and be at my Master's side for eternity.

But first my Revenge. However, I need access to my books and equipment in the Eyrie Laboratory to accomplish that. Recipes I remember however, and Demon will be duly entering them in the Black Book, under my instruction. Demon is also useful to cause rock falls within the caves and closing the door of my Eyrie—unfortunately too late to capture those three inquisitive, interfering men.

There are yet another two blank pages here but no more of what we now consider to be the scribblings of Demon, supposedly these are unknown to the Count.

The writings continue…

Today, I have learnt, through the auspices of followers of the Master, who keep me informed as to the actions of mankind, that are of interest to myself. The woman Suzanne is to visit Switzerland and will stay at the Hotel Orb de L'Or. She will no doubt be investigating, the life and times of Michael Deville's regression as Henri de Ville. Although I cannot enter the village in solid form, I am able to do so in my Shadow form, so I look forward to meeting that woman.

The space here presumably denotes time, until the arrival of Suzanne.

My Shadow stood close to the woman today. I spoke in her mind but she turned and moved swiftly away. Never fear though, I shall be near you at all times, until I am ready. She meets with the gatekeeper, Bart Slovinski, in his cottage and my Shadow is hidden from their gaze. Through my patient watching, I have today discovered that she is related to Michael Deville by marriage. Thank you, Master. Suzanne Deville is unaware that through her late husband; my son Henri in a previous life she is therefore, a member of my family.

She shall be the carrier of The Revenge of the Count."

~

"Those four hundred years of inactivity must have dulled the Count's brain," Boris said. "It took a bit of pushing from the devil himself, to wake him up."

"Quite." This from Father Emanuel. "Speaking of time, I think we have read enough for today. Let us lock away this Black Book. It has such an aura of evil that I put nothing else in my safe with it, lest they become infected too."

Bart's face showed relief that his stint as reader, was complete for a while and saying that he would start preparing their evening meal, departed, leaving the others to tidy the study before joining him.

Chapter 59

They sat discussing what had been revealed through the Black Book so far and concluded that mostly, the writings had merely confirmed what they already knew. Finally, retiring to bed after midnight, they all slept the sleep of the righteous and awoke the following morning, feeling fresher than they had done for several days.

After breakfast, the men made their way to the study, where Boris continued the reading.

"Ah! Your connection to Henri de Ville, through his resurrection in the form of Michael Deville, will enable me, The Count, to bring forth Henri, who will ensure your death, Suzanne. I will speak the words necessary and will command my Demon to advise me the instant you enter the Great Cavern. Then, it is only a matter of manipulating the body and voice of Henri de Ville, to lure you close enough for him to draw you to your death.

Here, there is a blank space, as I presume the Count to be awaiting news from his Demon. Then the writing continues, again presumably after he receives notice of Suzanne entering the Great Chamber. The Count would have completed his invocation to raise Henri de Ville and we all know the consequences of that.

Damn you, Henri! You fought me to the end, her end. However, you did not succeed, and my plan has been accomplished. Demon, of course, has no choice but to obey my instructions and duly released the Mist, to my control. That is my Revenge.

Now, my Shadow will watch the outcome throughout the world.

Here there is another blank page, then…

DAMNATION AND AGAIN DAMNATION!

The Gelberger tour guide was infected, yet survived. He was meant to pass the Mist to all within his household, thereby completing the task, allotted originally to Henri de Ville. It seems that not all of those infected, are killed by the Mist. Nevertheless, an exceptionally substantial number of humans has died, as planned, throughout the world and so far, no one has been able to discover the antidote, although worldwide efforts are in hand at all times. That antidote is secreted within my Eyrie Laboratory and can only be released at my command through the incantation, written in my ledger of notes and spells. That is of no concern however, for I wish my Revenge on the entire world—the extinction of those dwelling thereon at the moment.

~~

The writings cease here, my friends. Since we removed the Black Book from its secure hiding place in the Eyrie, the Count has been unable to instruct his Demon. However, at the very back of the book are what appear to be recipes, which are written by another hand, presumably that of the Count, when he still had access to his Eyrie. I suggest we have our lunch now, early though it is, then I think we should endeavour to transcribe, as best we can. Perhaps, if you both agree, I will type up our notes of these and provide us with a copy each, and for security purposes, leave one in Emanuel's safe."

This was agreed and Father Emanuel, once again ensuring the Black Book was locked firmly in the safe, they left the study. This time, after the usual prayers and blessing, Father Emanuel actually locked the study door, commenting that he felt the need of extra security.

Chapter 60

More coffee was drunk than food eaten, as they mulled over what had been written in the Black Book. It had mostly been a confirmation of what they already knew, or discovered whilst exploring the caves. Having made themselves comfortable, they moved back to the study, placing the book on the desk, so Father Emanuel and Bart, could work on trying to decipher the words written, whilst Boris typed directly onto his iPad.

"It looks as though some of the words might be Latin based, so how about I do most of the reading and Bart cuts in when they appear to be just a jumble?" Father Emanuel offered.

"I don't know about cutting in," Bart replied, "but it seems a sensible suggestion, so let's give it a go."

"Well, they seem to be some sort of incantation and as we are unaware of the danger of actually saying the words out loud, I will speak some and write down others, so there is no continuity. We do not want to invoke the devil or cast an evil spell. What we are looking for, is something that appears to be the antidote to the MistVirus, then, and only then, we will decide what must be done. Do you both agree?"

Bart and Boris nodded their acquiescence.

"Right, here we go.

When I wish to evoke the vapour to store in my tanks, I must say the words for evaporation. These are merely a few and I hold them within my head. The vapour itself, does not contain my Revenge. This can only occur as it is released from the holding tank, whilst casting the spell in the following words."

Bart interrupted. "So, it looks as though you have to speak the incantation aloud, and the vapour has to be released from the tank as they are spoken. Demon must have been instructed just when to release the mist, as the Count spoke the incantation."

"Nevertheless, I have no intention of taking the risk. So long as the words appear, in what looks like poetic format, I shall write them as they are on the page, duly translated and pass them to Boris, to insert into his iPad."

There was silence, except for the scratching of his pen, as he wrote the words of the incantation. First, Father Emanuel wrote a word, then leaving a space he wrote another, progressing in this manner, then filling in the gaps until it was complete.

Father Emanuel, quietly set to the task, in his neat script.

Machinate my Machiavellian Mist/Manufacture my Mist/Materialise my Mist/Motivate my Mist/May my Malignant Malediction Manifest my Mist/Throughout the World of Mankind

"You will now understand my reluctance to speak those words, as their meaning is obvious. Under no circumstances, is any of us to actually speak the words and preferably, not even one of them aloud, until we are ready to release the antidote.

The next so-called recipes are clearly more spells, or words to invoke them. However, at the moment, I can see no reason to make a note of them. I will continue to read other entries but will only write the incantations if they appear to relate, to that in which we are interested. Meanwhile, the recipes or spells, may be of slight interest, without the instructions to activate them.

This one tells how the Count cast the spell, to bring young virgins to the Convent of the Golden Orb, before the Gelberger family closed the caves to him.

First of all, I require the maiden of my choice, to be in a place of my choosing, for which the following incantation will bring her there.

Which item I will ignore." Father Emanuel made the sign of the cross above that single item, in the same manner as he did above each page, before reading what was written thereon.

"It continues…May my Lord and Master, grant me success in this endeavour. I conduct this procedure every tenth year, so far with little and subsequently, no success. I will manifest myself before her, in much the same way as I did later, during the regressions of Michael Deville and will say those words that hypnotise. *'Be still, my child, and hear me'*. After which, I will instruct her where the remainder of her life lies and the day and time to arrive. The sisters will welcome her and later, will commence the procedures necessary, for the impregnation and subsequent birth of my son and Heir."

"Should we include the incantation for the ten-year raping?" Bart enquired.

Boris and Emanuel replied together, with a loud and definite, "No!"

"So, again my friends, that serves to confirm our knowledge through the regressions of Michael Deville, via Suzanne." Knuckling his eyes, Father Emanuel said wearily. "My eyes are tired, for as you see the writing is faded and the words are what appear to be, a mixture of various languages, some of which are not any that Bart and I recognise. Maybe they are pre-history in origin but perhaps they are in a language, known only in the underworld of evil. Whatever, I have had enough for one day."

Saying which, he closed the Black Book and locked it in his safe until next time.

Chapter 61

"This will be the last day of going through the Count's ledger, and mighty glad I am to say so." Father Emanuel breathed a sigh of relief, although he was not looking forward to the final stages.

They had agreed to continue in the same manner as the previous day, so as Boris settled before his iPad and booted it up, Emanuel and Bart opened the Black Book.

The next two pages, held only the unknown language and the two following those were spells and incantations, concerning the controlling of zombies.

"Did he actually control the bodies of the dead?" Father Emanuel questioned. "Or perhaps it was people like Michael Deville, who were seeing their previous lives, as required by and through the Count or the Man in Black. This does not concern us, however, as we have no wish to perform anything from the recipes but a way to terminate the MistVirus, so I will continue."

There were other spells to sterilise cows and another to prevent the milk developing in their udders. Also, one to kill flocks of sheep, where it appeared that they had all haemorrhaged and drowned in their own blood. The eggs of chicken simply disappeared, and it was assumed they had been stolen, until the local chicken farmers met and discovered that they all had the same problem. From the notes, it seemed that these disappearing eggs were transferred to the convent, by some form of magic or as Bart described it, *some bloody evil spell*.

"So effectively, the Count was stealing the food out of the mouths of the villagers," Boris said.

"Here we are," said Father Emanuel. "The antidote to my Mist.

*First of all, there must be a sample of Mist in the tank No: 1, to a depth of 6cms, then…

*From Tank No: 3, transfer an exact amount of gel substance, equal to one half of the Mist in tank No: 1. The Mist should now change its colour from grey to bright blue.

*From tank No: 2, extract precisely three quarters of the red boiling liquid, equal to the total of the content of tanks 1 and 3 when combined, and pour it slowly into the bright blue Mist in tank No: 1, which will now change colour to bright red.

Under no circumstances, allow any of these substances to come into contact with your skin.

*Now, release the Mist, slowly, whilst quoting the following incantation.

At this point, I will again write the words, none of which must be spoken aloud."

Once again, Father Emanuel wrote as he had with the first of the incantations, and once again silence prevailed.

Anti-vaporous Mist Red of the Count/Anti-Mist Virus Mist Blue of the Count/Anti-Mist Revenge of the Count/I Command you to Evaporate and Cease the Count's Revenge/Throughout the World of Mankind.

Father Emanuel passed his translation to Boris, who immediately began to enter the words onto his iPad. These words were from the script of Father Emanuel and he assured his companions, that he had no feeling of danger in typing them as they appeared, and had no intention of taking the same precautions.

"Well, my friends, we have a great deal to mull over now. There are no more recipes, spells or incantations, thank goodness. I suggest we take a break for now and after partaking of some lunch, sit comfortably before the fire in armchairs, to discuss the final entries in the Black Book."

"Good idea. I'll print off three copies of all the entries."

"No, no, Boris," interrupted Father Emanuel. "There is no sense in risking the misplacing of any of the entries. However, I suggest that you print the final one and after we finish with it, I will burn each copy on the fire, thus ensuring that only the iPad will hold a record."

"I can't agree with that, Emanuel, for my iPad is just as likely to be stolen. I would appreciate it if you will secure one copy in your safe. One printed copy of all our notes, should be secreted elsewhere, for security. Meanwhile, I will keep my iPad close, and I suggest you get that damned Black Book, locked up in your safe again."

Bart suggested they relax, have some lunch and perhaps alcohol, to bring about that relaxation, then when in the mood to do so, continue their discussions later. So, on that note, the three retreated to the kitchen to prepare lunch.

Chapter 62

Much later in the afternoon, sitting around a blazing fire, the men once again considered all they had discovered in the Black Book.

Boris handed out A4 sheets, containing the spells and incantations appertaining to the raising of the mist and its antidote.

"I suggest to start, we all read the information on our copies and please remember, not one word of the incantations is to be spoken aloud. Although we all understand that they are not effective, without following the directions implicitly. I don't know about you, but I am not willing to take any risk, where the Count and his evil spells are concerned."

Everyone agreed and heads were lowered, as they absorbed what was typed on their copies.

"Okay, now let's indulge in a brainstorming session. Would you like to start, Emanuel?"

"A very difficult situation but one we knew full well, was to come at some point. Before we can tackle the antidote, we have first to return to that demonic Eyrie Laboratory, for it is only in that place we can activate the spell, to enable us to speak the incantation. So, to my mind, we have to prepare for yet another visit to the caves and this time, we need to be prepared in even more detail than the last time. The Count is probably aware that we have his Black Book and who knows, he may be listening to our conversation even now.

Bart, you wish to comment?"

"Thank you, Emanuel. I totally agree with you and with that in mind, suggest we do not make any plans at this time. Bear in mind, that the Count tried to pull Suzanne into his control when she first arrived in the village. She was somehow aware and walked away. That means that he has the ability to remain invisible, or as he describes it, in Shadow form. We must indeed enter the caves once again, where his evil cannot gain entrance. We will make our plans there."

"I had considered that each of us in turn, type our comments onto my iPad," said Boris, "but I agree with Bart, for if his shadow can listen to our conversation, presumably it can also read over our shoulders.

However, bear in mind, my friends, that the Count may also be able to receive information through his Demon, from within the caves. I think we would be advised, to make our plans within the sanctity of the church, if you agree, Emanuel."

"I do indeed, Boris. This is a subject that needs the power of God. I suggest we save that until tomorrow morning."

Boris made eye contact with his companions, then said, "I am going to the kitchen to make more coffee." Boris closed his iPad and tucking it under his arm, left the room. However, it was not the kitchen he entered but the small downstairs toilet. Once there, he hastily typed a quick note.

We need to be even more watchful of the mist, which for some reason, as yet unknown, does not appear to have the ability to enter through a crack, such as under a door. Strange is it not? Keep the conversation still related to the subject in hand but not in any way informative. Have you sufficient empty wine bottles into which, we can put something that looks like alcohol but is not? We can all drop into an apparent drunken sleep, in armchairs before the fire and hopefully remove the Count's attention. For a while, I think we should all remain close together, at least for tonight…What do you think?

Boris then returned to the kitchen, leaving his iPad, still open in the toilet.

Bart and Emanuel were already there, and the coffee machine was gurgling merrily.

"Boy, that smells good," said Boris, making eye contact with Emanuel and giving a small nod towards the door, through which he had just entered.

Father Emanuel nodded his understanding and excused himself. On his return, he raised his eyebrows in understanding and seeing that the coffee was ready, poured three steaming mugs.

"My, I needed that," said Bart. "Would you kindly pour me another, whilst I make room for it?" Going through the door in direction of the toilet.

On his return, he sat at the table, giving a sigh, and surreptitiously placed Boris's iPad on the chair next to him.

"We need to get to business," Father Emanuel said. "You go through, and I will get some wine. Take glasses with you please, Bart."

~~

"Hmm. Nice fruity Red this, Emanuel." Bart sipped his third glass of black-current juice. They discussed different wines whilst still imbibing, until at last they apparently dropped to sleep, until they felt it safe to assume privacy.

Father Emanuel stirred first. His movement roused Boris, who shook Bart to wake him from what had become, a deep and restful sleep. It was three-thirty, as silently the men collected sweaters and made their way quickly and quietly, through the tunnel leading to the church vestry.

Chapter 63

After praying, the men sat in the front pews to discuss their plans to enter the caves once more. It was agreed that Bart would lead this, as he was more familiar with the territory.

"We have first to decide which entrance we should use. Should we climb the Serpent's Tail and enter through the ledge or go more easily, through the main entrance, bearing in mind that this would entail our climbing up behind the waterfall, to make our way back to the Cathedral Cavern, where we have to be anyway. Both seem to me to be equally difficult but perhaps the main entrance is a little easier. We should go prepared, wearing our wetsuits and leave warm clothing for when we exit."

Boris and Emanuel agreed with the latter, and they discussed just what should be packed in their trusty backpacks. Finally, they decided they would each carry smaller packs containing food and two thermos flasks, one of which would contain hot coffee and the other hot soup. The larger packs could originally carry the smaller ones plus waterproof bags, in which to place their outer clothing, plus an extra sweater and socks. This agreed, Boris made a suggestion.

"I know we have studied the information on how to produce the antidote but none of us really have much experience in this respect. I would like to discuss the matter with Gerry and Meg and if you are willing, Emanuel, do you feel, with our help, able and willing to cope with extra guests at the Rectory? I don't know that they have any more experience than us but it would mean another two dependable people."

"I should be delighted to welcome your friends and it would mean an extra man of the church in our midst. We might be of different religious backgrounds but undoubtedly, we are both firm believers in God, our father. Yes, Boris, please let us invite Gerry and Meg to Switzerland, for a holiday."

Having spoken and made more plans, Father Emanuel prayed before the altar in Latin, followed by the Lord's Prayer, in which Bart and Boris joined. Then, they returned to the vestry, through the tunnel back to the Rectory. Once there, they made their way to a hot shower and bed for two hours sleep.

Chapter 64

In the kitchen later, the men sat round the table to a much-needed breakfast. Now much refreshed, Bart telephoned Villette on his mobile, retreating to another part of the house to do so.

Father Emanuel, retired to his study to answer emails and contact his verger, to discuss arrangements regarding parishioners who were members of the church. The priest would endeavour, through the internet, to give a short sermon of encouragement and say prayers, on a daily basis. The verger would sound out the parishioners and agree a suitable time of day for this purpose. Governments in many parts of the world had declared a lockdown of all communal meetings, which included that of church services.

Boris had remained in the kitchen. First, he loaded the dishwasher and tidied, as was his wont. He liked things to be where they belonged. Then making another pot of coffee, he set about phoning Gerry on his mobile. It was answered after only the second ring.

"Boris, we were wondering what had happened to you, not heard from you for a few days. Meg's been worried as usual. Is everything okay?"

"Yes, Gerry, and give my love to Meg. Bart and I were wondering if it would be possible for you to get over to Switzerland for a holiday before they stop all forms of travel. I know some flights are still operating and I have made a provisional booking, from Gatwick to Berne, for the two of you next week. Sorry if that isn't convenient; we shall understand but it will soon be impossible for you to get a holiday at all. Anyway, my friend, please discuss this idea with Meg and ring me back later. I assume that services in Britain are locked down, as they are here so—for the time being, clear?"

He broke off, leaving Gerry to hopefully fill in the blanks.

"No problems, Boris, I'll get back to you later today. Meg is out with the dog at the moment. She walks a lot these days and I even go with her most times. I think the twins are due home this weekend, so much to think about."

"Of course, if I remember correctly, Kathy reads World Religions and Becky Biological and Biomedical Science. That brings something else to mind, so perhaps if you could ring me after seven tonight, I need to sort out something with Emanuel. You will be staying with us at the Rectory by the way and I know you will get on like a house on fire with Father Emanuel. He's a man after your own heart, although perhaps a little less impulsive."

With that, they said their goodbyes and Boris drew his faithful iPad towards himself. There was indeed much to consider and another trip to the church seemed necessary.

A couple of hours had passed, so Boris put on yet another pot of coffee and shouted loudly. "Emanuel! Bart! Coffee in the kitchen. Now!"

They joined him within five minutes and with roused eyebrows, sat at the kitchen table as Boris poured three mugs of coffee. Bart added cream and sugar, the others stayed with black coffee.

"I know you can't hold a normal service, Emanuel, but I suppose you will be doing your usual prayers before the altar soon. I am beginning to get a real interest in your religion and would appreciate it, if you would kindly mentor me in this respect."

Father Emanuel raised his eyebrows again, a slight smile on his lips. "Of course, I would be honoured. Let us finish this coffee, then we will go to the church. I feel the building assists the words and intentions better in those conditions. Psychological no doubt, but very real."

Bart looked down with a shamefaced look. "Mind if I join you? I have fallen away from my faith over the years but what is happening in the world today, makes me feel a need to recover it." He looked up. "May I?"

"I shall be delighted, as will our Heavenly Father. Come."

Father Emanuel led the way from the room, with Boris and Bart following.

Chapter 65

Back in the confines of the church, Father Emanuel said, "So, what was all that about?"

"Can we pray first please, Emanuel. Something serious and possibly interesting, has turned up and I felt it necessary to discuss it in the sanctity of the church as we did yesterday." Boris shook his head with a worried look on his face.

Feeling more secure now, Boris told them of his conversation with Gerry.

"I apologise for inviting them to stay at the rectory, Emanuel, but we need to be together in this mission and I feel safer when we are here, closer to God perhaps. Although it is probably more in my head. Nevertheless, from the rectory, we can come through the tunnel into the sanctity of the church, where hopefully, the evil one cannot enter.

Anyway," he continued, "something Gerry said made me think of another important point, that might just make the difference between success and failure. He said that the twins are to visit next weekend. Now, if you remember, Kathy is studying World Religions and Becky Biological and Biomedical Science. Although we are reasonably competent people, none of us has the latter qualifications or experience, which may indeed prove to be essential, in preparing the antidote. I would, with your agreement, like to invite the twins to join us, providing Gerry and Meg are willing. Their studies, although they have not yet qualified, are likely to prove useful. This of course, will mean yet more guests at the Rectory, again if you are willing, Emanuel. What say you?"

"No problem, my friend. I agree with you that it is a good idea. However, we three have the only rooms with ensuite bathrooms, so the four guests would of necessity have to share the family bathroom, which is between rooms five and six. If they are happy with that arrangement, then let us prepare to receive them."

"Good. Thank you, Emanuel. I have already taken the liberty of making provisional plane bookings for Meg and Gerry, so will need to do the same on behalf of the twins. I had better do that as soon as we return to the Rectory. They are only taking half the usual passengers, to enable distancing between them. The provisional bookings are only held for twenty-four hours, so time is of the essence."

Bart had been silent through this conversation but now he broke in. "I suppose we can have the local shop deliver food to the Rectory, but such quantities might arouse suspicions as to what the local priest is up to. Perhaps, some items, could be delivered to Villette's cottage. She could say it was to make sure she is able to provide sufficiently for her mother."

"Alternatively," Father Emanuel said, "could we bring Villette and her mother to the Rectory? I should personally, feel happier if they were under the same roof as us. I tend to agree with Boris, about feeling safer with all of the people engaged in this mission, under one roof."

Bart beamed. "Great idea, Emanuel, I am more than willing to give up my room, as I am sure Boris is, to the two ladies. We can share room two and Sara and Villette can have my room. If they all choose to holiday with us, I am sure Gerry, Meg and the twins will be happy to share the family bathroom."

"Absolutely," Boris agreed. "The Rectory is becoming quite the hotel. Don't let us forget though, that we must get Villette and her mother, who you recall cannot move at any speed, from their cottage to the safety of the Rectory. Also, our visitors from Britain, must be transferred from Berne Airport to the Rectory. They will need to be aware of the Mist too. But in the meantime, let's ascertain whether or not our invitation has been accepted, before making any further plans."

So, the three men returned through the tunnel and whilst Emanuel prepared lunch, Boris once more telephoned Gerry, whilst Bart secluded himself to plan a way in which they could safely, transfer Villette and her mother to the Rectory.

Chapter 66

After lunch, Bart showed his ideas to transport the two women from the cottage to the Rectory. He had thought long and deep and to prevent having to give much verbal information, which might be overheard, had drawn a plan that he now placed on the kitchen table, beckoning the other two to stand closely around it.

Father Emanuel was one of the few people in the village to own a car. It was an old Renault, small but in good working order and shining. This car was rarely used but Father Emanuel kept it in the garage, ready for use when and if necessary. Bart's idea was to drive it to the cottage, having first made sure that Villette was aware of exactly what was going to happen. He would then return with his passengers back to the church lychgate, which Boris would ensure was wide open. The car being small, would just fit through it. He would stop at the church door, which Emanuel would be operating and then, with the passenger doors adjacent to it, they would help Sara and Villette from the vehicle, directly into the church. Bart and Boris would then, all being clear, remove any luggage from the car and once in the safety of the church, the two women could be led through the tunnel to the Rectory.

It might be necessary to leave the car parked in that position for the time being but as the church was temporarily closed, that would not matter.

Father Emanuel and Boris both gave a thumbs up and Bart folded his plan details. "Did you say we could have another blessing in the church later, Emanuel?" Boris asked.

"Certainly," was the response. "I need to explain the Latin prayers to you both, as you need to know for what reason you are saying these prayers and why they are best said in Latin. Let us rest before the fire in my study for an hour or so first, as I for one need to shut my eyes for a while."

~~

It was in fact nearer three hours when the men went back through the tunnel to the vestry.

"Can I get a phone connection from here?" Boris asked.

"Yes, but we should pray before continuing with our mission." Father Emanuel was in charge here, so the others followed him into their usual places before the altar. This time, Father Emanuel prayed in Latin as usual but followed with a translation, saying, "I trust that you may be sincere in your wishes to return to the faith."

"Right now," Boris said, "my wish is to speak to Gerry and see what arrangements can be made. Thank you however, Emanuel, for your consideration but may we return to that subject on another occasion please?"

Father Emanuel gave a nod and a smile. "There should be reception close to the altar and I suggest Bart makes his call to Villette from here, whilst you and I try to contact Gerry from the vestry, as I know reception there is good. If you have a problem, Bart, try the tower but make sure you close and lock the door when you leave. The door at the top is locked however, and I will not allow it to be opened."

Leaving Bart to make his call they returned to the vestry, where Boris dialled Gerry's number. He answered on the third ring.

"Hi there, I was about to ring you."

"I'm glad I beat you to it, my friend. We try and speak only from the sanctity of the church nowadays, as we aren't sure if we are bugged in the Rectory. Anyway, we have decided to try and get Emanuel's housekeeper and her mother, to the Rectory for safety but there are six bedrooms and I have another idea."

Gerry interrupted. "So have we. The twins think they may be of use because of the subjects they are studying and would like to join us for a 'short holiday'. Meg was against it, danger and all that but has been eventually won over. However, the flights might have proved a problem and I have a friend with a small plane, who would be willing to fly the four of us to Switzerland. Can you suggest a suitable place for him to land and take off, a field would do if there's no airport nearby? Oh, by the way you said you had an idea too, please tell."

"In fact, I was going to ask if you and Meg might be willing to consider asking the twins if they would be interested in helping. Bear in mind though, that this is not necessarily a safe venture, and that Suzanne lost her life because of it. Thank them for us. I'll get back to you later today about the landing strip. There is no airport close, but I think Emanuel might be able to come to some arrangement with the Gelberger family, to use one of their fields."

They said their goodbyes as Bart joined them.

Leaving Emanuel to discuss with farmer Gelberger, the possibility of using one of his fields for a small aircraft to land and take off again, Boris and Bart returned to the church to discuss their progress. Boris quickly told Bart of his conversation with Gerry, and Bart punched the air in delight that the twins were going to add their skills to the mission. Then, it was his turn.

"Villette was dubious at first, but Sara quickly overruled any objections and snatched the phone from her. She says they will receive a delivery of fresh vegetables and other supplies later today and that Villette will phone the shop to order extras. Emanuel is to do the same, put in a grocery order to be delivered today. Tomorrow morning, the two women will be ready for collection at five o'clock. It will still be dark, so I will be able to get them in the vehicle with a degree of safety. The baggage loading will depend on circumstances at the time but most important, will be to get Villette and Sara into the car. The rest will depend on you and Emanuel."

By this time, Father Emanuel had joined them and heard the important bits. He was also able to add his own good news that farmer Gelberger would arrange for a field to be clear, when it was needed for the aircraft to land.

Half an hour later, they were once more sitting round the kitchen table sipping mugs of steaming coffee.

Chapter 67

Fortunately, the following morning was dry and lightened by a full moon. Bart knew that Villette would be ready well before the appointed time, so at a quarter to the hour, he reversed the little car out of the garage and made his way down the road, past the church. As he thought, Villette and Sara were ready and waiting by the front door, luggage by their side. He scanned the area but could see no sign of mist. Bart hustled them to the car then returned to collect the luggage. He tried to persuade Villette to get in the car with her mother for safety, but she insisted that it would take less time to load the vehicle if there were two of them.

It was just after five o'clock when they had secured the cottage and Bart drove back towards the church. The lychgate was open and Bart drove through, Boris closing it immediately behind them. Then he ran swiftly to the church, constantly looking around for any sign of danger. Father Emanuel was standing by the door, ready to receive Sara, as Bart and Villette helped her from the car, taking over from Bart who returned to empty the vehicle with Boris' help. This was soon done and locking the car, the two men joined Father Emanuel and the two women in the church.

Villette settled her mother in the front pew and returned to help the men carry the luggage and food supplies into the vestry. Then they all returned to the favoured front pews and Father Emanuel conducted a small service. They remained sitting in peaceful silence, each with their own thoughts and no doubt all thanking God for this safe and uneventful journey.

"Thank you, Father, for that service," Sara said. "I cannot remember when I was last able to sit within the sanctity of this church, although I shall always appreciate the way you visit me regularly."

"The pleasure is mine, Sara," he responded. "I think it is now time to make our way from the vestry to the rectory and get you ladies settled into your room."

It was a slow walk, with the men lugging their various packages and Villette following with her mother. Finally, settling round the kitchen, coffee brewing, they breathed sighs of relief.

~~

Whilst Father Emmanuel unpacked the groceries, Villette helped her mother to slowly climb the stairs and reaching what had previously been Boris' room, they unpacked their belongings. The room boasted twin beds and Villette insisted that she and her mother were happy to share, feeling happier to be on hand should she be needed.

Bart and Boris had already made their choice to share the room next door. They had, in fact, chosen the former due mainly to the fact, that Bart felt better able to protect the women from this close proximity, rather than from the other end of the house or from the floor above.

Father Emanuel had provided bedding for the two beds in the room and Villette soon had them made. Sara breathed a sigh of relief as she lay on the bed nearest the wall and smiled as she looked at the picture hanging there of a Mother giraffe, with her miniature version at her feet. She was bending down with lips pressed against those of her calf and the picture was named *The First Kiss*. Sara declared that it was the best bedroom picture she had ever had the pleasure of sleeping nearby.

Her mother now sleeping soundly, Villette returned to the kitchen where with arms akimbo, she surveyed the mess of packaging spread around the kitchen. "Right, you three get out of the way, so that I can clear up this mess and prepare something for lunch. Mum is sleeping, she's exhausted after all the excitement this morning. When I have the food cooking, would you like me to make up the beds in your room, Bart?"

"Well," he replied with a smile, "I would indeed appreciate a hand with them. I am quite good at looking out for myself, but Boris is hopeless. We will leave you to it for the time being and go into the study, to make arrangements with Gerry and Meg for the other holiday makers."

"Thank you, my dear," Father Emanuel patted her shoulder. "I am so glad you are here in the Rectory. Two less people to worry about."

"From your lips to God's ear," Villette replied, kissing him on the cheek.

Chapter 68

It was after one o'clock when Villette went back to their room to wake her mother. Sara was in fact sitting on the edge of the bed, having just woken and had blown a kiss to the two giraffes. Sitting for a while was something she found necessary nowadays, to get herself together and indulge in a mind over matter process, to get in control of the arthritis that plagued her.

"Do I smell lunch, daughter of mine?"

"You do, Mum, can you manage, or do you need a hand?"

"I can manage very well on a level surface, as you well know." Then with a sheepish look, "I would appreciate it if you would go down the stairs in front of me though, dear."

Lunch once again, was served in the warm friendly atmosphere of the kitchen, tasty lasagne with a side salad, followed by raspberry ripple ice cream.

Later, they all went into the sitting room where Father Emanuel had lit the fire, which was now blazing merrily. He added some wood and with Sara comfortably in an armchair, the others drew the settee up closer to the fire. Bart and Boris sat one each end, leaving Emanuel the other armchair. Bart patted the settee between himself and Boris, but Villette chose to curl up on the rug, in front of the cheerful crackling blaze.

"When are the other guests arriving?" Sara asked.

Boris shook his head and made a zipping action across his lips before speaking. "Unfortunately, there was no reply from Gerry and Meg. I suppose they were employed with parish duties, so I will ring them later. They will need to book their flight soon though, as I understand from what I have seen on television, most airports will be closed to all travellers soon. Probably, next Monday," he added, with a finger to his mouth, passing a small note first to Bart who then passed it on to Sara, and so forth. It read, *I will speak to them from the security of the Church this evening, meanwhile keep conversation non-informative.*

A gentle snore came from the armchair, in which Emanuel had dropped off to sleep. Villette grinned at Bart and moved to sit next to him on the settee where the two of them followed suit, Villette with her head resting on Bart's shoulder. Sara, having already rested, opened her latest novel, and proceeded to read, while Boris played a game on his iPad. They remained in those positions until the fire had burnt low, and they began to feel the chill. Two hours had passed.

Villette was the first to stir. She stood, stretched, and proclaimed that she was going to make some tea.

Boris moved to stoke the fire, the noise of which woke Emanuel with a jump, while Bart hastened to assist Villette with the tea.

Sara didn't move. She had closed her eyes, just to rest them, shortly after starting her book and was still peacefully asleep and she remained that way until ten minutes later, when Villette and Bart entered with a tray of tea and cake.

Father Emanuel turned on the television news. Viewing was no more optimistic than previously. The MistVirus was still killing thousands throughout the world, by apparently squeezing the life from them. Climate change might be the cause of this phenomenon, was apparently considered a strong possibility. Although, no one appeared to be sure of this or indeed any other reason. However, governments worldwide were endeavouring to find a way to control the Mist and laboratories were working on a possible antidote, so far with no results. The presenter continued to put forward other possible causes, but the favourite seemed to remain with climate change.

"Oh, if only they knew," said Boris.

"People would not believe it and those that did would either panic or be the usual group of conspiracy theorists. Whatever, it would lead to riots and terrorism. This is the problem, only we know where the antidote is and how to prepare it. It is our mission, to finally remove the evil of the Count from this country and this world." So, saying, Father Emanuel turned the TV off again and, in all honesty, everyone in the room was relieved not to have to see and hear yet more tragedies.

Chapter 69

When Father Emanuel went through the tunnel to the church to do his usual check that all was still secure, Boris accompanied him. He would remain in the vestry to telephone Gerry and update him as to the latest progress.

Gerry listened, then it was his turn to update. "First," he said, "I am so glad you have those two women safely at the Rectory. Secondly, my friend tells me he is available for either Tuesday or Wednesday next, so if you can fix with the farmer for the use of his field on one of those days, we should all be together in a day or so. Can you let me know which day is most suitable for you please?"

Boris thought for a while before responding. "Either day will be okay, but can you make it early in the morning, say around four thirty to five? That is almost certainly why it worked so well with Villette and Sara. We didn't discuss our plans to bring them here to the Rectory, when we were in the house and we think that may be the reason, together with early timing, which proved to be to our advantage."

"Don't forget that if it is dark, the pilot will need lights to guide him in and that might be more noticeable than if we were to land in daylight," Gerry replied, "but I will have a word with my friend and get him to check the weather forecast for both days. I'll ring you later this evening to let you know."

"Thanks, Gerry, but be careful what you say. I might sound paranoid but somehow the Count seems to have a pretty good idea of our plans when we make them in the house, which is why I'm ringing from the vestry of the church. Nowadays, for that reason, we always have serious discussions about our mission, in the church. I will message you the co-ordinates when I get back to the study, so your pilot friend can fix his point of landing."

Saying their goodbyes, Boris joined Father Emanuel in the Nave. They sat in silence for a while, then the priest listened as Boris told him of his conversation with Gerry.

After a while both stood, genuflected before the altar, and made their way back to the Rectory.

~~

The remainder of the evening was spent playing cards, waiting anxiously for Gerry's call. It was nearly midnight before it came.

"Sorry, it's a bit late, old chap, but have you seen the moon tonight? It won't be full until Wednesday and hopefully, if the weather holds it's going to be light as day. I know you like to study eclipses and such, but this Earth Moon should be well worth a look. I shall be looking up there through my telescope right up to two or three in the morning. As I said, sorry to call so late but my enthusiasm ran away with me."

"Not to worry, my friend. I'm playing cards at the moment but will take a look when I win this hand," Boris said with a chuckle. "Give my best to Meg please and when you can manage a holiday, my cousin and I will be delighted to see you. Cheerio for now."

With a flourish, he put down his cards. "I don't know about you folks but I'm tired and need my bed." Giving a thumbs up gesture. "See you in the morning."

He retired, closely followed by the others. Bart helping Sara climb the stairs, commenting as he did so, "I could throw you over my shoulder and carry you up if you like, ma'am. We might get there quicker."

Sara smacked his arm. "Don't you dare," she said.

Part V

Chapter 70

The following morning after breakfast, Villette shooed the three men out.

"This place is a tip and I need to spend the next few hours getting it tidy again. Don't worry, Emanuel, I won't move any of the papers on your desk, in fear of you sacking me. Seriously though, I want to help Mother shower and get her settled down here first, so if you three would kindly take a long walk or something, lunch will be ready at about one o'clock."

With an acknowledging wink, Father Emanuel ushered his two colleagues towards the lobby, where they put on walking boots and warm coats. Before leaving, he prayed for safety during their absence from the Rectory, then made the sign of the cross over the closed door. Bart and Boris were now in full agreement with what Boris had previously looked upon with ridicule, and were happy to join in.

They walked through the wooded area, each man now carrying a spray bottle containing Holy Water. Should there be any sign of mist or vapour, they would immediately stand back-to-back and spray a circle of this around them, loudly proclaiming the Lord's Prayer.

The far side of the woods was adjacent to a fenced field, which was relatively flat and empty.

"This is the one farmer Gelberger has set aside for the aircraft. Let us walk on down to the farmhouse and have a word with him," Father Emanuel suggested.

The farmer's wife opened the door and welcomed them into her warm cosy kitchen. "I'll just make some coffee," she said, "and then leave you men to talk. Hot scones, cream and jam are on the table, so help yourselves."

Bart knew the farmer, so introduced his cousin. "This is, Boris, my cousin from England."

The two men shook hands and looking each into the eyes of the other, felt immediate trust and friendship, which was perhaps, an unfamiliar reaction for both of them.

Farmer Gelberger's gravelly voice spoke first. "Come on now, Father, what are you up to? You want to land someone or something by air in my Woodfield. I find it hard to believe that you are up to something illicit but you expect me to keep it quiet." He waved his hand round. "Don't worry, I can keep my mouth shut but I would like to have some idea of what's brewing."

Bart and Boris nodded their acquiescence to Father Emanuel and between the three of them, told most of what they knew, following the death of Suzanne. When they finished, the farmer sat back rubbing his head. "Look, my friends, I know you want me to keep this to myself, for obvious reasons, but if you are willing, I would like to bring my son Joshua into this mission of yours. Don't forget that he was the one to pull Suzanne out of the Bottomless Pool, with the help of others and he survived. We have never been sure how this came to be, but from what you now tell me, he may well be able to help. May I call him in?"

The other three exchanged looks, then they nodded. "Yes."

Joshua was a younger version of his father, tall with broad, strong shoulders and legs like tree trunks. Both had beards, although Joshua's was more evenly trimmed than that of his father. Much the same applied to the hair on their heads. Joshua looked as though he went to a barber, whereas his father's hair appeared more as though he chopped at it himself. He came through the kitchen door some half hour later, with a confident stride.

"You wanted me, Pa?" He said. "Sorry to be so long but had to finish off the milking. Old Tom is taking them back to Lowfield as you instructed. Anyway, now I'm here, what can I do to help?"

His father introduced him to the visitors and once they had sat back down with more mugs of hot coffee before them, proceeded to tell him about the mission, with a few interjections from the other men.

At the end, he tipped his chair backwards and said, "Hmmm. I have always felt there was something ominous about that drowning. Yes, it was this family that instigated the Christian carvings back in the thirteenth century, at the cave entrances. It is something we hold close to our hearts, and yes, of course this family will be delighted to help with your mission. To start with, I will be at Woodfield alongside you on Wednesday morning, to assist with the safe conduct of the passengers in the plane to the Rectory. Thereafter, if we may, I and my father would be proud to join you at the church, to discuss the plans for the extinction of this dreadful MistVirus. Whatever it takes, eh Pa?"

The return journey to the Rectory was once more uneventful, although whisps of mist could be seen in the churchyard and around the priest's old Renault.

Chapter 71

Villette had made up beds for the four expected visitors and cooked, cooled then frozen meals, in case it became difficult to prepare them. They sat around the fire and played cards, read or just chatted about inconsequential things, for the rest of the day. On Wednesday morning, by arrangement, farmer Gelberger telephoned and Boris took the call in the vestry. Later, with all present in the church, he relayed his conversation.

"The field is prepared, and Joshua will join us on the far side, at half past one in the morning." Boris raised his hand to stop Sara's question, knowing beforehand what it would be. "He suggests the far side rather than by the woods, as we shall have a better view should any Mist appear. The night is forecast to be perfectly clear, so no additional lights will be needed. If we all agree, I would suggest Bart and I, together with Joshua, will be ready to disembark the passengers as soon after touchdown as possible. The two of us will immediately get them back to the Rectory as quickly as possible, leaving Joshua to see the plane back in the skies, make sure all is clear and return to the farmhouse. On arrival here, will you Emanuel, be ready to open the door as soon as we arrive?"

Bart interrupted, "Also to make sure there is no sign of the Mist. Perhaps, you could flash a torch if all is clear, on-off, on-off. Should there be any sign of the Mist, then turn on your torch and leave it on. That will serve as a warning and enable us to see a safe route."

"Good. If there is any sign of the Mist though, I suggest you turn on the outside lights. That way, we get a better chance of seeing exactly where it's coming from. Anyhow, we're hoping we'll get away with our next lot of visitors, arriving as straight forwardly as we did with you ladies. Emanuel and I will leave our mobiles on for the duration, so if there is a problem, we have people at both ends to help."

Bart broke in. "With that in mind, although we have definitely decided to use the back entrance, perhaps Villette could stay at the front door as emergency standby. In which case, you also leave your phone open, my dear."

Father Emanuel agreed to this. "I will bless you before you go. Also, I will place two crosses either side of the front and rear gates and sprinkle Holy Water over the paths to both doors. Perhaps, it might be a good idea if you two do likewise, as you make your way through the woods."

This was agreed and saying prayers for the safety of themselves, Joshua and their guests, the five adventurers returned to the Rectory and their beds.

Chapter 72

The next day was spent checking everything was in order and preparations were made for the safe meeting of Meg, Gerry and the twins that night.

At one o'clock, Father Emanuel saw Bart and Boris out of the kitchen door, all the time glancing around to check there was no sign of the Mist. The two men entered the woods in single file Bart leading, spraying Holy water in front of them and Boris doing the same behind them, keeping a careful watch for Mist amongst the trees and bushes. On reaching the field, they sprinted across to join Joshua on the other side.

"Hello, Bart, Boris," he said. "I have on the advice of my father, made slightly different arrangements for the collection of your guests and safe delivery to the Rectory. Pa thought, to ensure that it is not possible for anyone, or thing, to be aware of what we're planning, he drives our large van to the field. We will load the visitors direct from the side of the plane into the van and he will drive you directly to the front of the Rectory, not the back as planned. From there, he will carry on to our field farthest away, where ostensibly he will see to an ailing cow, then return home. Meanwhile, I will ensure the plane takes off again and make my way back to the farmhouse. I trust you agree with this," he said with a wry look that made it obvious it was too late to disagree anyway.

"Splendid, Joshua, it's a privilege to have you on our side."

"Thanks, Bart. Is that a plane engine I hear?"

It was indeed the expected aeroplane and after circling the field, ten minutes later the plane touched down. The door opened almost immediately, and a small set of steps was lowered. Gerry was the first to descend, helping Meg just behind him and followed speedily by the twins. Farmer Gelberger had meanwhile, driven the van up to the steps and opening the side door, ushered the four visitors plus Bart and Boris, into it. Sliding the door closed, he climbed into the driving seat and returned to the farm track that led to the road, leaving Joshua to his task.

As soon as they were moving, Boris spoke into his mobile. "Did you get that, Emanuel, the front not the back?" He immediately rang off, trusting that the priest had indeed understood the quick message.

The steps returned to their place on the plane, Joshua waved at the pilot to take off again. As he did so, Joshua glanced around to check all was still clear. It wasn't. From the edge of the wood crept a single snake of Mist. Joshua took to his heels and ran, jumping over the fence rather than making his way along to the gate. The Mist followed getting closer by the minute, then as if pulled by a rope around its neck, was jerked back into the woods. By this time, Joshua was in the farmyard and turned just in time to witness this strange effect. He continued to the door of the farm and entered, giving a sigh of relief as he did so.

His mother was awaiting his return and saw the confused look on his face.

"Is everything done safely son, you look...?" she asked hesitating and looking frightened. "Is your father alright?"

"I don't know, mum, it was strange. The Mist was snake-like, chasing me from the woods across the field but when I reached the farmyard and turned to check where it was, it looked like something pulled it straight back into the woods. It was almost as though I was not to be its prey. Do you suppose that was because I survived the first attack of the MistVirus? Almost as though I now have an immunity. But Pa got away safely with the others, I don't think whatever that Mist is, realised I was not alone."

~~

Meanwhile, the van carrying six passengers, driven by farmer Gelberger, had arrived at the front gate of the Rectory. Bart exited first, searching around to make sure all was clear.

"As soon as we are all out of the van, you drive off. Don't stop for anything until you reach your field. Understand; you are nothing to do with us. Thank you, my friend, we owe you."

The farmer nodded and as Boris slid the door closed, did as he was bid.

Bart led the way to the front door, now opened by Father Emanuel and Bart stood beside him as he ushered the four visitors through, saying, "Straight through, don't hesitate, we'll sort everything out once the door's closed."

Which was when Father Emanuel leaned forward and grabbing Boris by the sleeve of his coat, dragged him through the door, where he tripped and landed on his face. The door slammed and he sat up as the bolts were drawn.

"Thank you, my friend, you obviously did get my call."

"Sorry about that. Are you alright?" Father Emanuel helped him to his feet. "Mist is creeping round from both sides of the house; I fear it is surrounding us."

Chapter 73

The Mist was indeed doing just that, surrounding the Rectory but fortunately, due to the quick thinking of farmer Gelberger, it was too late this time.

The evil that controlled the Mist had learned through some supernatural means, that something was planned, although being unable to enter the church, was not aware of what that would be. So, his weapon of revenge was set to watch the Rectory. When Bart and Boris silently sneaked out of the back door into the woods, the Mist did not notice, as it was secreted in the churchyard.

The Count in his hideout at the top of the Hotel Orb de L'Or, gave vent to his anger. CRASH! The antique inkstand shattered as it hit the floor, blue ink splattering the carpet. Sweeping papers from his desk, shouting and tearing his hair, the Count threw himself into the large leather office chair, then taking some deep breaths, straightened his hair and poured a large glass of brandy. Sipping it, he heard a sound unusual for that time of night. It was an aircraft and sounded as though it were landing. He banged his fist on the desk. Could it be connected to what those three interfering bastards were planning?

The Mist was controlled in much the same way as his Demon in the caves, the equivalent of a receiver being contained within the head, or front part of its body. From that leading Mist, its controller directed instructions to all branches of its kind throughout the world. The Count ordered it to search the woods and infect all those it found. It reluctantly, had to report that nothing and nobody had been discovered but that an aeroplane had just taken off from a field adjacent to the woods.

The Mist then advised its controller, that the son of the farmer was to be seen running back towards the farmhouse. The Count ordered it to catch Joshua, so it sped after him as directed. As he reached the farmyard, the snake of Mist felt itself yanked rapidly back into the woods.

"Go to the back of the Rectory, you fool. Surround the house to prevent anyone from entering."

So, it was that the Mist slid under the fence to the Rectory garden, and extending its length and breadth, drew close to the back of the house. From there, the head turned left and the tail right, travelling along the side of the house until it reached the front. Once again, too late.

Chapter 74

Meanwhile, back in the warmth of the Rectory kitchen, the number of people involved in this mission had increased from three to nine, plus farmer Gelberger, Joshua and his family, who were all now safely back at the farmhouse.

Becky was the first to speak. "What on earth was all that cloak and dagger stuff about?"

Bart put his finger to his mouth and shook his head and the twins shrugged. Villette rose from the table, checking the oven to see if the food was yet ready. Returning, she poured nine mugs of freshly brewed coffee, leaving those who wanted, to help themselves to cream and sugar. The twins looked at each other, then with a nod poured cream into their mugs, looking a trifle guilty at having done so. Gerry and Bart also added cream, plus heaped spoonsful of sugar, looking not in the least guilty. Having already added cream to her mother's coffee, Villette and the other three took their coffee black.

Kathy sniffed. "Now *that* aroma from the oven seems to me the most important thing for the moment. I'm starving. I guess we all must be, as we seem to have been travelling or getting ready to travel, since lunch time yesterday. I imagine, Villette and not you, Uncle Emanuel, has prepared the food, certainly Dad couldn't fry an egg."

"Don't assume, young lady, that just because your renowned Father is no chef, all of we males are similarly inflicted. However, in this case you are correct, Villette is my trusted housekeeper and cook."

"He's right, Kathy, I can't cook for toffee, but Bart is an excellent chef and from what I've tasted from his efforts, Emanuel is also skilled in the art. Well anyway, I have always been able to eat and enjoy what he has prepared," Boris cut in. "In all honesty, they only trust me to sort out the washing up."

Which drew laughter from everyone and served to lighten the atmosphere.

"Ten minutes, then the food will be ready. Would you two please set the table. I think it best if we eat right here, if that's okay with you, Father Emanuel,"

Villette said, rising from her chair and directing the twins to where cutlery and condiments were stored. And so it was, in ten minutes time, Bart had lifted the huge casserole from the Aga oven and placed it in the centre of the kitchen table. With the ladle, everyone helped themselves and tucked into Chicken Chasseur with a large baked potato each.

For a while, there was silence, except for the sound of cutlery on plates. Second helpings soon cleared the dish and with no encouragement, the twins cleared the table, making room for a large strawberry trifle, covered with whipped cream.

This time, it was Boris who cleared the table and loaded the dishwasher to capacity.

"I would like to show our visitors my church," Father Emanuel said. "I think you will not find it much different from your St Patricks, Gerry. We may conduct our services in a slightly different way, but we do worship the same God and hold similar beliefs."

They all followed the priest, through the tunnel to the vestry. This time, Becky and Kathy helped Sara, with one on either side, and Villette followed close behind. She was used to being the sole support for her mother and had to control her urges to take their place.

However, eventually, with Father Emanuel, Bart and Boris in the front row of choir stalls and the other six in the one behind them, the three men turned to face their guests. Father Emanuel spoke first, explaining the reason for meeting within the sanctity of the church. Then, having prayed for their safety, handed over the next explanations to his companions. Sara and Villette were already completely up to date but Gerry, Meg and the twins were only aware of what Boris had deemed safe to tell over the internet and telephone. As expected, there were questions.

The first came from Becky. "Are you saying that there is a laboratory in the caves and that is where the recipe for the antidote is held? If so, I gather it will be our job to mix these three things together, whilst quoting the words you mentioned. Mixing a gel substance with a mist or more accurately, a vaporous mist, is a bit of a conundrum, but I can work on that, then adding the liquid shouldn't prove much of a problem. However, from what I have been hearing, nothing will prove to be easy, for the Count, or whoever he might be, will do all he can to prevent our success."

"Quite," Father Emanuel replied. "Although the Count is unable to enter the caves we believe, in fact we know, that he has a Demon secured therein, that he can to a large extent control. However, it is our belief that this Demon is able to act on its own to a certain extent. This belief comes from the writings in the ledger, as not all appear to be either consecutive or in the same style of writing."

Bart took over from here. "This first meeting is just to get us all on the same page and to make sure you will know that nothing of our discussions, even amongst each other, is to be spoken outside the sanctity of this church. I would suggest that we now return to the Rectory, where we can speak about the church, it's services and so forth. Then we will make our way to bed. Tomorrow is another day and one during which, we can discuss our individual thoughts for our next move."

"I will appreciate it if you two would help me again. It is so much easier with one either side and you two are so well balanced." So, this time Sara with the twins, led the way back to the Rectory.

Chapter 75

Sleep did not come easily to anyone that night, with thoughts and possible plans rushing around in their heads. But when Morpheus finally won, they all slept dreamlessly, until daylight filtered through the drapes.

Breakfast was a dribs and drabs affair, with everyone looking after themselves. Thus, it was, that the kitchen was left in somewhat of a mess. However, with the assistance of the twins, Villette soon had everything stacked in the dishwasher and tidied away. Then whilst Becky and Kathy peeled vegetables, Villette prepared fish and prawns to make a fish pie for their evening meal. Meg, meanwhile, made a large trifle, having earlier made jelly which had now cooled, and poured it over mixed fruit and the sponges that had been soaking in sherry overnight. This was placed in the refrigerator to set, before the final adornment later that afternoon.

~

It was after 11.30am before they silently adjourned to the church for privacy, to continue discussing possible plans of action prior to re-entering the caves.

Becky was the first to speak. "Right. This laboratory of the Count. As I understand it, to achieve an antidote for the Mist thing, we have to first mix a gel from tank three, the amount being exactly one half of the Mist in tank one and add it to the Mist. Having done this, the colour of the Mist should change from grey to bright blue. This concoction in tank one will then be topped up with the boiling red liquid from tank two, which again has to be precise. In this case, I understand it to be three quarters of the total now in tank one. Was it on the final mixing that someone has to quote the verse or whatever, to ensure the antidote actually works? And just one more question. Is this rigmarole going to shut down the Mist thing throughout the world, or just around here?"

She paused and Father Emanuel chose to answer her questions.

"First, you are correct insofar as the mixing is concerned and we are hoping your knowledge of such chemical measurements, will help us achieve the end we desire. The words are to be spoken once the Mist has turned bright red when it is to be released from the tank. We have no idea what will follow this action; therefore, I wish you all to be outside the vicinity of the laboratory. I alone will open the release valve and quote the anecdote."

This brought a cry of dissent from all present and it was Sara who brought them to order.

"I understand what Emanuel is implying but, dear friend, you are needed in this community. I am nearing the end of my life and it would be more sensible for me to be the one to perform the final action." She stamped her foot and looked severely to the others.

"No" was the chorus of voices.

Gerry raised his hand to silence them. "Sara has a point, but I cannot agree with her. She is needed not only by her daughter but also by the community, in which I am sure she adds considerable thoughtful actions."

Boris cut in, "There are only three of us who should be responsible for this. We have involved the rest of you only to assist in the things of which we have little or no experience. And that, only because of your association with our dear Suzanne."

"Totally agreed," said Bart. "We three, were the ones to search the caves and discover the Count's laboratory. Therefore, we three should be responsible for releasing the antidote, in the manner prescribed. Your assistance is more than gratefully appreciated but we will definitely *not* put you in more danger, than that in which you are already involved."

Father Emanuel nodded his agreement. "We three know all the Count has done and the way he works. However, I feel that it is my place to release the Mist, if for no other reason than I am a priest and therefore, perhaps have a more direct route, as the opposite of evil."

Kathy added her opinion. "From my studies in medieval religions, I have to agree with Uncle Emanuel. This needs the intervention of a Christian Church leader, such as himself and/or my father. Now, neither of you have the experience of exorcism, so I recommend that the two of you read up on that subject, in depth. Yes, it will take time, which I understand is of the essence, but you should be fully prepared for anything that may happen during the mixing. You say that the Count has his Demon within the caves, whom he apparently controls, to the extent that it fulfils any writings he might require. You can therefore assume, that the Count can also control this Demon to perform other duties. In this respect, I believe that this can only occur if the Count is aware of our actions. Hence, our meetings being conducted here, in the church itself."

"She's right, you know." Gerry smiled at his daughter. "I feel we have enough to think about for now and think perhaps we should return to the rectory and do yet more thinking. Also, Emanuel and I need time to follow Kathy's suggestion."

"In that case," Boris said, "I declare today's meeting closed. Remember no voiced discussion that might somehow get through to anyone or anything, outside this group. We will all mull through what has been discussed and if necessary, write any notes that could be useful to future discussion. I do mean write, not type into our various phones, tablets or computers, just in case they can be hacked."

With that and much else in their minds, the group returned to the Rectory.

Chapter 76

The following day found them all in the church by ten o'clock, to continue their thoughts and plans.

This time, Father Emanuel opened the meeting with a prayer and Meg moved to the organ, on which she played and sang in her rich voice, the 23rd Psalm. The others soon joined in and even Boris, seemed to know most of the words. Then with the melody of the organ still reverberating throughout the church, Gerry requested permission from Father Emanuel, to lead them in reciting the Lord's prayer.

This done, he again asked, "Does anyone mind if I start this session?" There were no objections, so he continued. "I don't know about you, Emanuel, but I still need probably another two days, to complete my study of exorcism and probably another to write my plans as to how we might use it to our advantage."

"I also, need more time to absorb the subject, Gerry. It is not possible to skim over the subject, it must be thoroughly understood. If we do not know fully what we intend to do, who knows what could go wrong. I would suggest that you and I go over this together when we have completed our reading. Do you agree, my friend?"

The answer being definitely yes, Becky, who was bursting with the desire to be heard, waved her hands. Her mother tried to hush her, but Boris indicated that he agreed with the young woman and told her to proceed.

"Well, it's this mixture that appeared to be the problem, but I think I've solved it. Measuring the Mist can be achieved simply by dipping a stick for the depth of it. Then I asked myself why tank three is the first addition, rather than tank two. Then it dawned on me. Gel is perforce viscous or gelatinous, so how do we mix a gelatinous substance with a Mist? Did you three notice if it was viscous or a liquid?"

Bart answered, "I did not. However, I did notice the tanks were all labelled tank number 1, 2, 3, plus their contents, in this case gel but as to its consistency,

I really have no idea. I must confess our attention was mainly on tank 1, for obvious reasons."

Emanuel and Boris agreed with him, so Becky continued.

"I thought as much. Well, if it is gelatinous, we have to think again but it occurred to me last night that I use a gel on my hair and that is a liquid spray. Are you with me?"

Villette, Meg and Kathy all nodded agreement whilst Sara looked at her daughter. "Is that the stuff you spray on your hair?" Receiving a nod from Villette, she continued. "So that's the sticky stuff that leaves a mark on the leather chairbacks." On receiving a blushing nod from Villette, she said, "Hmmm!"

This brought a laugh from those present.

Becky said, "May I continue? As I said, the hairspray is in liquid form and only turns into a gel when it is sprayed from the canister. So, I thought about it, and this is my solution, if you'll forgive the pun. The measuring of gel versus Mist is the most difficult thing to achieve. As I said tank one could be measured by a stick, or ruler perhaps but to do that we need to see if it is possible to do this through the glass, because measurements must be one hundred per cent correct. As to the gel, if it is indeed a liquid, we have to find a way of collecting enough of it to fit into a spray bottle. To do this, we shall have to remove that exact amount from tank three quickly enough to prevent it turning to gel."

Bart commented here. "There were other tanks in that laboratory similarly labelled but apparently empty. Could those be for the mixing process, or do you think that will be completed in tank one?"

"Again, Bart, as we are not sure they are indeed empty or if they contain something invisible, we have no way of knowing until we actually visit the caves, to make sure of what's what. So, as the three of you seem to be in charge here, perhaps you could arrange a visit, for you plus my father, Kathy and I."

"This would seem a time to close this meeting and for Meg, Villette and I, to return to the Rectory to prepare some lunch, whilst you, the twins and Gerry make plans for a further trip to the Count's laboratory," Sara said.

Chapter 77

The meeting, now reduced to six, it was Bart who took charge.

"We know that the Count is, presumably due to the carvings at the caves entrances, unable to enter the system. We believe this to have been done between the thirteenth and seventeenth centuries, which was just before the Henri de Ville period. Also, because of his apparent ability to activate his so-called Demon, is the reason for holding these discussions within the sanctity of the church. We have learned that our plans can be disrupted, as though someone is aware of what we discuss. We have only a vague idea how this is achieved but have discovered that possibly the Count is unable to come within the walls of a Christian church, or at any rate this one."

"I've read the regressions and spoken to Suzanne about them," said Gerry. "It seems to me though, that the Count had no difficulty whatsoever, in entering the chapel of St Patricks, when trying to remove his son by Isabella. What I'm saying is, if he was able to do that, why not here nowadays?"

Father Emanuel answered him. "Like you, we do not know. However, one possibility is just that. We are in Switzerland; his area and he is desperate to continue his line. Henri was to be that line but in the safety of the caves, he realised that he was not in all conscience, prepared to follow the footsteps of his wicked Papa Count and so chose to drown. However, Papa Count still appears to have had some control of the spirit of Henri, probably in the same way as he has of his Demon. There is no other way he could have killed Suzanne. This could possibly be because of the hold he had of Henri de Ville before he drowned. The caves were closed to him, but these are just theories, and we seek facts. Sorry, Bart, do please continue."

"Suzanne was sure she felt the presence of the Count before she first had conversations with me. I believed her. Indeed, I warned her to make sure she was in the company of others and kept her hotel room door and windows firmly closed at all times. This would not necessarily have kept the Count out but would help to deter anyone he might have acting on his behalf. I believe that the Count in shadow form, walks wherever he is able within this area. No one will get real sight of him, so within the Rectory he is able to in effect, join our gatherings. However, Father Emanuel, is very careful to make sure the tunnel to the vestry is sanctified before entry and after we reach the church. He also ensures this is done when we leave the church."

Father Emanuel nodded. "I do indeed, exactly as Bart says, and more thoroughly than you would imagine." He smiled. "What Boris calls my praying and spraying thing."

"So," Bart continued. "We need to plan when and how to surreptitiously make our way into the cave system, as we wish above all, to avoid that being noticed if at all possible. The easiest way would actually be through the rear entrance of the church. It is rarely used and therefore kept permanently locked. I believe Father Emanuel has the only key, he told us the spare was mislaid years ago. Also, it is not so far to walk, therefore less chance of being observed. We can skirt around the car park and once in the caves, all we need do is make our way to the path leading up behind the waterfall. What say you, Boris?"

Boris took a deep breath, exhaling slowly, speaking breathily, "Well, I believe you once showed us a door leading directly into the graveyard, Emanuel, assuming that is the one Bart referred to. If we were to make our way into the church in the usual manner, as though coming for a service or whatever the Count has surmised, we do, we can exit through that doorway and make our way through the cemetery to the woods, and eventually, the carpark and the cave entrance. Something else occurs to me, the time. Early morning has been good for us when we attempt to venture out, so perhaps we should consider about four-thirty to leave the Rectory and enter the tunnel."

"Seems a plan," said Gerry. "However, the women must not appear to be woken or that may alert the Count something is going on. How long will it take to get to the cave entrance from the church?"

"Good point, my friend, but we have to make them aware of what we plan to do, so I suggest we leave everything on hold until tomorrow morning, having our usual prayer session in the church. We will then make arrangements, so our usual activities in the Rectory appear to be no different than usual. At a good pace, it should only take us about fifteen or so minutes to get to the cave entrance and once inside, we are clear to go."

With these words, Father Emanuel suggested they close the discussion for now and go get some food. "I'm starved and I'm sure you all are too."

The twins sniffed in unison, declaring they could smell it from here and without more ado, made their way towards the vestry.

Chapter 78

So, it was that plans were made that evening and on their return to the rectory, the group followed their usual procedures. Hot drinks were prepared and Villette carried her mother's hot chocolate up to her room, helping her to prepare for bed. She returned to the kitchen, joining the others round the kitchen table and eventually, they all slowly dispersed to their own beds by ten o'clock.

A couple of hours later when the house was in peaceful darkness, with everyone apparently sleeping, the six adventurers quietly gathered the items they had agreed upon into their individual backpacks, ready for a very early start. Time for a few hours sleep, hopefully, they lay on their beds waiting for four-thirty, when they would leave through the tunnel to the vestry.

Meg had been wide awake since Gerry did his packing. They had slept in each other's arms until his phone beeped but neither had really slept afterwards. They lay there whispering, about everything but what was to take place the next morning. Meg was so proud of her Girls. They had both achieved places at Cambridge University. Kathy was reading World Religions and Becky Biological and Biomedical Science. She and Gerry were very proud of them both and the twins, being inseparable so far in their lives, were extremely pleased that they were attending the same university. Since the moment they were born, just five minutes between them, these two had needed each other's support and found it difficult to be apart for any length of time.

"Promise me, you will take the greatest care of them, forever," Meg pleaded.

"I will care for them with my life," Gerry responded.

Then Gerry's phone beeped. It was time to move on to the next stage.

~~

The six investigators entered the tunnel led by Father Emanuel. He was followed by Bart, then the twins, side by side, with their father behind them and

Boris bringing up the rear. On entering the church, the priest drew them to the altar, and after saying a prayer in Latin, they prayed together for safe delivery and the blessing of God's protection of their task. Finally, checking that everyone knew their places for the next part of their journey, which would take them through the cemetery to the woods and eventually, to the carpark entrance to the caves.

Again, Father Emanuel led the way, through the small door and into the cemetery, silently praying whilst spraying Holy Water before him. He was followed closely by the twins, hand in hand, with Gerry behind them, then Boris. This time Bart brought up the rear, like Father Emanuel, spraying Holy Water behind them, enclosing their pathway against any lingering evil entities. They made their way in this fashion, keeping carefully to the perimeter of the car park, until the entrance to the caves was immediately before them.

Father Emanuel stood to one side, beckoning the others past him. Bart now took the lead through the entrance tunnel and into the Great Cavern. He led them to the path up to the waterfall. When they had nearly reached the top, he indicated that they should remove their top clothing for the trip behind the waterfall. Bart, Boris and Father Emanuel wore their wetsuits, the other three made do with tee-shirts and shorts. With dry clothes, safely packed in waterproof bags in their backpacks, the intrepid six continued their climb, roped together for safety. The twins appeared to have no fear of the dangers, presumably owing to their youth, but their father was no youngster and had no experience of such things as mountaineering. However, he had promised Meg to take care of their daughters and would do so, whatever the cost. Boris, sensing the fear in Gerry, was close behind him and this time, Father Emanuel brought up the rear.

They actually accomplished the treacherous balancing act along the ledge, with no difficulty and once clear of the waterfall, removed their wet clothes and donned dry ones once more. Then they were ready to continue to the Cathedral Cavern, where entrance number six would take them to the Eyrie Laboratory. It was possible to hear one another speak now, free from the noise of the giant waterfall, and gazing down into the Cathedral Cavern, Gerry and the twins gasped at the very glory of the scene.

Bart, however, allowed them no time to just hang around and exclaim.

"Come on, we are making good time so far," he said. "Let's get this over and back home in as short a time as possible, follow mc."

The girls ran their hands over the stalactites and stalagmites as they passed and declared silently to each other, that they would explore this cave more thoroughly later on.

They entered tunnel six and as the curve led them into the laboratory, the new members of the team had cause to gasp in wonder once again.

Chapter 79

"I suggest we rest for a while and drink some coffee," Boris said. So, as they relaxed in silent thought, Becky stared at the tanks, running through her mind, what she needed to do. As she began taking equipment from her backpack, Kathy put her hand on her sister's arm.

"Take care, Sis, don't forget that if you so much as touch the tank, the Mist will swirl, then there is no way you can measure it accurately."

"Don't worry, Kathy. You have your mumbo-jumbo, and we proceed as we agreed. Okay?"

They had spent most of the night under the bedclothes, whispering their ideas and had come up with a plan they thought might just work.

"Yeah. I go to T1 first, speaking in Tibetan, the prayers used by the monks to seal the interior of their monasteries from invading forces. The monks would draw close to the interior walls and kneel in complete and unmoving silence, whilst saying the prayers I will use, and those forces were unable to get within touching distance of the walls of the Monastery."

"Right," Becky replied. "I will be close behind and as you get as close as you can, saying the Tibetan prayers, I should hopefully, be able to measure the static Mist. I shall not be able to get very close to the tank, so must keep a steady hand, as I need to get an accurate reading from a distance. We won't know how far away that will be, until we actually do it but I'm hoping it will be exponentially less than the Monastery, because of the difference in size. I will get as close as I can, bearing that in mind. Otherwise, we have to rely on modern technology to get the reading accurate."

Kathy nodded, then with a thumbs up to the other four, they moved towards their first task.

It proved surprisingly easy; Becky held the digital distance calculator at what she thought, to be about the right length away from the tank, gradually lessening the distance, until she got a flash on the screen. Then moving a millimetre at a time, until an actual reading appeared, she nodded to Kathy, who continued chanting. Becky almost shouted as the measurement of first the height of the tank appeared on the small screen, then she altered the position of the instrument, to record measurements of the depth and width of the tank. As she slowly lowered the instrument, it finally gave a measurement for the height of the Mist, sitting at the bottom of the tank.

Kathy had meanwhile noted the measurements in a small notebook, as Becky spoke them out loud, still managing to continue chanting at the same time.

"Now to T3," she said, as Bart led them to their next task. "Yes, it is a liquid, so our next problem will be, to discover a way to drain off the right amount to add to the Mist."

"That might prove to be the most difficult one," Boris commented. "It won't be the quantity, for if you draw off too much, we just don't use all of it but how to get it from the tank into a spray might not be so easy."

"We'll worry about that later, when we have worked out the exact amount of Mist to compare it with. Meanwhile, let's find T2," Kathy said.

The main problem with the boiling red liquid was going to be just that, the fact that it was boiling. They must make sure that the vessels required to contain these two last items, were suited to the requirements. They were also well aware they had been warned that under no circumstances, were the contents of any of the tanks to touch their skin.

As the six sat drinking coffee and eating sandwiches, they discussed whether or not to try and work out the required proportions, whilst still in the caves or to make their way back to the Rectory.

Father Emanuel, decided for them. "We have had enough for today I feel. We got little sleep last night and have been on the move since a quarter to four this morning. Our bodies and brains need to be extremely clear and rested before trying to make complex mathematic decisions, for under no circumstances, is any mistake allowed. The dangers of that are too formidable to be thought of. So, let us return to the Rectory, shower, eat, rest and continue this mission tomorrow, in the sanctity of the church. Meanwhile, once outside these caves, no comments of our trip are to be mentioned, not even quietly amongst ourselves." He said this with a sharp look at the twins.

Six very tired people made their return journey through the caves. Back through the beautiful Cathedral Cavern, behind the waterfall, fortunately without any mishap, down into the Great Cavern and eventually to the entrance. There were cars in the car park now and visitors around the gift and coffee shops, as they slipped silently around its perimeter and into the woods. Once in the church, they said prayers of thanks for their safety and eventually, arrived back at the Rectory, just before midday.

Meg hugged her husband and the twins. "Did you have a good trek up that mountain?" she asked, hustling them upstairs to take a warming shower.

Chapter 80

The next day was a much later start than they had anticipated. Yesterday's expedition had taken more out of them than they realised and the six were allowed to sleep, until they were ready to wake up naturally.

The women, set too preparing a hearty breakfast as soon as they heard movement from upstairs, so when the six now refreshed people, appeared in the kitchen, it was to find the table already laid and coffee brewing. Finally, they completed their meal and refurbished their mugs with hot coffee.

"Well, after that delicious and much-needed meal, for which I thank you, ladies, I suggest we give thanks to our Lord in the church, for our rest and food," Father Emanuel said.

It was now nearly mid-day when the nine intrepid investigators, travelled once more through the tunnel leading to the vestry and so into the sanctity of the church. The walk had been blessed in the usual manner and once in the church, Father Emanuel gave his usual prayers for God's protection during their quest.

Kathy raised her hand, virtually jumping up and down in her desire to speak.

"I'm sorry, folks, but something occurred to me last night and I think it's important. We all know that various religions throughout the world, are basically a man-made ritual, according to the culture of that particular community." She took a breath and looked around to see if the others were following. "Ours is the Christian concept, but there are many versions of that, bearing in mind that the majority of these in the western world, are based on belief in God, the Father, Son and Holy Ghost, or at least, in a supreme God. However, there are sects such as the Wiccans, who believe in a nature-based form of worship, Mother Earth for example. This may involve witches and warlocks, that can be either so-called white or black magicians."

"But this, well, it's us versus the Count. So, how does your lecture on the religions of the world help us?" Villette interjected.

"That's the point, Villette. Exactly what version are we dealing with? The Count and his Convent of the Golden Orb, were obviously not believers in our God." Kathy stopped, then taking a deep breath continued. "No. That was not right. They did, do, believe in our God but not as the Supreme Creator. They believe Satan should be considered supreme and to that end, his representative on Earth should be the Count, his heirs and assigns. The Count refers to him as The Master. What I'm trying to say, is that we must deal with this through the eyes of the Count and his kind, whilst still sticking firmly to our own beliefs in right and wrong."

Father Emanuel and Gerry nodded, and her father said. "You're right, honey. I suppose you're thinking of the incantation. Whilst we have to use it to free the world of this MistVirus, we still have to cover ourselves with our Christian beliefs and prayers."

"Exactly, Dad. But we have to devise a way to do that, in a manner that will protect all of us. Sorry to take up so much time but I think it's important."

Boris stood. "This is not something that we can deal with on a boom-boom basis, plan today and carry out tomorrow. I feel that it might well take us a week or so to prepare and possibly more than one day to carry out. However, perhaps our biochemist could bring us up to date with her reckoning now. Becky?"

"Yeah. Well. I haven't worked out the math for the amount of Mist in the tank yet. I've got the measurements and will have to sit down with a calculator, to make sure it's accurate. In fact, I shall do it with two calculators in case one is a bit off. I shall also write the figures down and work it out in my head. Would you be willing to help me do that, Mum? You're good with figures, and I'd like your input if you're willing.

The liquid/gel shouldn't be too much of a problem. I have to get a tube into the tank and should be able to drain off into a container, like you did that day from your petrol tank, to fill the lawn mower when it ran out." They giggled at the remembrance of the look on Gerry's face, as he tasted the petrol. "I'm not suggesting we do that, by sucking. We'll have to get a pump or something to do the job.

The boiling red liquid will have to be removed in a similar manner. So, that's my next collection of tasks to be done."

"You've certainly got my help with the math, Becky, and in any way possible." Meg put her hand on her daughter's arm with a gentle squeeze.

Father Emanuel went next. "Both Gerry and I, are now going through the exorcism ritual together and we will follow up on what Kathy has brought to our notice. I suspect we shall be able to combine both things."

Gerry agreed with him and merely nodded.

Sara broke in here. "I know I am merely a potential bystander here, as there is little I can do in the way of climbing. However, I am able to read and it seems to me, that I can be of most help in assisting the two Men of the Cloth, by trying to combine what is necessary between Christianity and Satanism. Perhaps, you would help me, Villette?"

"With pleasure, Mama. And we three women will, if I may suggest, sojourn ourselves in the church and help protect your quest with our prayers, for the duration. When you return, we shall be able to assist you back to the Rectory and prepare food or whatever else you may require."

Bart had contributed nothing to these discussions and still silent, he led the way back to the vestry and through the tunnel. Before opening the door, he turned to the others. "We are in even more danger now, so under no circumstances should we go anywhere alone. Always there must be at least two together and preferably more than that. Becky and Meg, may I suggest that the math you discuss, if there is need to speak of what you are doing, should be considered and spoken of, as homework from the university." With that comment, he opened the door and they entered the Rectory once again.

Once more around the kitchen table with mugs of hot coffee, they relaxed to the best of their ability. Becky drew her notebook towards her and began scribbling figures.

The problem, Meg and Becky discovered, was a question of volume versus what the answer would be if transcribed to liquid. So, they worked it out in both, to be discussed at the meeting the following morning.

Now, for the next stage everyone was thinking.

Chapter 81

It was a long night for everyone. Villette helped her mother to bed at nine o'clock and stayed with her throughout the night. The twins were yawning by that time and after another ten minutes, declared themselves too tired to do any more homework that night and retreated to their room. Meg and Gerry followed soon after, leaving Father Emanuel, Bart and Boris still sitting at the table with glasses of brandy in their hands.

They sat in silent contemplation for nearly an hour, then Father Emanuel suggested they do the rounds, to check that the house was firmly locked and to bless all entrances.

It was midnight by the time they retired to the room shared by Boris and Bart, into which they had brought Emanuel's bed, so that no one was alone during the night. Bart had declared that he thought he would be better employed being in the same room as Sara and Villette and Boris agreed with a grin, that he thought he should be looking after the twins. Father Emanuel declared that the thought of sharing a room with a married couple, was not something he could approve of for a man of the cloth. So, it was that the Rectory was in comparative silence until six the next morning.

~~

By 9.00am they were back in the church. Gerry suggested they bring the desk and chairs from the vestry, so that they could sit together, rather than being spread over two pews, making it easier to discuss their plans. Boris and Father Emanuel moved the desk from the vestry between them, and Gerry and the twins grabbed a chair each. The others would sit on the front pew, with the desk being drawn close. Finally, the group looked towards Father Emanuel to lead.

"I believe it is the turn of Bart to chair this meeting," he said. "I feel he has a better knowledge of the caves and the history of this area than any of us.

However, this morning Meg passed me a note, asking me to bring the Count's Black Book with me." He withdrew the ledger from the bag, in which he carried any paraphernalia he might need, placing it on the table between them. "Please, Meg, would you explain."

"Well, Becky, Kathy and I, concentrated on the math homework yesterday and found it almost impossible to compute the measurements. Then Becky remembered noticing some pipework in the laboratory and it occurred to her that this might be connected to each tank. That brought another thought to my mind. Maybe we should be working in algebra, not the usual mathematics. First of all, though, we need to go through the subject in the Count's ledger. There may well have been something we just skipped because it was too difficult to take in at the time. Hence, I asked Emanuel to bring the Black Book with him today." She stopped speaking, leaning over to open the book. All eyes were now on the page concerning the laboratory. "Perhaps, Becky should continue from here, as she is better at explaining these things than I am."

"See the drawings, there are lines drawn underneath the tanks that may well be pipework. Obviously, we can't be sure of that until we are in the lab again, but that's where clever old Mum had her bright idea. Do you want to tell them, Mum?"

"No, dear, you're doing fine."

"That's why we need the book. Mum thinks our idea of measurement, is not the one the Count means. We spent so much time trying to work out the measurements of each component, in liquid content and height measurement when added to the tank. But what if," she took a deep breath. "What if the measurement should be that of the Mist, when the other two things are added. See what I mean?"

Heads we shaken, except for Kathy and Meg, who both nodded vigorously.

"It was just 6cms from the bottom of the tank to the top of the Mist. If we add half of that amount 3cms, we get 9cms and if again we add three quarters 6.75cms, we get a total of 15.75cms. See, where I'm coming from? We need to mark on Mist tank 1 each of those measurements, which makes it much easier, especially if that *is* pipework, I sort of remember.

Think of it algebraically."

Taking a pen, she wrote on the pad before her: x + c + b = a. She looked sheepishly at the other members of the team. "That might be wrong thinking but it's just an example.

I've had another thought too, regarding the gel. We can assume that once it's piped from tank 3 in liquid state, it will become viscous on entering tank 1, like when it's sprayed onto our hair. Now gel is obviously heavier than mist and will therefore sink or be fed directly underneath it. Again, we only have an assumption, as we know the Mist is capable of squeezing the life out of humans. It actually pulled Boris' boots from his feet. Therefore, as they say, *assume makes an ass of you and me.* However, if whilst in the tank, it is just uncontrolled Mist, the gel will form a base on which that Mist rests. I believe that the only difference will be the change in colour, from grey to bright blue and the rise in measurement to 9cms. The addition of the boiling red liquid will or perhaps should, be fed onto the top of the Mist, which is why we have to look very carefully at the Black Book to hopefully, clarify things."

"Thanks to Becky and her team for a great presentation. You have given us much to consider." Bart brought the discussion to order, and opened the Black Book to the pages covering the directions for terminating the MistVirus.

~~

They gathered around the ledger.

"Does anyone mind if I photo this on my phone?" Boris was the one with the query. "I ask because you will all realise, that some of us will need to go back to the laboratory, to check if it is indeed pipework and if so, where any connections might be."

No one objected and Becky did likewise. Kathy copied the directions in her notebook, saying, "I think we need to double cover ourselves in this, so that if anything unforeseen happens, then we have back-up so to speak."

"Right," Bart continued. "Three of us should make the trip back to the laboratory, myself, Becky, because she is our biochemist, and either Emanuel or Gerry, as I feel a priest is necessary in that environment."

"Agreed, and it should be me," said Father Emanuel. "The religious side of things so far as the caves are concerned, has so far been in my hands and I feel that to try and vary it, no disrespect intended, Gerry, my friend, would be unwise. We can't be sure, but any variation in the way we act, so far as protection is concerned, may open a loophole that would enable the Count's Demon to intervene. Even if Gerry were to follow exactly the same routine as myself, the difference in his voice tone may prove dangerous for us."

"There is one thing you might like to check when you're back in the laboratory," Gerry said. "I wandered around the lab when we were there and focused on the boiling red stuff. In my opinion, it is not just red water but actual blood. Which begs the question as to where it originated. Is it human blood or that of an animal? Perhaps, it is from the women the Count impregnated and subsequently died in childbirth. Perhaps, it is from the Counts 100 themselves and is many hundreds of years old. Whatever, remember that although in tank 2, it is the third and final addition to the Mist tank and therefore, must be of substantial importance. If possible, and I realise it is most unlikely, perhaps we should try to get a sample, to check its components."

He took a shuddering breath, "Becky, I don't want you to put yourself in any more danger than we are already, but I felt it was something I should mention."

"Oh, my goodness. You have certainly given us even more to think about, Gerry. At this point, I will recommend closing our meeting for today. We will return here tomorrow morning, to finalise our plans."

So, they returned to the Rectory.

Chapter 82

Back in the church the following day, it was decided that Bart, Becky and Father Emanuel, should make the trip to the caves. They would, as previously, leave early in the morning and the others, would remain at the Rectory or in the church, until their return, which they hoped would not take them a whole day this time.

~~

They were ready at five o'clock the next morning, for what they hoped would be a short journey to the cave laboratory.

Kathy hugged her twin, "Take care of you for me," she said.

"Of course, darling Sis. I've got Bart and Uncle Emanuel with me, so what can possibly go wrong?"

Famous last words, thought Gerry, who had overheard his daughters talking. However, no discussions of the subject within the Rectory, so he quietly escorted the three to the church, in the early hours of the morning. He made the usual blessings as he locked the door behind them and having prayed in his own way before the altar, silently returned to the vestry, through the tunnel and back to his bed in the Rectory.

Meg was awake and as previously arranged Kathy was with her, with a nod and a kiss, he put his arms around them and they tried to relax, thinking of Becky.

~~

The three reached the cave entrance, having gone through the usual procedure to get there. Becky personally, thought this was a waste of time but was too polite to say so. They continued uneventfully, to the laboratory where having removed the measuring equipment from her backpack, Becky proceeded to mark the Mist tank from the top of the Mist at 6cms, then 9cms and 15.75cms.

249

The Mist, swirled angrily within the tank, as it had as Bart pressed his forehead against the tank, when they first discovered the laboratory. This done she joined Bart and Father Emanuel, inspecting the pipes that were indeed, running beneath and attached to the bench.

Tank 3 appeared to be a straight run directly to tank 1, its connection entering in the centre bottom of the tank, into what looked like a 5mm spray. The connection from tank 2 was on the far side of tank 1, about half way between the 9cm and 15.75cm lines, which Becky had drawn on the front.

Bart drew a scale map of the pipework, laying on his back under the bench, whilst Becky photographed it with her mobile. She then took photos of the three tanks with their connections and her own marking on the front of tank 1. When they finished, Father Emanuel, who had been exploring the region leading to the Count's Eyrie, suggested they sit for a while.

"Time for the good old coffee and sandwiches," he said, then continued. "When we get home, I will get your father, Becky, to bring the others to the church, so we can tell them of today's accomplishments. I may have found something that might help us, but prefer to only tell once."

So, it was that they made the return journey and were safely back in the Great Cavern.

Then, the Bottomless Pool seemed to erupt, their torches all went off and they were surrounded by the ghostly gleam of the eruption and roar of the waterfall, as it flowed into the midst of it. Around them, rocks fell from above.

Becky thought of her words to her twin, *what could possibly go wrong?*

Chapter 83

"They've been gone for ten hours now. It should only have taken them at the most six." Meg was sounding panicky and from the look on the other's faces, they agreed with her.

"Come," Gerry stood, moving towards the door. "Let's go into the church and pray."

~~

Back in the cavern, Bart drew his companions together against the mountainside, as far away from the pool as possible. They had backed against the walls alongside the waterfall, standing with their hands over their heads as the larger rocks broke when hitting the ground, sending fragments in all directions. They looked at each other, listening to a voice, which, considering they could not hear each other clearly was strange. This voice was absolutely clear and as all three confirmed later, each one of them could hear every word.

I am Henri de Ville. Come close and I will tell the secrets of Papa Count. You think you know but I know them all and will tell if you come close to the Bottomless Pool.

Then another voice joined it, also quite clearly heard.

Help me. Help me please. This is Suzanne. I know you are there, Bart. We still have much to discuss. Please come to me by the pool. Help me. Help me please.

"Hold onto each other and do not let go for any reason." Father Emanuel, spoke directly into the ears of his companions.

Then the voices stopped, the fountain of water ceased and gradually rocks only fell occasionally. With Bart leading the way, he steered them, keeping close to the mountainside, towards the tunnel leading to the entrance, as quickly as possible. Once in the car park, he continued to lead them round the outskirts of the area and into the woods.

"Now, keep together and let's get to the church as fast as possible." Taking his mobile phone from his pocket, he rang Gerry's number. "No. Don't speak, just get to the back door leading to the cemetery and be ready to open it when I knock three times, then twice. Unless you hear that sequence do not, I repeat do not, open it." He rang off saying to the others, "Now run." Within ten minutes, they entered the cemetery, reaching the church door a few minutes later.

Bart knocked and it was immediately opened by Gerry, who stood to one side to allow the three to enter helter-skelter.

Villette, Meg and Kathy had been despatched back to the Rectory, to make flasks of coffee and sandwiches. They returned shortly, bearing not only food and drinks, but dry clothes and blankets, in case they were needed, which indeed they were. The two men retired into the vestry to change, whilst Meg and Kathy fussed over Becky behind the altar.

Apart from welcoming words, nothing had been said about the events in the cavern or Bart's strange phone call. Now feeling warm and comfortable, sitting around the desk, Boris spoke.

"Do you feel up to telling us about your adventure now?"

"Bart was wonderful getting us out of the waterfall cavern as he did." Becky piped up.

"Please tell us what happened," said Sara. "We only know from Bart's phone call to Gerry that something was amiss. What's this about getting you out of the waterfall cavern?"

"That was no problem, I know my way around those caves, especially the large caverns, like the back of my hand," he replied modestly.

Father Emanuel, told of the extinguishing of their lights, the great eruption in the centre of the Bottomless Pool and of the two voices they heard. Becky told of the bravery of Bart, as she insisted on referring to it, when he rescued them by leading the way from the caves and their probable deaths.

"When we get back to the Rectory, I will get Boris to download what I have on my phone but meanwhile, I believe Becky has the drawings she made in the laboratory. If they are not spoilt by the wet." Bart smiled at her with raised eyebrows.

"No, I kept it in a plastic cover." She placed the notebook on the desk, opening it to reveal her sketches made in the laboratory.

They all looked at the placement of the pipes and discussed what might be the safest way to open the valves and close them again at precisely the right moment.

"Uncle Emanuel discovered something near the Eyrie, that he would not tell until we were all together. Please do tell us now," said Becky.

Father Emanuel pursed his lips, sighed and rubbed his eyes. "Time has passed, strange things have happened and I begin to wonder if something is playing with my mind. Do you remember the lever we found, that opened the door to the Count's Eyrie? Well, when I was exploring, while the other two were examining the pipework and making measurements, I wandered over in that direction. The door was open, just a crack. I confess my cowardice in that I was too scared to peep through the crack and just passed by. However, it occurred to me that the Count's Demon might dwell within that cave and the fact that it was open, might mean that it was out there in the laboratory amongst us which presents the possibility, that our interests whilst in the laboratory, could well be passed to the Count. I think it is something we should seriously consider. Any comments?"

"Yes." It was Boris who answered. "Considering what happened in the waterfall cavern, this is a real possibility. Do you recall your strange dream, Emanuel? Well, it occurs to me, that we may be able to seal the Demon in that Eyrie. If the door was partially open, that would mean someone or something within needs to open it to exit or enter. Agreed?"

Nods from everyone confirmed.

"We need to enter surreptitiously and if the door is closed, we carve Christian Crosses across the opening. That should prevent the Demon keeping an eye on what we do within the caves. It may well be able to still communicate with the Count but not to tell him what we are doing. I'm no expert but I've carved my initials on many a desk at school and hearts with initials on the odd tree."

"Dad's quite good at it too," said Kathy. "I remember him trying his hand at the Monumental Mason's in Worcester." The twins giggled at the memory and Meg shushed them.

"Can we call it a day for now please?" Sara asked.

Which, being tired, was something they all agreed upon.

~~

Villette and Meg shared the job of preparing dinner, while the other members of the group took showers and changed into their nightclothes.

Chapter 84

Meg woke to find herself alone. On the dressing table, was a note from Gerry.

GONE FOR A WALK-SEE YOU LATER xx

Gerry, together with Boris and Father Emmanuel, had set off really early that morning for the caves. At four o'clock, Bart had accompanied them to the church and seen them cross to the woods once again. This time, they were carrying the tools required to inscribe the carvings they intended to make across the doorway to the Eyrie. They had discussed their strategy in the vestry after dinner, while the women cleared up and Meg and Villette took their showers. It was decided to keep it to themselves and to let the women sleep. Gerry decided to leave a note for Meg that he knew she would understand. Bart would remain in the church so it would appear, if anyone might be interested, that the four men had taken a walk together before breakfast.

Meg showed the note to Villette first. They had become friends over the short time they'd known each other and Meg felt she had found a friend in whom she could trust. They whispered over the sizzling pan of bacon as Meg explained in a few words, what the note meant. Then she showed it to Sara, who instantly understood, as did the twins when they finally appeared in the kitchen, ready for breakfast.

~~

Meanwhile, the three men were back in the laboratory. They breathed sighs of relief to see that the door to the Eyrie was firmly closed. Boris and Gerry, as they quietly as possible and speaking in whispers only, when necessary, removed the tools from their backpacks. Father Emanuel sprayed incense over the doorway, praying in Latin. His voice was firmer than he thought possible, expecting it to quiver in rhythm with his hands. There was a slight rumble but the door did not budge. The walls seemed to tremble within the laboratory, again there was a deep rumble but still nothing opened the door. Father Emanuel continued to pray, as Boris and Gerry hastened to carve. They commenced with one on either side of the door opening, each making a downward tail of the cross then joining it across the bottom. Then they carved from the centre of the tail, a cross strut, about 30cms down from the top, so sealing the entrance. Father Emanuel blessed the cross, as Boris and Gerry made a similar one, on the other side of the doorway.

After they felt secure with this work, they broke off for some coffee and sandwiches, thoughtfully made by Bart.

"Now for some real carving," said Gerry. "Anyone can carve straight lines." He proceeded to show his skill. Above the door, he carved an Angel, with arms outstretched, touching the cross-struts of the crosses on either side.

Again, Father Emanuel sprayed incense and prayed, this time ending with the Lord's Prayer, in which the other two gladly joined.

"Well, that should keep the Demon from interfering with our task," he said. To which Boris showed crossed fingers and a grimace.

"By the way," Gerry enquired, "did we find a way of letting the Mist escape once it's blended? I imagine Kathy was thinking of just opening one of the pipe valves but perhaps we should check, to see if there's a special exit somewhere in the tank."

"Fancy us forgetting a serious thing like that," Father Emanuel exclaimed. "Let's examine it before we leave."

They found what they were looking for in the top of the tank. It was a small sliding opening, rather like those to take batteries on telephones and about the size of a mobile phone.

"Well, that has made today's expedition a useful and I think very successful one." Bart said, as they made their weary way back to the cave entrance and home to the Rectory.

Bart was waiting for them at the rear door as they hastened across the cemetery. "Not now," he said, ushering them into the church. "We will discuss everything and make our plans after breakfast, in the usual way."

He locked the door behind them as, Boris led the way through the tunnel back to the Rectory kitchen. It was nearly midday.

Chapter 85

The women looked up as they entered. Father Emanuel shook his head.

"My, that smells good," Gerry commented. "That was a most refreshing walk but I'm cold, so if you would please give me ten minutes, I think I'll have a quick shower first."

"Good idea," Meg retorted. "You don't smell quite so good. Perhaps, you had all best get showered and changed. We'll fry the eggs when you come down."

Whilst they sat enjoying their breakfast later, there was much discussion about the walk they had supposedly taken and the beauty of the countryside.

Once everything had been cleared, they all returned to the sanctity of the church, to plan their next move.

"It occurred to me," Gerry told them, "that there had to be an exit for the vapour, other than through the original entrance valve."

The twins looked sheepish but were reassured by their father that it was not a problem. The three men explained what had been discovered and as everything appeared to be in order, settled down to planning the next stage.

It was the first week of October and as Kathy pointed out, the tenth month.

"Religions throughout the ages have been a matter of ritual," she reminded them. "Therefore, it seems to me that we should release the Mist on the tenth day of the tenth month. My reason for thinking this, is tied in with the Count's ten-year impregnation of a virgin. If that number was important to him, it might well prove to be important to us. Anyway, that is on Monday next, just five days from now. It's up to Uncle Emanuel to confirm my reasoning but I feel we should go into the caves on Sunday the ninth, so we are prepared for what we need to do well in advance."

It was agreed and each person would be allotted their individual task in the preparation. Again, it was agreed that no mention of what they proposed would be spoken of, unless they were actually in the church, as that was the only place, they felt to be secure. These meetings would take place at the usual time, when from conversations between various individuals residing at the Rectory, it was to be assumed they held services of some kind or perhaps cleaned the church, in preparation for when it was proclaimed open for services once again.

Meg insisted on accompanying the group, when they went to the laboratory in the caves, to evoke the antidote to the Count's Revenge MistVirus. Gerry did his best to dissuade her, but in the end, gave way, perfectly understanding his wife's desire to be with her family, during such an important and potentially dangerous exercise.

It was therefore, decided that Sara and Villette, would remain in the Rectory until they heard from the group, that they were on their way home with the mission accomplished.

Chapter 86

The ninth of October found them once again in the Great Cavern, with Bart leading, followed closely by Boris and Gerry. The twins went next, then Meg, all three clinging to each other, with Father Emanuel bringing up the rear. The walk along the ledge behind the waterfall was made in single file, all roped together for safety. From there, they hastened to the Cathedral Cavern, where they removed their wet outer garments and once again in warm clothing, crossed to the entrance that led to the Count's Eyrie and Laboratory. So far, the trip had proved relatively uneventful.

Father Emanuel was delighted to see no evidence that the doorway had been disturbed but nevertheless, blessed and sprayed it with incense. He then gathered the other six people around him and they held a short service, followed by the blessing of the three tanks and the laboratory in general.

As none of them felt comfortable to spend more time than necessary in the laboratory, they returned to the Cathedral Cavern. Meg placed the flasks and food on the altar-rock.

"Come on, we must eat and this is the obvious place to put our things," she said.

That seemed to pull them all from an almost trance-like state and soon they were chatting, whilst consuming food and hot drinks. Eventually, with sleeping bags spread in as comfortable niches as possible, they slept. Boris woke first and roused the others with his version of a trumpet call. This, although not exactly appreciated, served its purpose and after drinking from their flasks of coffee and eating a ham sandwich each, they proceeded back to the laboratory.

Once again, Father Emanuel checked that the Eyrie door remained undisturbed and performed his ritualistic service before starting on their mission.

~~

Gerry stood with Becky by tank 3, where Boris was in position to open the valve when Becky gave him the signal. Father Emanuel and Kathy took a position where they could see clearly, the valve into tank 1, which Bart would open, and Kathy would commence her Tibetan prayer. The twins exchanged nods and both valves were opened simultaneously. Within three minutes, the liquid from tank 3 began to flow into the tank containing the Mist, settling in gelatinous form beneath it.

Kathy was watching the level of Mist rise and as it reached the 9cms mark shouted, "Now!" Father Emanuel immediately closed the valve.

Everyone moved to the place behind the second bench, which they had overturned, as Boris had insisted, they keep behind it as some sort of protection, should that be necessary. The Mist, when they looked, had now turned bright blue.

"Hooray," Becky sounded exultant. "So far so good, it has done what the book said. The tank 3 stuff has gelled and the Mist has changed colour. Let's have some coffee, then do the next bit. The sooner we get out of here, the better pleased I'll be."

Meg hugged her daughters, saying, "Shall I watch the measurement for the next step?"

There was a chorus of 'no' and Boris declared that they would keep the same format as before, on the grounds of unchanged ritual.

So it was, Boris opened the valve to tank 2, containing the boiling red liquid and Bart opened the one that would direct the liquid into the Mist Tank. It flowed unerringly into the tank, apparently sitting on top of the Mist. Kathy said, "Now." And both men closed their valves. Tank 1 now contained a measurement of 15.75cms. As they watched, the boiling red liquid seemed to envelop the Mist and to mix it with the gel at the same time. The contents turned to a bright red vapour as they watched, then was still.

To everyone's surprise, Kathy raised her hand. "This is where the religious aspect comes into effect," she said. "I want Dad and Uncle Emanuel standing side by side and about a metre from tank 1, with Mum standing just behind and Becky and I on either side of her. I'm sorry, I don't know why but it just seems right. Uncle Emanuel will read, no, chant please, the incantation and Dad will hold the Bible, open at the twenty-third psalm, which he will start reading aloud when the incantation is complete. I'm sure he knows it by heart but please, Dad, have the Bible open at that page. Okay?"

He nodded his agreement, saying, "If that's what you think is right, love. First, though let's put our stuff by the exit tunnel, we should get out of here immediately the readings are complete."

That strategy was unanimously agreed and once everything was ready for a speedy exit, they settled into the formation suggested by Kathy, to complete the ritual.

"Time to release it, is everyone ready?" They all nodded a yes, to Kathy's question. "Right, let's go," she said.

Both Bart and Boris stood side by side by the tank of red Mist. They had decided to remove the small panel together. As it opened, the Mist swirled upwards and the two men stood back as Father Emanuel chanted the incantation.

Anti-vaporous Mist Red of the Count/Anti-Mist Virus Mist Blue of the Count/Anti-Mist Revenge of the Count/ I Command you to Evaporate and Cease the Count's Revenge/Throughout the World of Mankind.

The red Mist was still streaming from the tank as Gerry read *The Lord is my Shepherd I shall not want* as quickly and reverently as he was able.

The tank was by that time empty, and that was when everything seemed to explode.

Chapter 87

As they completed the ritual, Gerry turned and ushered his family to the exit, followed by Father Emanuel, with Bart and Boris close behind.

As the tank emptied, the red Mist gathered in a straight, upward flowing stream. The tank in which it had been contained exploded and the straight line of Mist went through the roof of the laboratory like a missile. As it disappeared from view, the mountain seemed to implode, leaving a crater the size of a caldera.

~~~

Back at the Rectory, Sara and Villette jumped as the house shook. The sky was lit by a bright red flash, which was more than a flash for it lasted several minutes and then came the **KABOOM, CRASH** and **RUMBLE** of an explosion.

"Dear, God, what is that?" Sara said, shaking with not only the shock waves but absolute terror.

"I don't know, Mum, but let's get into the tunnel leading to the church, it's underground and might offer some protection."

The two women fled as fast as able but the tunnel was shaking from the shock waves too. They stayed there huddled together, waiting for what might come next.

~~~

Meanwhile, news reports were appearing with messages of BREAKING NEWS on television, as announcers were advised by their directors, of the amazing destruction of a small village in the mountains of Switzerland. Later, some programmes were cancelled to enable coverage by TV reporters, who had speedily made their way to the area and taken photographs from helicopters, while other news presenters tried to speak to survivors in the area. They could all report seeing the red missile-like flash rise into the sky. Some reported seeing the flash, followed by what appeared to be a spaceship but these people were unable to describe it in any detail.

"It just seemed to follow the red flash. It was so fast, up then it turned east and was gone."

~~

Ten Days Later

"This is Archie Praed and today, I am presenting a special edition of Inexplicable Strange Events. In this case, the collapse of a mountain in Switzerland. On the screen behind me, you will see pictures of the devastation."

He was silent as the camera rolled, showing first, what the mountain with the peaceful village below looked like, before the collapse virtually obliterated the village of Billenbach. The presenter continued.

"As you can see on the plateau at the mountain top, was the Hotel Orb de l'Or that used to be the Convent of the Golden Orb. The farm belonging to the Gelberger family, together with the gift shop, café and car park, for the use of tourists visiting the caves, which were licenced to the Gelberger family, were completely obliterated. Only the church remains standing, with minimal damage and next to it, the shell of the old Rectory. Why we ask ourselves, amongst all that devastation, is the church relatively undamaged?

After the break, I will be joined by the two sons of the Vicar of St Patricks, who with his wife and twin daughters, are amongst the missing."

"Welcome back. Let me introduce the two sons of the Vicar of St Patricks. This is Edmond Cameron, the eldest son of the Reverend Gerry Cameron, whose first wife sadly died, during his birth. I believe you live in Canada, Edmond."

"Yes, and it's Ed please. I've been there since I was twenty, I have a wife and two children and farm one hundred acres, rearing cattle."

His accent tended to confirm the time he had spent in that country. The presenter turned to the younger son. "You are Adam, first child of your father's second marriage and at the moment are studying at Yale University."

"That is correct." Adam said no more.

Archie Praed turned once again to Ed, with whom he felt more at ease. "Your parents and sisters were taking a holiday in the mountains of Switzerland, if I understand correctly. Do you know why they chose Switzerland rather than a venue with warm sunshine?" He smiled self-deprecatingly.

"No idea. Adam probably knows more than I do."

"Can you help us here, Adam?"

"Up to a point but I'm not sure it is safe to do so. You see they, my parents that is, had a friend called Suzanne Deville, who was a journalist on that weekly magazine, *International Viewpoint*. She had a book published, *Dark Regressions* and it was for something connected with that book that took her to The Golden Mountains. She was drowned in the Bottomless Pool, which is in the first cavern, the Great Cavern, where the waterfall goes into the pool." He took a breath. "That was the reason they were going to Switzerland and Kathy and Becky went with them because of the subjects they are studying at Cambridge. I would have gone too if I hadn't been in America."

"Did your parents not believe that Suzanne Deville's tragic death was an accident? The local police seemed satisfied that this was the case."

"Sorry, I am not prepared to discuss that. I am studying law at Yale, so don't have much time in the way of conversation with other members of my family. My brother and I would prefer to be allowed to resume our lives in peace from now on, if you will excuse us."

Ed concurred with his younger stepbrother. "If you will excuse us now, we feel enough has been said on this matter. Thank you for being so obliging."

And with that, the two brothers rose from their seats, leaving poor Archie Praed to cover the sudden exit. They exited the building through a back entrance that they had previously discovered, breathing a sigh of relief.

Chapter 88

Trying to remain unflustered, and making a pretty good job of it, the presenter continued.

"So much for the family members. After the next break, I will be speaking to the editor of *International Viewpoint*."

More advertisements and music...

"This is Archie Praed back with you and my guest this time is Paul Holiday, head of editorials of the magazine *International Viewpoint*. Good evening, Paul, thank you for agreeing to come on this programme. I believe that the owner of the magazine, Boris Slovinski, was staying with his cousin in Billenbach and appears to be listed amongst the missing. First, let me ask you about the reporter, Suzanne Deville, who was drowned whilst visiting the caves in Billenbach. I understand that she wrote a story that was serialised in *International Viewpoint* and later published as a book."

"That is correct." Paul Holiday looked as though he might be as unforthcoming as the two Cameron brothers.

"Can you give us some idea as to what the book was about Paul?"

"Not really. If anyone is interested, they should read it."

"Okay, I can see your reluctance," Archie began.

"No, you can't." Paul Holiday's voice was an octave higher. "You have no idea of the danger connected to those involved with those regressions. With Suzanne, the Convent of the Golden Orb, the Great Cavern and above all," he lowered his voice to almost a whisper, "the Count or Man in Black. Suzanne was scared of him. Is he real or just a figment of her imagination? I don't know, but for sure I am going to be very careful. All the people connected with that book of hers are apparently dead and I have no desire to join them." Paul shuddered as he came to the end of his speech.

"Fine, your choice, Mr Holiday." Archie Praed suddenly became formal.

"Can you tell us what the prospects are, of *International Viewpoint*, which you represent, continuing?"

"At the moment, I intend to continue as always. I have been running the magazine since Boris went to Switzerland and shall continue to do so. Once we know Boris' wishes in respect of *International Viewpoint*, decisions will be made and you will no doubt, be told, so that you can broadcast the latest information."

As the pictures of the collapse of the Golden Mountains, now a huge caldera and the devastated village, appeared behind the presenter, Paul Holiday was escorted from the set.

"Well, that is indeed another Inexplicable Strange Event, I might even preface that title with the word Extremely."

He concluded with his regular ending for this programme.

"Good night, all and sweet dreams."

~~

The News Programme Later That Day

"Meanwhile, another thing that has been allegedly connected to the caves and the Bottomless Pool, was the so-called MistVirus. You will have no doubt seen the television news reports concerning this mist or vapour, which appears to be able to squeeze the life from its victims." The news reader leaned forward in his seat. "Information is coming from all parts of the world, that no more deaths due to this factor, have been reported, since the destruction of the Golden Mountains. Also, there have been no signs of the snake-like mist since that time. Could it be connected?

Keep alert and should you notice anything of specific interest, please email me on the address at the bottom of your screens."

Epilogue

The Cameron brothers were back at the Rectory of St Patricks, watching the DVD they had been given of the programme in which they had appeared, two weeks ago. They had felt unable to discuss the matter after their return and as there was now only a week before they needed to return to Canada and America respectively, considered there was some obligation to do so. A Memorial service was to be held the following day and neither of them knew how that would affect them.

However, they knew what they felt at that particular moment, staying at the home in which they had been brought up by parents who had loved them. It was a sad, lonely emptiness, and they sat with arms around each other as they watched the final picture of the devastated village.

"Look! Do you see that?" Ed paused the picture and pointed.

There, standing on the path leading from the church, was the figure of a man. He was dressed in black, with a priest's collar of crimson, and on either side, slightly behind him, stood two female figures in the apparel of nuns.